LONELY RIDERS

MICHAEL D. DENNIS

This book is dedicated to Katherine Elizabeth for your inspiration and love. To Finn and Nova for filling my heart with your existence.

And I saw a new heaven and a new earth: for the first
heaven and the first earth were passed away; and there was
no more sea.

Revelation 21:1

CHAPTER 1

It was Valentine's Day. Elise would be home soon, and I wasn't done making dinner. I considered myself an amateur chef from all the jobs I'd had in restaurants in nearly every neighborhood of Los Angeles, from East LA to Venice. I'd been fired from most of those jobs for not seeing eye-to-eye with my bosses. I'd still managed to pick up a few skills with a knife, and knew my way around a kitchen.

Our loft downtown had more open space than most of the restaurants that I worked in. The gas burner stove I used was a relic that Elise and I had found on the side of the street off Santa Fe. The old Sears emblem was rusted, but the pilot clicked. I'd hauled it up to our place with the help of a few homeless guys who had wanted to make extra money. It worked fine. It just needed spit and elbow grease to get it back to a presentable shape. After a few days, I got it to a point where I'd have felt safe eating food cooked on it. There was always the slightest smell of gas, but only when I ran it. I figured there was a small leak in the line. I'd duct-taped most of it up and that had pretty much solved the problem. But it wasn't a big deal.

The inside of our place felt like a time capsule from the past. The 1990s were a special time in my heart. It was the end of the century, which felt like more than just an end to an era. I still laughed at how everyone had prepared in case the world exploded as the Mayan calendar had predicted, like all the prophets and talking heads on the news had jabbered about for the years leading up to 2000.

I had always been more worried that the end of the '90s meant an end to grunge rock, marijuana, and flannels. It didn't go down like that. After people realized the world wasn't in fact ending, they started to act crazier, like they'd missed the big spectacle. And the good news was that flannels were still in style, so I wasn't alone. In fact, they just became trendier and more expensive. Even better news was that marijuana became more popularly accepted, too. I kept my Nirvana poster up and had Sub Pop Records drink coasters to reminisce.

I wanted to make this Valentine's extra-nice for Elise. Even though the world wasn't going to explode into flames, I hoped. I thought all the predictions had just gotten the year wrong. I was an old-school romantic. Yeah, I know that sounded cheesy. Elise loved that I was into vintage everything and would only buy clothing from secondhand stores. She was way more connected to the modern world. She stayed up on fashion trends, partly because it was her job, but also because she considered herself a tastemaker. I hadn't even known what that word meant before I'd met Elise. She flipped my whole perspective upside-down. The crazy difference in our opinions just made our conversations more interesting and our curiosity about each other stronger.

I was an anarchist, though without enough of the drive or commitment to really protest the government. I conducted most of my arguments silently and never got motivated enough to take to the streets. I had never listened to my parents and argued with anyone who thought they knew more than me, so pretty much everyone I met for more than a few minutes. If alcohol and any other recreational drugs were involved, forget about it. I would be chastising any opinion that didn't completely align with my own. I idolized punk music innovators like Johnny Rotten, Iggy Pop, and other grunge rockers like the Melvins that had formed from the shadows in the underbelly of the world. Their revolutionary music fit with my own outlaw mentality. I liked to think being opinionated and revolutionary was part of my charm.

But deep down, underneath the layer of my hardened exterior, I was a sweetheart. I would do anything for the ones that I loved. My center was all soft and gooey, but I kept a layer of studded protection around it. You had to in Los Angeles, or you would get your heart and spirit broken every second. I opened myself up to Elise. I should say she opened me up, and I felt naked.

This was Valentine's, an overly commercialized holiday, but I decided to make it mean more to Elise. She deserved to feel taken care of, and I really admired her for who she was. She was a true artist. Everything she touched, she made more interesting. Her first present to me had been a vintage jean vest she'd remade with rivets and patches from local punk bands from the LA scene. A Germs patch was sewn over the right-side chest pocket. I could tell she'd cut that out from a T-shirt. It had been the first present I'd ever really liked in my life.

Elise would look at everything and see how she could make it better using her own two hands. She was "crafty," our friends would say. I think that was one of the first things that made our relationship stick. Yes, she was gorgeous.

Her small ski-slope nose, soft pale skin, and bobbed platinum hair clearly pulled me in, too. She would accent her perfectly symmetrical face with red lipstick, which was also my favorite. Her thick hips would pull me in and seduce me from underneath every pair of acid wash jeans. Elise's whole vibe ran deep into my subconscious desires, being a child raised on MTV music videos and a slew of blondes wearing too much makeup who all imitated the legendary Samantha Fox. She had been the most iconic blonde lead singer during the start of MTV and had ignited a hair trend that was never forgotten in Los Angeles.

Elise was perfect to me, though. She was an evolved, more modern version of Ms. Fox, probably a little too good for me when you got down to it. She didn't require all the caked-on makeup but used it to accent her style more than purely relying on her natural beauty. Someone with her intelligence and good looks could do anything they wanted in this city.

We had only been together for six months, but we were soulmates. We'd known it the first time we met. We were finishing each other's sentences and talking about how much we loved artists who really expressed themselves without fear like Chris Burden. We talked about how Burden walked into a gallery in New York and had his friend shoot him in the arm.

"What if he'd missed?" we would laugh.

Elise and I talked about how much more expensive an artist's work gets after they die and how capitalistic your art really becomes in the afterlife. It was a little twisted, but the conversation fit us.

Yeah, you could say we were born to love each other and bound together as fate would have it. After our first date, we went to a motel situated off the 5 Freeway, a real shithole. But it didn't matter; we pretended the flow of cars was the sound of the ocean, and we slipped away into our own world. The ecstasy we experienced that night as we had endless amounts of sex was unparalleled. Our bodies predicted each other's movements. Every orgasm we had made us fall deeper in love with each other.

Within a week, we moved into a loft apartment in the Arts District downtown off of Third and Traction. It was a great spot, you know—old freight elevator, exposed beams, the smell of steel, and polished concrete floors. She'd said she "couldn't picture life without me."

And then she would tell me, "Because you love me right. The way I need to be loved."

Valentine's was the day to shower your loved one in spoils, as prescribed by the tradition. I'd indulged tradition and made her favorite dinner, halibut with a homemade tomato-and-crushed-almond sauce on top. She loved to eat that sauce by itself, on bread, on anything.

She'd once said, "I could eat cardboard with this on it."

It was a real sweet thing to say and let me know it didn't matter what I made; she would always compliment me, because that's just how kindhearted of a person she was. If she didn't like something, she would just smile during the whole dinner and take little nibbles here and there. That was the dead giveaway. If she liked it, she was in the clean plate club within a few minutes, finishing her food before I made her a second whisky ginger.

Elise was always seeing the best in everyone, cherishing the inconsequential details of the world, and putting a magnifying glass on them that had a beauty filter built into it. Her world was crystallized in a coat of sugar that no one else could see at first, but she could get you to witness it if you really listened to her vision. And I did. I drank her Kool-Aid. I gulped it down. Shit, I bathed in it.

I hadn't bought her roses, because she was too unique for that. I'd gotten her these white lilies. They looked almost dyed because the white was so bright, I only found them from this local florist just outside the flower district. They were so soft, so elegant, and had this flowing edge that reminded me of the softness of her pale skin. I hadn't bought her any presents; I gave her a poem about when we were standing on the First Street Bridge. The place where we'd first said, "I'll love you forever." She'd said it over and over again, and we'd kissed so deeply that day. Even now, I could still feel her lips all over my mouth. Her lips were strong, but sensual. We fit together perfectly. Our bodies, our spirits, everything. Our relationship was fucking magnetic; no matter how the world tore us apart, we would be reunited.

There was no real end to it, or at least that was how it felt. Our love was unconditional.

I heard the freight elevator grinding up the brick shaft to our floor. I lit the candles. I held the bottle of her favorite champagne in my hand, ready for her entrance. My heart beat rapidly and the wait for her seemed never ending. I counted the seconds aloud. I used my fingers like I was doing basic arithmetic. I thought if I counted slower on my left hand, adding up the time, it would calm my nerves. It didn't. I was so eager to please her. It was nice to feel like it was the first time we'd met all over again. I don't know what made that day feel so different.

She walked in and looked around. She smiled.

"Hi, sweetheart. Happy V Day," I said softly.

"What is this?" she asked.

"I made you dinner. Got you champagne. The one you love. The orange label."

"Thanks, Kyle. I mean it, you're the best."

Her words weren't that convincing, but I took the compliment. I could tell something was bothering her. She dropped her bag on the floor and held me close and kissed me with so much passion it almost felt like anger. Her skin was colder. She had goosebumps on her arms; my fingers gripped her tightly.

"The fish!" I was lost in her.

I ran to the oven and took out the food and separate baking pan lined with the red sauce. It wasn't burnt. "Thank god."

I plated the food. It looked good. I went back over to Elise and she was sitting down on the ground hunched-over.

"I lost my job," she finally said.

She was defeated. Her green eyes, with amber-colored streaks, had a tendency to completely press the pause button on my own internal world.

"I... I'm sorry."

I didn't know how to answer. Elise had always had a good-paying job. She'd been working her way up in the fashion world right out of school. Her parents had money, a lot of it. After her father died from cancer when she was eighteen, her mom made sure she always got what she wanted. She'd gone to the best design school in New York before she moved out here for her job with this insanely well-known luxury hat company.

"It's all right. I just don't like to feel, you know, not wanted when I give my all to help other people."

"Yeah, always so giving. You're a rare human."

"I know I am. Heart of gold."

"Well—you have something else going for you, too." I looked at her ready to devour her.

"What's that?" Her mood changed.

She nodded with a dirty smile, and then jumped on top of me. I caught her in the air. I lifted up her thighs and pinned her against the wall. I licked my fingers and slid her panties

8

to the side and played with her. I fingered her and took her thong off, and then we went to the floor. She yanked my shirt over my head and undid my belt and pulled my pants down. The door to our apartment was still open, but I didn't care if the neighbors watched us.

"I want you inside of me so bad," she whispered.

She pushed me onto my back and climbed on top of my face. She needed to feel in control of her own pleasure.

I wanted to give her everything she wanted. I licked and sucked on her, until she was ready and slid back down onto me. I pushed my hard cock inside her. She started to ride me, moving back and forth on top of my naked body. Her dress was pulled up around her waist so her thick ass could slap against the insides of my legs. I was so hard. She pulled her top down and squeezed her nipples underneath her lace bra. She turned her head from side to side, her hair snapping around her face. She turned me on so much it hurt.

"Deeper, daddy." But I slipped out. She grabbed me, jerked me hard a few times and put me back inside of her.

"Oh my god, baby! I fucking craved you," I said.

This was not the cliché Valentine's Day lovemaking. Elise wanted to fuck my brains out and release the negative energy from the day's events. I wasn't complaining. I watched her focus the energy on her hips and satisfy the ache she had inside. She popped them up and her ass slapped down again hard against my pelvic bone. She started to pant, "Uh-huh, yeah, that's, uhhhh. Cum with me, daddy." She didn't need to say anything more. I was cumming inside of her. In all the times we'd had sex, this was the first time I'd ever cum inside her. It felt incredible, like it was never going to end. I didn't want her to get off of me. I wanted to live inside her and glue our bodies together with our cum.

Then she fell off back, knocking the bottle of champagne over. The white froth started to bubble out of the end of the bottle and onto the floor. Elise dragged the bottle over and took a long sip, downing it. She rolled over and let the alcohol trickle out from her lips into my mouth. Her lipstick was almost all smeared off. The champagne was cool on my sweaty naked skin.

I got up and shut the door, hearing voices down the hallway. I reached down beside me to pull Elise up, but she pulled me in closer to kiss her lips again. I did, and I held her body against mine for a few minutes before getting up.

"I'll warm up the fish."

"OK," she muttered.

"Let me finish..."

"It's OK, let's just eat it right here on the floor." She knew what I was going to say.
I grabbed the flowers and set them down next to her.

"For me? You didn't have to. I know you don't like lame-ass traditions." She put on a cute accent and blushed.

"Yeah, but I know you kind of do."

10

Elise got up and grabbed the flutes and filled them up. She sat back down and set them on the floor, our makeshift dining table on our shag rug. I brought the plates over. The top of her dress was still hanging off, exposing her slightly. Her mascara was smeared down the sides of her face in crescent moon shapes from the tears. Even in this state, she was so beautiful.

"I'll get another job." I couldn't help but say it.

I didn't want her to have to work, but gigs had been few and far-between recently. I was picking up anything I could.

I pictured coming home after a hard day's work in a distorted *Natural Born Killers* kind of way, and seeing Elise wrapped up in our oversized California king bed snuggled up under the covers, candles burning. It was a little more peaceful of a scene than the one Oliver Stone had painted in that deranged love story, but I wanted the same bond, the connection that was so deep in our souls, not even death could pull us away from each other. Our life was less driven by horror, but we would still watch it together in bed and link our hands like a wannabe Mickey and Mallory Knox.

Once we got in that bed, I never wanted to get up. It seemed like all our troubles would fade away. We would lock them out, buried under the covers. It felt so good in there the rest of the world crumbled.

Our bedroom was filled with the aromas of candles, tobacco, vanilla, and sandalwood all swirling in the air. Beneath that overload of smells was the hint of sweat from her body. The thin layer of sweat that absorbed into the sheets from her being there, so cozy, not wanting to move, just diving deep into her immaculate thoughts about the details of the world. Her scent was more of an aphrodisiac than the candle fumes. It intoxicated me and turned me into a savage beast. I was addicted to her.

I would just lie there and watch her eyes. They would flick up and down, taking it all in. I could see her analytical mind picking apart every last detail of the room. She would get up when she had exhausted creating stories for all the inanimate objects. Like the woodcarving she'd picked up from Bali, the mug with old stale coffee stains in it, or each thread of the fake Persian rug and how the strands interlaced to form intricate patterns. She would walk naked over to the window. It was my favorite part about watching her. I could appreciate her entire body, not just sexually, but the silhouette. It was more erotic, the way the light bent through the spaces between her legs and underneath her arms. It was the negative space that was so alluring.

She would stand at the window and curl up on the sill and take one of my American Spirits out of the pack. She didn't really like smoking except when she was on that windowsill. She would look at the way cars parked outside the building, and she had a story for every person who drove those cars, too. Whether she saw them or not, she would concoct their elaborate fake lives. It would get so in-depth that she would tell me she was worried for them because their husbands were abusing them, or they were having financial troubles and resorting to exploitative things to make money. She was like an invisible saint on that windowsill, looking down on all her people.

Elise wanted to save them. That was a common thing for her to say: "I wish I could help them." It was always a new person, a new cause, and I swear she would give them our last dollar. It was a great thing. But it would make me feel shitty that I didn't have the money to help her fulfill her philanthropic dreams.

It was the only time I felt inadequate with Elise. She was a good lover to me. And even if she was a daydreamer, so was I.

I couldn't remember how many times she'd watched birds flying by that window and said names for each of them. This was her way of being part of the larger cosmological world, and to me, it was so insanely sexy that I would die without knowing what she was thinking about.

"I'm going to get another job." I repeated and broke the silence of my fantastical daydream. And took a bite of fish.

"No, you don't have to. We'll figure it out."

"I guess."

But we'd never had to deal with this. She'd had a good-paying job since we'd met.

I thought about all of our bills and rent. The landlord, Pascal, was a real dick. There's no way he would give us any leniency on rent. He'd inherited the building from his wealthy Italian parents and managed the café downstairs.

It was a cool artsy place that had a blues piano player come every Friday to do a couple jams and make the elitist art dealers and architects feel cultured. Once, we'd even seen Frank Gehry there. His doodles adorned every book on display at the restaurant, an architect student's wet dream. To me, they looked like scribbles, but hidden in those lines was a masterpiece. I never really liked eating there because even though we were tenants, they rarely gave us a discount on anything, not even the day-old baked goods.

I'd asked once, "Do you have anything freshly baked?" The cashier looked at me funny.

I thought she knew what I was talking about, but still maintained the act as if they were actually decent. "You can try the blueberry scones. You'll need to buy a coffee, too, though, to choke it down." She winked at me. I went ahead and shared in the fun about the lack of freshness in their pastries. It hadn't completely been a joke, because it was true.

I had a good heart. And believed that we were all connected subconsciously, and that we all had a deeper purpose. I just hadn't found mine.

I knew I had to find something to do for work. Selling weed or putting all of our possessions up for sale wasn't the answer. All the hustles I had on the side were not enough. I needed a chunk of cash to get us ahead while Elise looked for another job. That could be a long time, with the job market the way it was. She was smart, creative, and an amazingly beautiful person. And you had to go beyond just superficial attractiveness if you wanted to land a job that wasn't waiting tables, slanging drugs, or climbing up and down a pole at night. Despite all her incredible values, the job market was tough, and we had to prepare that it could take a while before she landed one that fit her true career ambitions.

I never felt fully dedicated to a job or anything other than being in the moment. In the kitchen, you made sure you got the work done with speed and then got paid out nightly, weekly, whatever. Point was that I had been, and was still always, out for me in my jobs. Get in there and do what you gotta do to survive and live good. I didn't get the whole selfless thing, but Elise was a Capricorn, so she took it to a whole other level, caring about other people's problems.

For her to lose her job created an even more confusing state of manic depression. Elise could take a tailspin from this. I prayed it didn't last too long. I didn't pray to God. I just prayed to a higher power, the universe, I guess.

I knew that right now, the only thing she was thinking about was what she'd do next. How to get that new job? I knew she was already thinking about the other brands she would be interested in working for. She was picturing their company culture, if she could navigate her way to the top, and how long it would take her to run the show.

We ate in silence for a few minutes. It felt right, the silence, our breathing, and incongruous sips of the remaining champagne, before we hit the hard liquor.

"I can get a real job." Elise just looked at me with tears in her eyes.

"I'm going to take a shower." She got up and started toward the bathroom. She stopped midway and walked back over to me.

"Thank you for the beautiful dinner. And the flowers. All perfect."

"I love you. And I mean it. I'll find a solid gig. I promise. Until you get back on your feet, you know, in that CEO role you deserve." I winked and tried to boost her up.

She looked at me in disbelief.

"Bye, daddy." Elise gave me a small kiss and walked down the hall.

It had been a little while since I'd gotten work in a kitchen, but I meant what I'd said. I would be willing to get a real job. I just wasn't sure what. I'd had solid success selling marijuana for the last few years, and occasionally a little cocaine at the local bars and to the servers at the restaurants I worked in. It paid my share of the bills.

I picked up the plates and shoved the leftovers in my mouth. I washed it down with the remaining dribbles of champagne. It wasn't enough moisture to offset the fish. I looked at the kitchen counter where we kept our makeshift bar. The half-empty bottle of Johnnie Walker Red had my name on it. I picked it up and unscrewed the gold plastic cap. I was surprised to find the safe pour insert was still inside the mouth of the bottle. That was normally my first move, to pop it out after I'd opened a handle.

I took the butcher's knife and stuck it in the hole, loosening and popping the insert out along with fish scales that were on the knife. It hit the cabinet and bounced off. "Gretzky denied." I used to love the Kings. Now I barely watched them. Instead, I had become a collector of the plastic inserts from alcohol handles.

The swig I took was long and deep. It burned and felt so good to wash the fishy taste out of my mouth. It filled my stomach with warmth. It was a warmth that nothing else could replicate. A few other drugs would fill you up with a warm feeling, but left only permanent stains of shallow emptiness. Alcohol was like a hug from a teddy bear inside my belly. More like a thousand tiny little teddy bears. My mouth tingled and the scent of alcohol burned through my nostrils. "Ahhh, so good."

I started to clean up and then decided to dig through the newspapers in the corner of the room. Stacks of them had become a collection at this point, after neither of us bothered to take any of it down to the trash. I looked for the most recent one and flipped open to the classifieds section. I didn't know where else to start. *Damn, she's taking a long-ass shower.*

I flipped through to the jobs section and scanned the listings. "Pool cleaner needed" and then "Work from home – MAKE MILLIONS!" It was one bullshit job and scam leapfrogging the other in the listings. *What the fuck am I going to do?* I was lost. The shower finally turned off.

Elise was taking her time, and then I heard a loud crash. The sound of glass shattering was unmistakable. I sprinted to the bathroom door and yanked the handle. It was locked.

"Elise?" I didn't hear any movement. I slammed my hand down on the handle, trying to break the push-button lock. The lever just snapped back against my fist.

"Fuck! Elise, open it." I pushed my shoulder against the door and started to bang against it harder and harder. It wouldn't budge.

This sparked me into action, and I stood back and kicked in the door right next to the handle. My foot went right through the hollow fake wood door and into the other side. I pulled half my leg out from the large hole. There was so much steam in the bathroom that I could hardly make out what was happening.

I bent my arm inside of the hole and unlocked the door from the inside. There was blood and glass all over the place. Elise was sprawled out on top of the broken glass of the shower door.

I picked her up. She was unconscious. I carried her out of the bathroom and grabbed a towel in my other hand. I laid her on the towel face-up. Her body was covered in blood and water. I couldn't trace the source of the wound. I grabbed her phone, as it was closest, and dialed 9-1-1.

The operator asked, "What is your emergency?" I didn't know how to answer. I was in shock.

"Fuck."

"Sir."

I couldn't speak. The muscles in my mouth didn't work. Like in a nightmare, I was paralyzed. I could only watch Elise's chest move up and down, affirming that she was breathing, and I sighed the slightest relief.

"There's blood everywhere. She needs medical attention."

The operator didn't seem to get the urgency and started asking me basic questions about my girl.

"Calm down, sir, and tell me what happened."

"It's a fucking emergency." I couldn't calm down. My nerves were flying.

"Please describe the emergency."

"She fell in the shower. There's blood everywhere," I repeated myself, hoping the operator had dispatched an ambulance and stopped playing these mind games.

"I'm sending an ambulance."

"OK, right now!"

I answered the questions mechanically until I regained view of the scene in front of me. I wiped the blood from her face, off her mouth. It smeared from the moisture, causing it to run. The cut was coming from the skin near her collarbone. I couldn't stop it from coming out. Every time I wiped it, more blood escaped.

I took off my T-shirt and pressed it to the wound. My favorite vintage white Iggy shirt was sucking up the dark blood.

This wasn't the first time she'd had an incident from pills. She'd had a problem ever since the day we met. It had never gotten this bad. I thought that our love would help her get over it.

Helpless, I kept counting the seconds until help arrived. I wasn't qualified for this. The thought crossed my mind of having to stitch her up myself with the sewing kit she kept by the bed.

I heard the sirens coming down Third Street.

The EMTs came running into the bathroom to find me holding Elise.

"What happened, sir?"

"I think she just passed out in the shower," I said. I knew she'd probably taken pills, but I didn't want to say that.

"Has she taken any drugs?"

"Maybe."

"What's her name?"

"Elise."

"OK, please step back."

Elise was still partially naked, so I grabbed a towel and tossed it over her body.

They patched her cuts up and started to move her to the gurney.

"Elise, Elise. Can you hear me? I need you to nod your head yes if you can." There was a slight twitch from her head.

They got her on the stretcher, covered in blankets and in a neck brace.

We headed out the door and down the hallway.

CHAPTER 2

On the way to the hospital, we hit so many potholes, I was afraid they wouldn't be able to hold the IV in Elise's arm. The stand with the saline bag was rolling across the ambulance floor. The ambulance almost clipped a couple junkies who had a fire going in the middle of Skid Row.

We pulled into White Memorial Hospital off Boyle. They slung her out and right into the ER. The ambulance guys got her in there with ease. They had done this thousands of times.

They wheeled her off down the hallway.

I paced around the entrance to the ER. My heart was still beating uncontrollably. I couldn't catch my breath. But I pretended to be cool. I supported myself against the wall. My eyes scanned some of the printed literature posted on a bulletin board with thumbtacks. I tried to stay collected. I swallowed a few times. My throat was so damn dry.

I knew she'd be OK. I wasn't a fucking idiot, and I realized we must have looked like a couple pill-poppers who were taking too many prescriptions and reenacting a sex scene we saw on an HBO series. Roleplay in the shower did take it to another level because of the danger factor. I was sure that was what the intake report said.

After what felt like an hour, the doctor finally came out, still drying her hands on brown paper towels. She tossed them in the nearby stainless-steel trash can and approached me. She disposed of her scrub cap, too.

"You must be Kyle."

"How do you know?"

The doctor looked down at her chart. "Your wife," she paused, "or your girlfriend has been mumbling your name over and over again. Plus, you're out here pacing around tirelessly."

"Ummm, yes, I am. Is she all right?" I choked the words out.

"We have stopped the bleeding. It's a minor cut. She is getting stitches, and we'll need to monitor her overnight to make sure she didn't do any damage to her brain with such a hard fall."

"OK, can I go see her?"

"Not yet. We are still stabilizing her. She took a lot of narcotics, too. Her heartrate was dangerously low."

"Right, stabilize." I shook my head.
"Do you know how she accessed the painkillers?"

"I'm not sure. I know we keep a few in the bathroom, leftovers from past dental procedures."

"She took whatever you had left. All of them. Has she ever tried to commit suicide before?" she asked.

"Suicide. No way. She didn't, she couldn't have!" The question killed me.

"All right, relax, sir."

"Yeah, sorry, Doctor. Can I see her?"

"You can see her in about an hour."

"OK."

I didn't have much else to say. I wanted to thank the doctor, but it didn't seem like the right thing to do. I also wanted to break down and cry, thinking about Elise. More about the mental pain she must have felt, rather than the physical. She was driven to extremes like that. Her depression always kicked in when she thought she'd failed. She couldn't stand that idea. I should have been more sensitive and seen this coming. Failing—it was the only pressure that never really stopped eating away at her since she'd been a kid.

Maybe that's why she had the problem with pills for so long, but I didn't want to tell the doctor that this was a pattern. I was worried they would take her away from me.

I needed to clear my head, so I went outside and lit up a cigarette. The first inhale felt so good. I hadn't had one in a few days, and I started to feel lightheaded. A man in a suit motioned to me. "Hey. You got an extra smoke?"

I looked at him, analyzing the quality of his suit. He looked like a federal agent or a detective from those crime shows. Too clean-cut, no American flag pin on his lapel, though.

24

That was the dead giveaway. But he did have a symbol on his jacket. Instead of a flag, it looked like a small, gold cross pin. *A man of God, I guess.*

"Yeah, sure, buddy." I was curious. I never saw a guy in a suit smoke anymore. These days in Los Angeles, even the business world was health-conscious, doing juice cleanses after finishing a hostile takeover of a rival company.

"Are you waiting for someone?" he asked.

"My girl, she's a little beat up."

"Oh..."

"Not like that. I didn't touch her. She's stabilizing."

"What happened? If you don't mind me prying."

"Nah, it's cool. She got in a fight with the shower door."

"Sounds painful."

"Fuck yeah, it was."

"Is she going to be all right?"

I couldn't tell if he was genuinely concerned for her wellbeing or just making small talk. Either way, it felt good to talk to someone.

The amount of information I was giving him was more than I disclosed to most people. I was vulnerable, and opened up to a complete stranger. He was so easy to talk to. It felt like I'd known him for my entire life.

"I think so. It was crazy. We were having dinner one minute," I paused, "she takes a shower, and next thing you know, she's bleeding out on the floor."

"That sounds crazy. Did they say when you could go in to see her?"

"Yeah, they said in an hour. Looks like we might be staying overnight. A sleepover at the ER on a Monday. Party time."

"Not the best way to spend a Valentine's Day?"

"Not at all." I almost forgot it was still Valentine's Day.

"You hungry?"

"Yeah. I got time to kill. Pacing around here isn't doing me any good." I hadn't had much of an appetite until he'd asked.

"Great. I know a place down the street that serves twenty-four hours. It serves Chinese food and donuts."

"That seems nasty. Doesn't sound like a winning combination to me."

"That's what I thought until I tried it. Trust me."

"Why not! It'll expand my palette."

We walked down to the end of Boyle Street until we hit Cesar Chavez Boulevard. The restaurant was tucked away next to this auto repair shop. I think they even shared the same parking lot out front. There were a few vagrants hanging around outside, and one customer parked out front eating ravenously inside an oversized Ford pickup truck with the window half-cracked.

The restaurant was decorated like a 1950s diner. Red, plastic-covered, ripped vinyl stools with steel legs. A row of white melamine board tables, chipped and defaced, was against the wall on the edges of the small place. I looked up at the menu and didn't see anything that piqued my interest. The menu was pieced together with magnetic letters, and every few words were misspelled. Most of the combination plates included variations of a noodle dish, like chicken lo mein and a donut for about six bucks. It wasn't a bad deal, though. I just had trouble convincing the grumbling in my stomach that everything was going to be mellow after this concoction. I figured it would be fast, because I needed to get back to Elise.

This guy ordered with precision, like he had been here many, many times before.

"Combo number three with a cup of coffee."

"Yes, sir," the cashier responded. Then he looked at me. He was an older Asian man in his sixties, but still had a sense of youth about him. His skinny mustache was patchy above his lip. The twenty-four-hour-a-day work schedule probably kept him on his toes and forced him into insomnia because his eyes were bloodshot.

"I'll have what he's having." I eyed combo number three and saw it was chow mein, orange chicken, and a maple bar.

It sounded nasty even while saying it in my head, but it was too late. He was already ringing it up.

"Oh, and a cup of coffee, too," I added.

"OK, sir. You want anything else?" I shook my head. "Thirteen dollars, please." I reached to grab my wallet and his hand stopped mine and pulled out his billfold. It was a nice thick fold of money held in place by a silver-and-gold money clip that had another cross on it, with words etched on it. It looked fancy, but I didn't want him to see me staring.

"I've got this one, buddy." He handed the cashier a twenty and told him to keep it.

"Thanks. I mean, I've been a little hard-up."

"Not a problem." We went to one of the empty side tables and sat down.

"Your coffee, sirs."

"I'll grab them." I popped up and got them both. I added a generous pour of granulated sugar from the glass container on the counter, a few single-serving half—and-halfs, and gave it a swirl with a plastic straw. The coffee was thicker than the normal cheap stuff you would expect from a place like this.

"You want anything in your coffee?"

28

"No, thank you, just black." I handed him the white Styrofoam and sat down, clutching mine in between my hands.

"It's cold tonight." I broke in with the typical cheap LA conversation anyone who lived here could relate to.

"So, you guys will be out of there tomorrow. That's good news."

"Sure is. I just don't know. Feels like whenever we get ahead... ahh. Never mind, I don't mean to get into my personal bullshit. I don't even know your name."

"I'm Michael. It's nice to meet you." He shook my hand casually.

We had already spent a good amount of time together for strangers and were now sharing Chinese food and donuts.

"Good to meet you. Name's Kyle. Kyle Whalen."

"So, you were saying..."

I didn't really remember what we were talking about.

I didn't want to look desperate, because this guy seemed to have his shit together. The suit, tie, even his watch all seemed to fit the cookie-cutter picture of success. I was sure his parents were proud of him, if they were still alive. I always wondered what kind of family life someone like that had. Raised by perfect parents. That was what I pictured. Got home from school and Mom was baking chocolate chip cookies; the house smelled like you could eat it. Dad got back and put his briefcase down, picked up the newspaper before dinner and asked his kids how their day was. Yeah, that was pretty much how I pictured this guy Michael's life had been growing up—the whole nuclear fifties family.

"My girl, Elise... she lost her job today, and I think that's what triggered this whole thing. It's why we're sitting here right now."

"Oh, I'm sorry to hear that. The job market is tough."

"I hate to admit it, but she's been the breadwinner this year."

"Nothing to be ashamed of. What do you do?"

"I'm… self-employed."

"Sounds like it has its perks."
"It can be good. But I gotta get back out there and pick up extra side work."

"You're looking for a job?" The bell from the counter clanged a few times.
"Order 2411," the voice from behind the counter said. "Two number three combos."

"Looks like our order is ready."

Michael got up and grabbed the two red trays. He slipped them onto the table. The smell was intoxicating. It was the whole sweet-and-savory thing. It got me every time. The fifth taste, umami, they called it. Yeah, this smell had to be umami.

30

"It actually smells really fucking good," I said. Michael kind of looked at me like I'd said something wrong. There was an awkward moment of silence.

"You were skeptical?" he said, stuffing a maple bar into his mouth.

"Yeah. A little."

"How could you go wrong with this combination?" He paused. "I'm just kidding! I think most people are freaked out by the concept. I love it, though. Gives me my fix. I can't resist when I'm in the neighborhood. It's one of my last vices, I guess. The MSG and fried donuts are a weak spot for me."

"How often do you eat here?" I asked him. He stopped sipping his coffee again and looked up at the television in the corner. It was a rerun of an LA Galaxy soccer game.

"I'm sorry. What did you say? Oh, how many times... I'd say once a week, at least."

"Do you work for the hospital?"

"Yeah, something like that."

His answer was vague, but I didn't really care anyway—this wasn't a job interview. We started to gobble down the chow mein. It was delicious. I took a scoop of it and put it on top of the maple bar and took a big bite. I, too, was getting high from all the sugars and MSG. I could see his point and now shared the same weakness. It felt amazing.

Michael was just sipping his coffee and eating methodically, a bite here and there. He motioned to the cashier and asked him to turn up the volume on the TV. The sound broke the awkward silence between us. I finished my plate and realized I had been so damn hungry. I drank down the last remnants of my coffee and swirled it in my mouth, trying to dislodge pieces of food left behind. The grains of sugar that didn't fully dissolve were gritty between my teeth. I stood up and got water from the cashier. He gave me the tiniest Dixie cup, filled to the brim. Half of it spilled on my hand, but the rest was enough. It did the trick.

"Let's get out of here." Michael finally spoke. Looked like the game on TV was over. We bussed our own table.

"Say, I know it's not really my business, but you said you need a little extra work?"

"I could use it for sure, man."

"Listen, I have a company. It's kind of in the healthcare business and we're always looking for extra workers."

"No way! That would be great. Shit, seriously? I would really owe you. My girl will be so happy to hear that."

"No problem."

We started to walk back down Boyle toward the ER. We passed another small medical building with tinted glass and a matte gray exterior. It looked a little run-down, but still modern with all the glass panels.

"I'm parked in here."

"Is this the employee lot?" I asked.

"I guess you could say that. Our offices are in this building. It's separate from the hospital. We are a little more, how would you say… innovative and experimental."

"Oh, OK, got it! Should I meet you here?"

"Yes, but send me a message first. Here is my card. Can you start Friday?"

I thought about it, and realizing it was only Monday, I just said, "Yes."

"That's perfect. Call me by Thursday. My cell number is on my card." He handed me a vertical card. I slipped it into the back of my jeans.

"Take this, too." He handed me a professionally printed pamphlet. The paper felt thick and there were a lot of pages.

"See you, Michael. Thank you."

"Make sure you read it. And good luck with your girlfriend."

"Thank you, really, thank you... I needed this more than you know."

He was already walking away toward the gated parking lot on the side of the building. I stood paralyzed by the excitement, and then my stomach started making weird noises. I ran back to the hospital entrance.

CHAPTER 3

The hospital bathroom was spotless, which was a relief. It was so much nicer than most public restrooms. Although with my stomach beating like a drum circle, I would have used a Home Depot bucket and a rag. I ran to the first available stall. My mind felt as full as my stomach did. My internal plumbing system was backed up all the way to my brain. I ripped my Dickies open and the clasp-fastener fell to the floor, chinking as it ricocheted under the neighboring stall. I dropped my pants as quickly as possible before my geyser burst into the toilet.

"Ahhhhhhhhh..." It echoed.

I let out the loudest audible sigh of pure joy. I'd barely survived that late-night snack, but I'd lived to tell the tale. I really paid the price for all that umami I got to experience. I'd show up to my new job a couple pounds lighter, that was for sure.

I pulled out the pamphlet. There was the same symbol and pronounced gold font on the front that looked like Sanskrit to me. I thumbed through the pages and saw a lot of math and geometric drawings, like mandelas. I tried to read a bit, but my stomach hurt so bad I put it down on top of the toilet paper holder and tried to get the poison out of me. I needed to focus.

There wasn't any graffiti in the stall, which was pretty rare. I liked to read the writings of someone who thought they were clever while going to the bathroom, or wanted to leave their mark. It was like a calling card to show you'd been around. I thought about what I would write. *Hmmm, I would probably go with the classic 'For a good time call...' But whose number would I put down there?* I didn't have to think too deeply—it would be my new friend Michael.

I took out his card and looked at it. It was too professional, and he was doing me a favor by hooking me up with a job. I'm sure he would be shocked with the abundance of phone calls he would get from the restroom guerilla marketing campaign. I laughed silently to myself.

My stomach started making noises again before I could get off the toilet. "Uh-oh." The combo platter number three wasn't done doing damage inside my stomach. It sounded like a rubber band snapped in my bowels, followed by gut-wrenching pain. This was going to be a much longer trip to the bathroom than I'd expected. The word came back and kept going through my head: *umami.* "Damnit, umami." And then, *Elise.* Her name repeated.

I finished up, grabbed the pamphlet, and washed my hands diligently. I looked in the mirror. My eyes had sunken into my face a quarter-inch deeper than before.

"I look like shit." I had to say it. Even though no one was in there to hear me, I started to break down, tears filling my eyes.

I splashed water on my face. The water was heavy—it got into every crevice and seemed to just sit there on my face. I took a few of the single-use hand towels and patted my skin.

I left and headed back to the ER, where I saw the doctor from before. She was talking to one of the other nurses, shaking her head.

"Hey, Doc." She looked up at me.

"What can I do for you?"

"Can I go see her?" I tried to make my eyes a sad shape. I wasn't good at getting sympathy, but I figured it was worth a shot. I couldn't bring the tears I'd had in the bathroom back to the surface, but the remnants of water droplets on my face probably looked like I'd been crying.

"Of course, you can. She is doing fine. We have removed the breathing tube since she's breathing unhindered. I believe she is sleeping now." The doctor looked at the nurse for affirmation. The nurse bobbed her head in agreement and pointed down the hallway. I could hardly wait another minute to see her. It felt like forever.

"She's in the third room on the right, number 426."

I nodded and walked down the hallway. Shrill screaming came from another bed. I didn't like the sound. When I reached the third bed—or really space, because it was just a shower curtain divider between the hallway and the bed—I peeked in before entering.

There she was, eyes closed, my baby. Sleeping now so peacefully, her mouth red, lips cherry. As I got closer, I realized when they'd removed the tube inserted in her mouth it had caused a light rash on her cheek, and in the corner of her mouth was a sore. At least they had removed it now. I was so glad I didn't have to see her like that.

I considered how I should have been by her side the whole time and not out grabbing Chinese food and donuts, but she would've wanted it like that. She was the kind of girl who wouldn't let you in the bathroom to hold her hair or caress her back if she got sick from a long night of drinking. Those nights always started with sake bombs and ended with scotch and a joint. Then, soon after, the spins always kicked our asses like a deranged formula. *One part sake, one part whisky, and the rest is history.* Fuck, that sounded good. A nice little mind-eraser.

I found a stool tucked away under the multiple digital screens and consoles next to her bed. When I moved it, it squeaked something awful. "Shit, I'm sorry, angel," I said, hoping the piercing sound didn't wake her up. It didn't.

She lay there sleeping. I just watched her chest float up and down in the hospital gown underneath the folded, starched, white sheet. The pattern of her breathing seemed normal and relaxed. It started to calm me, too, until my breathing matched hers.

I cupped my face in my hands, knowing she would be OK, but she would wake up and be so embarrassed. Then she would remember that she had lost her job and just want to get back to our apartment and start drinking again. I had sobered up now, too. Drinking again sounded like a great idea.

I knew how she would act. First, she would pretend like it didn't matter when we got home, and maybe even talk about how she would start a new hobby like she'd always wanted to, or volunteer at the Midnight Mission. Her thought process was predictable because I could feel her emotions—the real ones hiding under the surface—like we shared the same inner organs tied together by pain and alleviated by wild passion, even if only temporarily.

We were each other's best drug.

I slid my hand under the white sheet and down the side of the bed railing to find Elise's hand. It was soft on the top, but inside her hands were tougher than most women's from working on designs and patternmaking. I could feel her pulse in my hand, and she tightened her hand around mine. I didn't know if it was out of impulse or if she could sense my presence, back by her side.

I should tell her about Michael, the job, and the donuts and Chinese. I could still feel my stomach gurgling. My head slung down against my chest, and I passed out.

Commotion was all around me when I woke up. They were checking Elise's pulse and putting all types of other tubes in her arm.

"What the hell is going on?" I leapt up off the stool.

"Sir, stand back. Everything is fine."

"It doesn't fucking look like everything is fine!"

"OK, get him out of here," the doctor said.

One of the ER nurses maneuvered me out of the room and down the hallway. "Hey! What's going on?" I tried to get an answer from him about what was going on, but he ignored me and went back to help the doctor. I looked up at the clock on the wall; it was already five in the morning. We had been doing this all night, and now she wasn't all right? I started to panic with the last bit of nerves and adrenaline I had left.

My thoughts were split between logic and carelessness. I ran back down the hall to see Elise. The orderly caught me as I ripped the shower curtain back. I saw them using the defibrillator on her. Her chest exposed. Her nipples bared to the whole hospital staff. I was awestruck and disgusted by the sight. But the worst was the sinking feeling in my stomach that I might lose her. I thought of all the things we hadn't done. All the shit I hadn't said, and mostly, I wished I'd been better to her.

I paced around aggressively. One of the RNs had to hold me back from breaking into the circle of scrubs surrounding her like a huddle. Then, her body rolled back and forth and popped up in the bed as if she'd been resurrected.

"She's aliiiive!" I said.

She immediately fell back down again into the bed. The staff looked at me as they covered Elise's body, continued to give her oxygen, and monitored her vitals. She was back. She reached her arms toward me, and I fell through the huddle of scrubs and right onto her body. I kissed her rapidly all over her face, like sexy machine-gun fire on her lips. The bed railing was jabbing into my rib cage, but it didn't matter. After what felt like hours, the staff left and said they were transferring us to another room for one more night, just to make sure her heart didn't give out again from all the trauma.

"Hi, baby." We were finally alone.

"Kyle." She said my name so softly, I could barely hear her. Her mouth was so dry her tongue couldn't get through it. It still sounded good to hear her voice. Her voice made her alive again.

"You need water?" She just nodded.

"I'll be right back." It was hard to leave her again after all that. My heart was still pumping rapidly. I could feel the vein in my neck popping out.

I went down the hallway and just used the water fountain to fill her pink-and-white, plastic water pitcher. I looked down the hallway and as the elevator door closed, I thought I saw Michael again. *Hmmf. Maybe he's visiting someone else here at the hospital?* The thought slipped away, and I went back to Elise's room.

I woke up again. I looked around and forgot where I was for a second. Then I remembered and it hurt again. It felt late already, day two. Time was passing in waves now. The glimpses I got of the outside world through the entryway of the room were the only indication of time. Elise was already asleep when I got back to the room. I put the water down on the sliding tray on wheels beside her bed. Then I decided to put on the TV and watch it on mute. The only thing that really made sense was an old rerun of *Wheel of Fortune*. I played the game in my mind while Elise slept calmly. She woke herself up snoring a couple times—her head would shake a little, her nose would twitch, and then she would sigh and fall back asleep.

She looked peaceful, the emotional hurt pulled out of her by the medicine. Elise's spirit was back to being soft.

I remembered the first night we'd met. I'd seen her at Little Pedro's, the bar down the street from our apartment now. A funky electro pop band had been playing.

Her blonde hair was longer then, and she was dancing alone. Her face illuminated in fractals of the yellow-and-magenta lights reflected off an old disco ball. Her wild moves were so free. A light seriously radiated from inside of her, sent a beam straight into my heart. Maybe it was cheesy, but it felt so good. And the voice that so often got garbled in my head told me, "She's the one."

I walked over and started to dance, which I'd never done very well before. I loved music, but would just be a wallflower, drinking and drugging. She took my hand and was kind enough to move my body, so it looked like I had that rhythm built into me, too. It seemed like we were moving together through the vibrations from the speakers. Our souls were in sync.

That first night, we'd drank ourselves into the next day at a motel. We hadn't left each other's sides since.

"Baby, when we leave here, we'll go back to that moment. I promise."

I looked at her. She didn't move, but I pictured her smiling and engineered a smile in the image of her I had in my mind. It helped me deal with this process, this night of chaos, and the multiple near-death experiences.

I started thinking through all the things that had led up to this night. I wanted to figure out a way to reverse it and prevent it from happening. From the moment she'd walked into the loft, the overcooked fish, the sex on the floor, and champagne. Everything seemed so perfect, except that she'd lost her job. It meant that all the physical pleasure was faked. It hadn't been real because she had been in so much pain inside of her own head, it couldn't have been true. It made me think that maybe I couldn't fix the nightmare she had inside of her, and maybe she couldn't cure my pain, either.

CHAPTER 4

I woke up early in the morning. The nurse came in. "Here are her discharge papers. When she wakes up, have her sign these and you can go." I couldn't really respond because my mouth had such a nasty aftertaste, like burnt bacon grease. It was all I could focus on. I coughed into my hand and nodded instead. The nurse's V-neck scrubs had weird multi-colored bears on them that reminded me of the Grateful Dead.

Elise wasn't a big fan of the Grateful Dead, but she would let me relive those psychedelic memories and play my records as loud as I wanted. She was so cool like that. And in return I would take her on hikes in Griffith Park up to the observatory. She loved that kind of outdoorsy stuff. At the end of the hike, we would go sit in the planetarium and make out under the artificial starry sky. The air-conditioning in there always felt so good after that long hike up the dirt pathways to the top. The top of all of LA. You could see every corner of the city from that spot. They had those old viewfinders, too, that you popped a couple quarters in, and the periscope opened. The dark shade was lifted, and you could examine the minutiae of the city.

My trip down memory lane was cut short as the nurse came back.

"Sir, we need this room. Will you wake her up, or we can, so you can get her home?"

"I'll do it. Jesus, lady." The drastic shift in urgency was like a loud cartoon alarm clock banging those oversized metal bells. There was an invisible clanging in my head as a flurry of drastic movements ensued.

"Elise, angel. Wake up, sweetheart." She rolled over.

Globs of spit had collected and looked like salt crystals in the corner of her mouth. I took a piece of paper towel and dipped it in the water cup and wiped it off. She opened her eyes. She shook her head back and forth in denial.

"Come here." She pulled me in close.

"Baby, we have to go."

"Where? Where, Kyle? Let's sleep in."

"We are in the hospital still." She opened her eyes wider. They were so red as she looked around, trying to register everything.

"What happened?" she asked. "Let's go. Please, Kyle, I want to go." The panic was setting in.

Elise wrapped her arms around me, and I lifted her to get her feet on the floor. I grabbed the white plastic bag containing her belongings and went down the hallway. She walked slowly, staggering a bit. I supported her weight on my body. Without her heels on, she barely made it to the height of my shoulder. She leaned in, nuzzling closer to me.

We made it to the front entrance when a nurse, the same demanding one, caught us in the hallway. "Sir, you need to have her sign this."

Elise looked at it and looked away. She was acting like a child. She agreed to sign the paper after a long, awkward silence. She tucked her head back into my chest. I took the clipboard and held it for her. She autographed it and then initialed the couple of pages. I handed it back to the nurse and the gatekeeper let us go.

"Please get me home."

"OK. I'll look for a taxi. There's one." It drove off as I lifted my hand to flag it down.

"Not even at the hospital in LA can you get a stupid taxi!" As she finished yelling, another taxi drove up, which was a huge surprise. I opened the door and Elise climbed in.

Before I could get all the way in the car, I heard a familiar voice. "See you Friday, Kyle." I looked up and there was Michael in the same place as before, when we'd had a cigarette. He was having another one.
"A hundred percent." I nodded and got into the taxi. I had almost forgotten about the other night. It was like a dream. It just didn't feel real. It all seemed so intangible and cloudy.

"Who was that?" Elise was starting to become more coherent.

"Who?" I didn't really feel like getting into it yet.

I shrugged off the comment. I wasn't ready to tell her about it, and she didn't really press it. Elise slouched into the corner and closed her eyes. On the ride home I realized we probably didn't have any food in the fridge. I told the cabbie to pull over at a bodega on Spring Street. I ran in and grabbed the essentials, a twelve-pack of Negra Modelo Especial. I needed a beverage to sip on today that wouldn't get me too drunk, but would provide temporary relief.

The bodega was one of the shittier ones, but I liked it. I knew how to navigate it, so it made things simpler and cut down the time. I got the other items on my mental list: eggs, a premade ham sandwich, granola, and yogurt. I snagged a couple napkins, too, and packets of yellow mustard. I took out a couple twenties crumpled up in my pocket and gave them to the cashier. It was all I had left to my name.

I walked back out, and the taxi was gone. I looked around and didn't see anything.

"What the fuck!" I immediately panicked. I ran up and down the street, looking for the cab.

I started running back toward our place. My heart was racing, trying to find Elise. I still didn't see the cab anywhere.

"Jesus." I was scared and worried about Elise.

It was only about six more blocks to our place, but LA blocks were long, especially when you were lugging a twelve-pack in a heated panic.

I made it about halfway down the next block and there was the cab. It was pulled over on the side of the street. I could see Elise. Her body was hanging out of the passenger's side door. She was throwing up into the gutter. I ran with a stagger because of the extra weight I had from carrying the beer and the plastic grocery sack.

"Elise, baby, I'm here."

"Get your girlfriend the fuck out of my cab, buddy," the driver shouted at me.

"Why'd you fucking drive off? Calm the fuck down."

"Your girlfriend started screaming at me to take her home. I told her you were in the store."

"Yeah, right, man." I responded with my middle finger.

"Whatever, buddy. Just get her out of my car before she gets puke on it." He started to pull the cab forward to show he was serious. I grabbed Elise; her body was dead weight, so heavy it was like she'd doubled in size. I could hardly get her out of the taxi.

"C'mon, daddy. Let's go." She spat in the street.
I grabbed a crumpled-up five-dollar bill and loose coins. I threw them at the protective glass between us and the driver. He floored the cab, the door shutting on us.

"Where were you?" Elise was still pretty out of it.

"I jumped out real quick to grab the essentials. I knew you'd be hungry."

"I woke up and you were gone."

"I'm sorry, angel. Here, get on my back, we have about two blocks left. I can't have my girl walking on this dirty-ass street." Elise gladly jumped on my back and wrapped her legs around me.

"Let's get you home to bed."

It must have been a sight to anyone downtown. Even the people outside the Midnight Mission looked at us like I was running off with an escaped mental patient. When that crowd gave you that look, then you know something wasn't right.

After a block, Elise said, "Whose beer is that?" I kind of laughed to myself.

"Mine, it's mine." She just rested her head back on my shoulder and tried to sleep.

I could feel she was relieved to finally be close to home. I dropped the beer and eggs in the front entrance and carried her the rest of the way up the stairs to our unit. I set her down for a second to find my keys. She leaned against the doorframe and rolled onto her back against the wall.

We walked in and I helped Elise get into bed. She nestled under the covers and stared off into space.

This scene was probably the opposite of what her mother had ever wanted for her. I remembered when I had first met her mom, she'd looked me up and down with such disapproval. I couldn't imagine us ever getting along. We never did, either. I knew she wished her daughter had gotten in bed with a super-successful businessman who could support her and the rest of her family. Well, I wasn't that guy. I just played it cool when she flew into town and came by the loft. I kept my answers simple and not overly wordy to avoid leaving holes in the story, vulnerabilities for her to rip apart, or a philosophical argument about my career ambitions.

I went into the kitchen. I didn't know what time it was, but it didn't matter—I needed a drink. I took a few pulls off the large handle of Johnnie Walker that was left and chased it down with a fresh Modelo. It didn't taste right, so I sliced up an old lime we had in the fridge. It had been exposed to the cold air in the fridge too long and the skin was hard and felt reptilian. Still, the juices inside were enough to enhance the flavor of the brew. It tasted good. Now the flavor was right, the brew was *muy sabrosa.* I could always hear my old friend Ernesto say it when we'd have a brew after work.

I was satisfied by those thoughts and the booze and went and sat down on the couch. I needed to think about what had happened, decompress from all the shit, and just let go the same way Elise had. I popped the cap off another Modelo with the butt of my pocketknife, did an air-cheers to the memory of Ernesto, wherever he was, and then started to fall asleep.

I woke up thinking I heard the shower and my nerves sparked into action. I jumped up and realized it was just the trash truck driving by in the middle of the night—whipping the air by our building, the breeze carrying an odor of other people's garbage. It was a nasty smell. One you could almost taste.

The smell of human waste was almost pleasant after all the shit I'd dealt with in the last few days. It made me feel comforted because it was familiar.

I walked into the bathroom. Glass was still covering the floor, and streaks of Elise's blood had congealed there. I grabbed the cleaning products from underneath the kitchen sink and started to get to work on the floor. I smeared powdered bleach on the blood spots and brushed the glass pieces into tiny piles.

The collections of glass were hard to pick up with the paper towels, and one of the shards stuck me right in the index finger. It wasn't cut open, so I squeezed it, and when the blood started to come out, I sucked it like a five-year-old, fascinated by it. I never liked the taste of blood, but it was always nice to know we all bleed. It weirdly tied me to Elise, our blood mixing on the floor as I cleaned up the rest of the mess.

I went back into the kitchen and took a few more swigs off the whisky bottle. I couldn't bring myself to go into the bedroom. I felt like a foreigner in my own place. I knew Elise was sleeping, finally, and I didn't want to disturb her. I finished the bottle of Johnnie Red and downed another Modelo. My head started to spin.

I went into the bedroom and passed out next to Elise. Her arm slung over me and she held me, my back facing her. I didn't remember falling asleep. I just remembered staring at the clock, an old rockabilly 1950s cat clock, the tail swishing back and forth.

I had trouble sleeping. I was happy Elise was home and we were back together in the bed, but I couldn't get comfortable. I wasn't drunk enough to sleep, and didn't want to keep drinking or I knew it would be tough to wake up the next day. The night at the hospital kept replaying in my head every time I dozed off. I would wake up briefly and check to make sure Elise was still next to me. She was.

The smell of eggs filled the bedroom. It was so powerful, it overwhelmed the multiple scented candles and the flickering sensation from the ones we'd forgotten to blow out. Streams of smoke were rising from them. It painted a large cloud shape on the ceiling of the loft.

I was still in my clothes from the night before. I hated that. I felt so restricted and lazy. I didn't even remember falling asleep. I hardly remembered finishing off the bottle of Johnnie and making it to the bedroom. My shoes were off and a blanket was draped over me. Elise wasn't there, and I was sure she'd tried to tuck me in before going to make breakfast.

I started to shut my eyes again when she entered carrying a tray with all the best breakfast foods on it, including her famous French toast. She'd always talked about that, and her banana pancakes, since the first day we met, but this was the first time I got to sample its brilliance.

"If that tastes as good as it looks, fuck!"

She smiled. "Wake up, my savior, my hero," she said. It wasn't facetious. She truly meant it. She was feeling like her old self again. Elise fixed the cushions behind me to prop me up in the bed so I was better positioned to devour this amazing home-cooked breakfast.

I consumed the food voraciously. Elise tried to give me a kiss in the process and I did, getting smears of the Vermont maple syrup on her lips. I licked it off her lips a little.

"Haha! Looks like you were doing coke and not eating French toast." She grabbed her compact mirror from the side of the bed and showed me all the powdered sugar on my nose. We laughed. I was no *Scarface*, but I had my share of memories with my face horizontal to a mirror and snorting lines of cocaine.

It added a certain realism to Elise's comment that we both related to, and it lightened the mood from the night before. She was good at doing that. She always knew how to change the energy of any situation and defuse whatever bomb might be ready to go off in my head.

"You trying to fatten me up?" I joked.

"A little pudge wouldn't hurt you."

"Yeah, right, you don't want me to be chubby."

"Maybe I do, so I like a little extra squish."

"It was worth the wait—you've only been talking about this French toast for all of history. Now I'm worried the pancakes will be so damn good we'll exchange our vows over them," I teased her.

"That's a mouthful. Don't make any false promises this time, but do you really like it?" She wasn't usually this insecure, and I realized she still felt bad about the night before. This breakfast in bed was her way of wiping the slate clean.

"Elise, this is the best food I've ever had. And I'm so glad that you're OK."

She was embarrassed. She hid her face; she looked so sexy when she did that. I reassured her.

"It's OK now. My girl is back." I tried to make her feel better.

"You're not mad at me?"

"Hell no! I was just scared. I'm mad about you."

"You're so cheesy sometimes, but I love you. I do."

We laughed the rest of the night off. It felt good to laugh with a full stomach; I could feel it soaking up all the alcohol in my body. Elise took the tray as soon as I finished the last bite of French toast and put it on the ground.

She took off her pajama bottoms and was in her thong. She wasn't wearing a bra underneath her white ribbed tank top, and her nipples were showing through. She crawled under the covers and slid down my body, unbuttoning my jeans. I was already turned on. Her tongue felt so good on my cock.

I could hardly resist exploding in her mouth, but I wanted to feel her, be inside of her and reconnect.

I kissed her neck. I licked her earlobes and whispered in them, telling her, "You're my one. You're my sexy queen." I licked down her stomach, between her thighs, and ate her pussy until she came in my mouth. I climbed up her and went deep inside her. She pulled me in closer, locked her legs around my back, until I filled up her body with my seed.

We made love.

It was different, for some reason. There were none of the crazy positions this time, the angsty wild sex we'd had throughout our apartment in every room. This time we looked into each other's eyes the whole time even after I came inside of her.

After, I lay awake thinking about it. *Why hadn't we ever had sex like that?* It didn't make me question our love—the bond—it was more a third-eye perspective of the different sexual positions we'd tried this year, easily adding pages to a Kama Sutra book. Then my focus broke and another thought hit me like a fuckin' brick to my head: my meeting with Michael. The whole weird experience replayed like a montage, and in the end, I remembered what I had to tell Elise.

"Elise?" I waited. There was a long pause. I thought maybe she'd fallen asleep, but she turned over and looked at me. Her eyes were soft again, pensive and beautiful. They always swallowed me up in the morning, her skin perfectly pale-white. It almost glittered in the sunlight from our bedroom window.

"Yes, what's up?" She tried to be serious, but I could see her mouth quivering in the lower corner. She was on the verge of being playful, grabbing me and jumping on top of me, trying to tickle me to tears, even though I hated it. But she didn't. She lay there, solemn.

"What is it? Tell me."

"I don't know if you remember, but I got a job..." I stared at her, unblinking.

"You did? That's great. What is it?"

"It's a medical job—I think." I didn't really remember the details, or how to describe it.

"That's a good business. People make a lot of money in that field." She was really encouraging.

"Really? I thought you'd be upset, you know, feel like because you didn't..."

"I'm happy. I'm glad to take a break. I had time to think in the hospital and am just grateful. Grateful to be here, with you."

"Me, too." We kissed again and rolled over.

"What day is it?" I looked up at our Van Gogh calendar and saw the days with *X*s on them and made it as far as the fourteenth. I thought about how we'd missed a couple days.

There's no way Elise crossed off yesterday, not in her state of mind.

"Damn. It's fucking Thursday already. Michael wants me to start the new job tomorrow."

"On a Friday? What the hell? What kind of job starts you on a Friday? Is this a scam? A crazy place that's going to harvest your organs and stuff?"

"It's not in Tijuana, babe. It's right here in downtown, next to the hospital."

"Well, it's still weird they're having you start on Friday. That's random. Every job I've had starts on a Monday."

"I don't know. I guess they really need the extra help. Shit! Which reminds me—he told me to message him today about the details. What time..." I looked at the clock and it was already past four-thirty in the afternoon.

"Damn! It's so late." I thought it was still morning.

I could hardly remember what time we'd woken up, but the dismal light made me think it was much earlier. I searched my pockets in my jeans on the floor next to the bed. I found the crumpled card with his name, "Michael Bartelsman," in an elegant font on a nice hearty cut of pressed, white paper. I noticed a gold cross in the upper corner that I hadn't seen before, embossed in the card. His handwritten phone number was on it, and I tried calling, but the number was busy.

I decided to call the number again. There was a long pause before it started to ring through. It rang and rang.

Finally, it patched through, and there was a prerecorded woman's voice that sounded both real and completely cyber-phonic. "Name, please. First and last." I said my name, "Kyle Whalen." I pronounced each syllable with exaggeration in case it was a shitty voice-recognition system they had. I paused. A few quasi-analog sounds were audible in the background, faint but there.

"Please state who referred you, and the date of first assignment." I was confused—not about who referred me, but "first assignment"... that shit didn't make sense. I really didn't know how to answer.

I continued to get through the systematic Q&A session with the robotic woman on the other line. After a couple more questions I was home free. She said, "Please report for your job details tomorrow, Friday the eighteenth at eight a.m." *Damn, that's an early call time.* I wasn't overly bothered since I had slept all day, anyway.

I needed more time with Elise, but when I hung up, she was gone. I threw on my pants and a dirty white undershirt. I trotted down the stairs to see if I could catch Elise before she took one of her hour-long sabbaticals from our relationship. They were rare, but these last two days were also very rare.

Elise wanted to run from things, while I was more inclined to think through the tough shit in my life, and then come home and let her hold me close and stroke my hair. Elise had been doing this her whole life. She'd confessed to me that when she'd been growing up and things would get too difficult for her emotionally, she would run outside to an area under a tree, where she would carve things and sit for hours by herself. Most of the time, it had been about a crush she had on a boy, but other times it had been darker.

We had different routines that ended in a similar release of our frustrations and sorrows, when we would get back to the apartment and have amazing make-up sex.

I reached the street and saw the owner of the cafe, Pascal, instructing one of his line chefs to take out the trash and other bullshit work before getting back in the kitchen. I looked at him, my heart starting to beat faster, and even though Pascal and I never had any type of real contact except when he was taking my money for rent, he knew that I was looking for Elise. He pointed toward the bridge.

"Thanks, man," I shouted, not knowing if he heard me. I bolted toward the bridge. I sprinted, the air colder than usual on my face. I would normally be sweating my ass off at this point, but I wasn't. I felt a cold fear creeping inside me instead.

After the close call with Elise, where her life almost slipped away the other night on our bathroom floor, I didn't know what she was planning on doing. The fear continued to manifest past the point where I could predict what would happen next.

Crazy thoughts flooded my mind. *Would she hurt herself again? What the fuck?* I never thought so cryptically about

Elise. Now the thoughts consumed me as I ran at a full
sprint to the bridge.

CHAPTER 5

I reached Elise. She was standing up on the railing of the First Street Bridge, a hundred feet over the Los Angeles River. She started to walk toward me as if balancing on a tightrope. I was afraid to say anything, but I couldn't help it.

"Angel!" I ran faster and faster. I couldn't catch my breath. My face felt hot. When I got close, I slowed down and panicked. I approached with more caution than I was used to. I was so exhausted; trying to say something reassuring in this moment was so far beyond me.

She spun around in my direction. I gulped down spit into my dry throat and tried to take another deep breath in. I thought how in this one second, my life together with Elise would be drowned below us forever. The only Elise left would be in the form of stories, living memories, told by me and her mom. Elise's mortality had never been clearer to me than right now. The impermanence of our relationship, and of life, was belligerently stabbing me in the heart.

"Hi," she said calmly. So calm that it was eerie. I couldn't make out her facial expressions. It was too hard to see through the flares of the setting sun. In the background, the orange glow of a winter sunset wiped away the horizon behind her body.

I went a few steps farther to see her face. I had to get closer. Close enough to see her, to feel her. I needed to witness the granular contortions of her face. It was like reading tea leaves. I knew she was in pain. Not physically—her brows furrowed, and I knew she was deep in one of her analytical black holes. I'd had a solid track record of pulling her out of these since we'd met. I tried everything I could. This wasn't the time to hold back. I let my heart pour out to save her.

"Sweetheart..." I entered her personal space as gently as I could.

"Why are we doing this?" she asked me.

"What do you mean, my love?" She shrugged and looked at me.

"It just feels too real now." I eyed her. Was she testing fate? Challenging it?

"It is real, us, all of this." I tried using logic. It didn't seem like it was working.
"I don't want it to be real. It's a funny thing." She didn't finish her thought.

She looked over the edge at the oozing river in the concrete trench below, leading all the way out into the Pacific Ocean. She dipped her foot down below the railing on the other side. She slipped. My heart sank. She managed to catch herself out of luck more than skill. My heart was beating so fast I thought it was going to pop right out of my chest and explode blood all over the concrete.

She turned again toward me and fell forward into my arms. It felt so good. The relief.

Her body against mine made me feel like we were going to make it, together. Parts of her exposed skin between her clothes touched my skin. She started to cry against my shoulder, her body contorting into me.

"I'm a failure. My dad always said I would fuck things up."

"Your dad didn't know shit. He didn't! Look what you've made for yourself."

Elise looked up and saw the sun continuing to set over East Los Angeles. She took my hand in hers and calmed herself down with long, deep breaths. Her tight grip loosened and I felt her come back into our shared reality.

I reached out with my free hand, pulled her in, and kissed her with intense passion. She kissed me back, pushing her tongue into my mouth.

We made out until the sun fell, and the chemical coloration in the sky faded into night. The darkness cooled everything down quickly. The smell of sulfur from the retired oil fields below dissipated, concealed by the cool air temperature.

Walking back to the apartment, we still held hands. We were becoming one again—our rhythms aligned and each step was symmetrical. We were silent most of the walk back, just listening to the vibrations from inside the heart of the city.

"Thank you for saving me, again." I looked at her and then held her closer to me.

"You're my girl."

"Yeah, well, your girl is a mess right now."

"You are still perfect. Perfect for me."

"I love you, Kyle." She said it half-heartedly. Maybe she was just exhausted emotionally, but I just didn't feel it. The hair-bending, goosebump-causing words were not there. I took it in anyway. I knew she was going through her own internal battle, and this wasn't really the time to explore the meaning of love.

"How long will this last?" I didn't know what she was talking about. "Me being so depressed?" she continued.

I didn't know how to answer that question. Depression wasn't something she wanted to admit was rooted in her permanently. A genetic mutation inside of her DNA. She wanted to believe she was this fun-loving, free-spirited gypsy. I preferred that she was so insanely deep that the slightest words she spoke seemed so complex. It was her soul that I embraced and supported in her endless internal battle with herself. I always cheered for her to win.

I hugged her close to me when we got into our apartment. I knew it was better not to say anything. We were home. I needed to be supportive and cherish her without driving her away again. Then Elise pulled away and went into the kitchen. She poured almond milk in a pot and put it on the stove. She warmed it and then took it off, poured it in a mug, and put two heaping spoonfuls of wildflower honey from the farmers' market into it.

She was back to being herself, cupping her mug with both hands by the window, staring out. Her hands were always cold, and she needed the hot milk to bring her whole body back to a normal ninety-eight-degree body temperature. Her hands looked almost purple, standing by the window. Her skin was bleach-white, almost like she was a ghost.

I couldn't help thinking about the next day. I was laid out on the couch, feeling antsy. I had a nervous twitch in my left eye, a muscle spasm that happened whenever I thought too much. It was underneath a scar from an old bar fight, and I always figured the nerves had been damaged below the surface of the skin. Elise would make fun of me and kiss it when it would twitch uncontrollably.

"I'm going to stay with you tomorrow, baby." I thought about it and really didn't think I should leave her in this fragile state.

"No, Kyle. I'm fine now. I know this means a lot to you. It means a lot to me, too."

"Really? I swear, I can stay. I don't care, I just want to make sure you are all right. We can cuddle all day, watch movies. Whatever you want."

"I'm happy for you. For real. It's a big opportunity."

Elise wandered over toward the bedroom. She passed by the couch and leaned over and kissed me softly over my left eye. It was her "I'm going to bed, come soon because I can't fall asleep without you" kiss. I was deep in thought, and I knew it would escalate the level of all the whirling questions if I joined her now. After she walked by, I could still smell her perfume, and the scent of her skin. It clung to the air around me, and her presence had never felt so strong and still so invisible.

The thought soon passed, and I opened my eyes. I had fallen asleep and was still on the couch. "Oh, fuck, what time is it?" I looked outside of the windows to see the light was barely visible, and it was raining. I looked at the time on the kitchen clock. The bright-green numbers were blinking twelve, which meant the damn power had gone out in the middle of the night. I went into the bedroom and saw Elise curled up on my side of the bed. She was holding one pillow tightly to her body like it was me.

The clock on the wall was still battery-powered and read 6:30. *Good. It's early.* I crawled in bed behind Elise and wrapped my arms around her for a minute. I didn't close my eyes. I didn't want to pass out and miss my first day at the new job. I hesitated again, thinking about leaving Elise. She seemed so peaceful, and I wanted to believe in my heart that she would be fine.

Just in case, I did what I never thought I'd do and called Elise's mom. She didn't answer, even though she was always up early. I left her a message asking her to check in on Elise. I didn't tell her the details, because I knew Elise would be pissed at me, but at least I felt better knowing she could be there if Elise needed someone.

So, I got up, made a pot of coffee, and went downstairs to jump on one of my motorcycles and head over. Early bird catches the worm type of thing.

66

Taking the freight elevator down to the basement was the better option in the morning mist. I slid open the wood, sealed the plank doors back up, and went down to the bottom floor. My motorcycles were always in shambles. One missing handlebars, the next without a tank. I kept at least one that was running fine. I decided to take my Shovelhead. I'd tried to make it look like one of Harley's newer models by painting the tank matte silver and adding chrome, but it still looked like a Mad Max special.

I pulled the choke on and kicked it a few times, and it started up. The exhaust triggered a car alarm in the garage. "Fuck! How about that wake-up call." The neighbors who bothered to put their car alarm on in a gated underground lot deserved it.

I peeled out of the building and onto Second Street. The rain was light and the road was slippery. It never rained here. When it did, a fucking nightmare happened on the road. Everyone drove like morons anyway, so add a light mist and the shit hit the fan.

Flying through the Second Street Tunnel underneath Hope Street, the exhaust of the Harley sounded good. Third gear was a little sticky. The pipes started to heat up. It warmed the inside of my right leg. The smell of gasoline and oil burning in the air while traveling over sixty miles per hour was unlike anything else. I was navigating these mundane channels of life, but by the other side of this tunnel, I would have a new life, a better one. I would finally make money. My spirits were high.

The meeting with Michael at the hospital had opened a doorway. I wanted to provide for Elise, be a man. I'd never had a role model for what a father should be like, but if we had kids, I'd be a good one. I knew that much, and it felt so fucking brilliant to know what having a purpose felt like. I let go of the clutch a little quick, and the bike almost jumped into the car from the opposite direction that was making a left turn.

I pulled up to the building where I had seen Michael get into his car. The gate was still locked. *I must be early.* I waited and kept the bike in neutral, just in case it didn't start again on the next kick. After a few minutes, a van pulled in; the gate stayed open, so I shifted into first and pulled in. I parked near the front entrance of the glass building. I could see people inside. The commotion made me feel good, like I was in the right place. The building was in a lot worse shape than I remembered. The iron gate was nearly falling off the hinge. There were large cracks in the stucco that were filled in but not painted over. Maybe it was just the morning light that illuminated all the blemishes covering it, or because I'd been in a state of panic the other night when I'd first seen it.

I took off my helmet and gloves and went to the front. I expected the door to slide open, but it didn't. I saw a call box with a scanner. I placed my thumb on it. Nothing happened. I wiped the moisture from my finger and tried again. Still nothing. I noticed a small button and pressed it. I didn't hear anyone answer, but the door opened.

I went into the lobby. There were a few modern chairs and an old, ratty sofa along the wall. The place smelled weird.

It was a mix between sterilized hospital equipment and the musty air of dirty baby diapers. The interior was even more worn than the outside of the building. There was a huge leak coming from overhead in the corner. It must have been there awhile, because it had stained the crème-colored ceiling panels a rusty brown. Underneath the dripping water was a Home Depot bucket to catch the rain. It was nearly full.

The reception desk was covered in an array of lights behind the dated glass squares popular in the 1970s. The luminescence from behind the glass was cool-blue and felt more like a cigarette advertisement.

"Sign in, sir," a voice behind the counter said.

"Oh, yeah, sure."

"Name?" she requested and stood up. She was taller than I'd expected and had on thick glasses. I could hardly see her eyes through the bottlecap lenses.

"Kyle, Kyle Whalen." She scanned the other adjacent sheet for my name.

"Here you are. Please sign and date these forms. The signature pages have all been marked to save time. Once you're finished, Mr. Bartelsman's assistant will be out to get you."

"I'll just sign them right here. Don't want to be late. You know, first day and all."

"Not to worry. I recommend you look over the forms, especially the release ones and the nondisclosure."

I didn't really care about what I was signing, but I still took her advice and decided to look over the forms.

Even with the leak and spackle all over the walls, this place was more legitimate than any kitchen where I'd ever worked. There was real opportunity here, getting in at the ground floor. I wanted to tell the receptionist that, but didn't want to come across like a lowlife. Probably better to take the forms and sit down. I did and quickly marked up the pages. A few of the pages had disclaimers about "voluntary conditioning" and "preparation" for the portal. Those were the only things that stood out. The rest seemed like typical legal jargon and I didn't really think it meant much other than that I was able to carry out the responsibilities of the job.

When I was finished and about to stand up, a cute Asian girl in a lab coat came out.

"Mr. Whalen." She had spotted me.

"Yes, that's me, the one and only."

"Great. I'm Annie, Mr. Bartelsman's assistant."

"Cool." Realizing it was unprofessional, I corrected myself. "It's a pleasure to meet you."

"Thank you."

Annie led me down a few other hallways behind automatically sealed doors. "You can wait in his office until he arrives and orients you with the daily routines."

"This must be where all the top-secret experiments go down," I joked.

"Can I get you something to drink?" She ignored my humor.

"Coffee would be excellent." I was speaking in a misplaced surfer tongue. It didn't even sound like me. I was nervous.

"OK, coming right up. Do you want it black or with cream?"

"Cream, thanks!"

I waited in the office, sitting upright in his faux-leather club chairs. I could tell they were fake because my skin stuck to the vinyl. Michael's office was a stark contrast to the rest of the place. It looked more like an archeologist's office. Someone who had been traveling the globe collecting all types of tchotchkes and organizing them in an abstract narrative. He had a large drawing on the wall that looked like a huge circle with a couple Tesla coils scribbled in the middle. The paper it was drawn on was yellowed from years of wear and exposure to light. It was straight out of an archeological dig.

Annie was back in minutes, before I had the chance to browse around any further and look at the different artifacts so distinctly displayed all over the shelves.

"Thank you. Whew! I needed a little extra boost."

"Not a problem, number nine three si..." She stopped abruptly.

"I'm sorry?"

"Oh, nothing. Mr. Bartelsman will be in by nine o'clock."

What she said made me unnerved. But then it passed. The coffee tasted exceptionally good, maybe too much cream but the beans were roasted perfect. Didn't have that sour or burnt taste you normally got in the cheap Folgers roasts that I bought from the grocery store. I was a big Folgers guy, too. It was a consistent brand. Probably not all fair trade and locally roasted like this cup of coffee. These were super-bitter artisan grounds.

Michael finally walked in. He was rushing around and then paused when he saw me. He leaned forward and shook my hand. He was wearing the same style of suit as when I'd met him. He looked identical to then, like a perfect replica of my memory. Same suit and same gold cross lapel pin.

"You made it," he said, surprised.

"Didn't think I'd show?"

"The bets were against you, but I'm glad you did."

"You guys remodeling?"

"Ha! This building is old. It used to be a hospital. You're right, though. It needs a bunch of upgrades. Most of our dollars go straight into R&D and equipment."

72

"Gives a new meaning to industrial." He laughed and then started flipping through the paperwork his assistant Annie put on his desk.

"I see we have all your paperwork. Do you have any questions for me?"

"What exactly do you guys do here?" The question had been eating at me since I'd arrived. It looked medical, but not anything like what you'd expect from a real hospital or laboratory.

"You read the pamphlet I gave you, right?"

"Oh, yeah, of course." I didn't hesitate. Even though I pictured the book sitting on top of the toilet paper holder.

"Well, do you believe in past lives?"

"Hahaha! Really, man?" I paused and stared at him in the eyes. He wasn't laughing. "Um, sure, I guess."
"What if you could travel back in time? Do the things you never got to do? See the loved ones that you wanted to make things right with? A chance to start again."

The picture he painted sounded amazing. I was skeptical, but remained open-minded. I probably should have read a little bit from the information he gave me in the book.

"What's the catch?" It also sounded like total bullshit.

"No catch. It's just not proven yet. So, it's not based on fact. Everything we do here is experimental, to push the envelope through innovation."

"Sounds a little sketchy. This isn't the moment where you tell me this is an organ-harvesting clinic or something, right?" I wasn't totally sure, so I half-jokingly had to ask the question. Elise had planted the idea in my head.

"Of course not! We do everything aboveboard here according to modern medicine; we are just opening the door to new dimensions. In fact, we think we have discovered a way to cross over, like a portal."
"Holy shit! Are you fucking serious?"

"Are you sure you read all of the info I gave you?"

"OK, you got me. Not the whole thing. So, you're serious?" I redirected the questioning.

"I am. It's called a wormhole. Imagine if there was another layer of reality that people couldn't see with the naked eye. Maybe it's the dimension of God or the Devil, for all we know. We have proven it exists, and now we want you to tell us what it looks like."

"Are you bullshitting me, man?"

"No, I'm not."

"Sounds cool and all, but how long until I get back?"

"We just want you to take a short look inside to the other dimension."

I nodded, but I was not convinced. It seemed unbelievable. I thought about it for a long minute. I thought about Elise. How proud of me she would be.

"This job better pay a shitload," I said.

"We are a very well-funded organization. In case I didn't mention it before, we have an important group of private financiers. We will take care of you handsomely by the end of this, you have my word on that."

"Can you be more specific? Is this hourly or a big chunk?"

"Let's say five thousand a week to start."

"Holy shit. Seriously?" That was more money than I'd made in a month.

"Yes."

"All right, let's get this party started."

"And who knows, you could save the world... I'm kidding," he said with a funny smile on his face.

It was a crazy notion, but I was so intrigued. I had to know what was on the other side. Now the curiosity was eating me up. It was probably a bunch of bullshit, but who cared? If they were going to pay me to take a quick look around, then what the hell. Could I go back and fix all the mistakes I'd made in my life? I thought of Elise and all the things I would have done differently. God, I loved her so much I wanted it to always be perfect with us. It never was, and now I could fix that. I could go back and totally change who I had become. It was a second chance, like being born again. I could do it right with her, so she wasn't so depressed.

In walked a beautiful woman. Her thick strings of black hair pressed so straight and coiled up into a neat bun on top of her head. Her eyes were hard to see behind the thick lenses of her tortoiseshell-rimmed glasses.

"Ah! Doctor Jessica Rosen. Perfect timing."

"Hi, Kyle. I'm going to be here for you every step of the way."

"Then I'm in good hands." I felt possessed by her stare.

She looked at me curiously, but in the same way a predator studies the movement of another animal.

"We have a lot of ground to cover, but we'll start as you get closer to going into the other side."

"Anytime, Doc."

"Here. Take these." She handed me what looked like acid gel tabs to hallucinate.

"What are they?"

"They'll make this whole process a lot easier."

"OK, fuck it!" I threw them on my tongue. They absorbed right away and I washed the residual film on my tongue down with a little bit of coffee.

"So, I get paid every two weeks, right?" I looked at Michael. I focused my attention on the job.

"Sure, we can do that. If you have your banking information, we can set up a direct deposit now. We can also mail a check to the address you put here on the forms."

"Yeah, mail a check. I've had minor problems with my bank. I'll probably switch banks anyway now that I'm going to make solid money."

Before I finished the cup of coffee, I started to feel a little nauseous. *Should've eaten something this morning*, I thought. I continued to sip down the brew.

"I feel weird."

"Don't worry, Kyle. You're in good hands."

Then, my vision started to get blurry. The room started to spin, and that was the last thing I remembered.

PART II

CHAPTER 6

I watched the overhead lights pass in succession. Each light had the same luminescence. The repetition felt like a primitive form of hypnotism. I was sleepy and barely conscious. The hallway looked just like a shitty version of the hospital across the street. I had an itch on my nose. I tried to lift my hand to scratch it and couldn't move it. I looked down and saw it restrained by nude-colored straps with silver rivets and leather. They were locked down tight. I couldn't move any limb on my body, including my head. It was also strapped down to the gurney.

The bitter taste of coffee and a chemical-residue aftertaste was still on the tip of my tongue from the drugs. I saw the doctors and nurses on all sides of me, pushing me down the hallway. I tried to speak, but the words didn't come out. My internal dialogue was running rampant, but the muscles in my jaw wouldn't expand to form the words. I could feel the drool starting to leak from the left corner of my mouth. One of the nurses wiped it with a blue paper towel.

"Hey, hello. I'm not ready," I mumbled, the words barely traveling past my lips. More drool came pouring out, and it dribbled down my face and fell on the pillow.

We went through double doors accessed by a security key card. I heard the beep chime after the card was scanned and the steel locks clicked and released. It was loud and metallic.

The medical professionals, or whatever they were, spun the front of the gurney around and pushed me through the last door of the hallway. The room was lit by a few spotlights on stainless-steel tables in the center. *It's a fucking operating room. Holy shit!* I jerked around and used whatever was left of my muscles and attempted to escape.

I thought about how I was going to slip out of there and get access to a phone and call Elise. I pictured myself grabbing one of the nurse's phones from their pockets and calling her on the landline at the loft that rang through the old phone mounted on the beam in the middle of the room. I could see her answering it—she cried when I told her what was happening.

I felt their hands underneath me. The nurses and doctors transferred my slack body to the table. The reflections from the surgical instruments gave off a reflection like a solar flare. The doctor grabbed my arm and twisted it so my palm faced upright. I felt a sharp sting in my wrist as a pneumatic device inserted an object underneath my skin and cauterized the incision.

"I better get a big Christmas bonus!" I blurted out in a slur. None of the personnel hesitated in their next motion. It was like I didn't exist to them.

The intravenous line into my arm was cold. I could feel the fluids being fed into my veins. My blood was pulsing, and I couldn't escape.

I wanted to get the hell out of there and feel the sun on my face again. Let my beard grow, just to rub my hand on the stubble with the California sun glowing down and beating against my skin. Another night of binge-drinking and flying up the coastline on a motorcycle, the air burning my red eyes and the tears dripping down my face as I ripped past eighty on the speedometer. With my girl Elise on the back, wrapping her arms around my waist. That was all I needed right now. My girl, her body pressed against mine. The simple contours of her body so intelligently designed that led to her very core. It was a map I used to follow with my hands past each turn and every bump. It was my happy place, and it would make Elise contort and moan sheepishly with pleasure when I would lick between her legs.

Time started to pass slowly. I woke up day after day and endured the same routine in the lab. The days started to become endless and time didn't have a beginning or an end. It was impossible to discern how long I'd even been here now.

Those days with Elise seemed distant, and faded into a cemetery in my head. I didn't know how long I'd been here; it could have been weeks or months. Right when I got close to having a memory seem real again, a white-coated scientist shot me up with another serum. I knew it entered my bloodstream when my left eye twitched, my eyelids felt heavy, and the light blurred. When I looked out again, I didn't remember who I was anymore.

I didn't even remember my name until they reminded me of it. Saying my name with the last name first felt unnatural, and on my wrist was the remains of the cauterized incision. It had keloid and was raised above the skin as thick beads of a scar. I didn't think they wanted me to forget my new identity or place in this experiment, or maybe they just wanted to keep track of me. I did know why we were here—it had to be for the portal Michael seemed to get so excited about back in his office.

"You will now be starting the program. You may not know what is real and what isn't," a voice dictated through an earbud shoved deep in my ear canal.

They lifted my arm up and scanned the microchip in my wrist. It activated and projected a green spiral image. The doctors eyed it. I leaned up to look at it, too.

"It's your DNA helix."

"Fuck." It's all I could say.

"We can track changes in your strands—think of it like a new age hospital bracelet. We have all your info and data number nine three."

"Six." Yeah, I remember.

"Whalen, Kyle."

There must be others. I knew I couldn't be the only one, just based on sequence alone. There had to be a number one dash something, plus a long barcode, too. What they did with him or her, I had no fucking idea. I hoped it wasn't a cyanide bath at the end of this, if I didn't complete the experiment. What if one of the higher-ups here decided I wasn't responding well to their treatments? Shit, they might as well fill the next syringe with a formulation to permanently turn out the lights. I wouldn't know the difference. I finally gave up.

I submitted to the journey.

I remembered going to the first day of the job, but something seemed different. I remembered sitting down with Michael in that artifact-filled office. The pitch to be part of the experiment was legit. It didn't seem like I was going to be operated on. I used to not really care what happened as long as I got paid, but now I was scared I'd never see Elise again and live my normal life. Now, if I walked out of here with all my limbs still attached and the good part of my brain working, I'd be fine. I'd be able to buy Elise and me a house. Go for the whole white picket fence thing. That fantasy seemed so fake now, and my only mission seemed to be to figure out how to get out of here.

I woke up screaming. Mostly, "Elise!!! Baby, help me. Help me!" My cries went unnoticed, and if they lasted for longer than a few repetitions, the injection to make me sleep came quickly at the hands of one of the technicians.

I didn't even know if I was in Los Angeles anymore. The bright light above me could have been alien mothership beams taking me up into outer space—instead they were just bright bulbs that never went off.

I didn't sleep, not even when the lights went out. The silence started to speak to me, "Come with me, Kyle. Don't be afraid. Come find me when this is over and you can see the end in sight."

It was a demonic voice, too, one that was deep and guttural. The voice didn't stop until the lights came on the next morning and one of the guys in lab coats checked my pulse. His hand was cold and clammy. My oxygen level must have been low because he put a pressurized nosepiece on me to aid my breathing. The tubes were uncomfortable, but had become part of me.

I felt more mechanical than human now.

I planned to grab the scientist and choke him to death in between bed rotations and sponge baths. If I could get him close enough before the guards were called, I would hold a syringe to his neck and use him as my human shield to get out of this place. I just didn't know if I'd be able to function again—you know, work within the rest of society. I might offset the balance, or maybe they were infecting me with a contagious virus that I was going to spread all over. "Nah! Doesn't make sense. They wouldn't go through all this for an experiment that freaking basic."

"What was that?" the scientist responded.

"Oh, I didn't say nothing." He looked at me strange and grabbed his clipboard and started to make a few notes. It was hard to distinguish between my interior thoughts and the words that came from my lips.

"Hmm. Hmm," he muttered and went back to his beaker of clear liquid.

"You take all those super important notes? Here's one, 'This liquid diet you have me on here gives me serious indigestion.'"

"You can't have any food in your system when you go through the portal," he said.

"Well, when does that fun little slice of the experiment finally happen? I think I've been patient enough."

"Please remain quiet, Whalen, Kyle." There he went again with disorderly name-calling. They treated me like a cell inside a test tube. They pricked and prodded and when they got this molecule talking back, they seemed confused.

I started yelling, "I'm a human being. I'm a human being! You can't treat me like this. Fucking psychos, motherfuckers, give me a break. Pay me what you promised and let me get outta here." The injection came and all went quiet again. My vision was milky. I could still see the light up green hologram with my analog identity and DNA.
They studied the manipulations in the visual projection of my cellular composition.

I woke up again. The scientists were scurrying around. Seemed like one of the other specimens like me had gone all crazy and died on them. You could only push a person so far before they totally snapped. Maybe I was their prized patient because I had the highest pain tolerance. Surpassed the others and reached a new threshold. It could also be that I was next on the list to die in the portal.

I hadn't seen them kill anyone, and I wasn't sure what the scientists did with the bodies, but they disposed of them in a medical way, that was for sure. Or maybe once they went into the other dimension they never came back? Or maybe they went into the incinerator or worse. I never wanted to be burned or drowned. Any other type of death seemed cool with me.

Feeling isolated while you were still around a shitload of people was worse than being all fucking alone. You had no effect on their reality, and yet felt controlled by their mere presence. All they did was administer drugs; a robot could do that job, probably save them a couple bucks.

A few times a week, tours of people wearing these matching polo shirts would wander through the dingy lab and hover over me. They had matching symbols, a cross or similar, slightly modified, on their chest over their hearts. It was the same little pin Michael always wore on his suit. They were probably the ones who invested in this place. They walked so robotically, like they were all in sync with each other.

Every couple of days, Michael would show up in the lab. He was the only one who would talk to me. He would ask me how things were going, and if I was excited about going into the other dimension. He assured me it wouldn't be much longer. I thought it would make everyone feel more comfortable if he didn't visit. It was better they didn't look at me like a human being, but Michael did. He gave me hope. It was better to just remain another test subject who had desperately volunteered to the mercy of experimental scientists.

The only reason I looked forward to seeing Michael was that he was always accompanied by Doctor Jessica. She would spend time with me after Michael would leave and we'd have a session. The sessions would last forever. It was the only time I felt free again.

"I loved our session last night Kyle. A lot of pain was released."

"Yeah, I don't remember, but I feel better today."

"I'm sure you do." She wrote a few things down. Shined a light into my eyes to check the dilation.

"I think I'm ready."

"I'm going to give you medical clearance today."

"Then can I go home?"

"No, then you're ready." She made another annotation and then squeezed my hand before walking off.

I sighed. I didn't want to go in anymore. I wanted to leave.

They sure as hell didn't have to keep a twenty-four-hour watch on my ass. I was totally affixed to this table, might as well take a couple deadbolts and screw them through my shoulders into this gurney.

The main room was quiet today. The train, as I called it, because it was a white pod that took me to the video screen, was faster than usual, too.

I noticed there were only a few of the other regulars—you know, one through eight—on their beds. "Where's everyone else, Doc? They get vacation for good behavior?"

The doctor was in his late fifties, wore scrubs and thick horn-rimmed prescription glasses, and today didn't have much of a sense of humor. He shrugged off my sarcastic poke.

"Well, fuck me. When is my vacation again? I think they scheduled it for next month, but that really doesn't work for me." The doctor eyed me again, but still didn't respond, and it was getting irritating.

"I have this thing, you know. It's a big thing that I gotta do with my friend—it's with my wife."
The doctor finally looked at me for a prolonged period. "But you're not married," he said.

"Shit, you're right. I almost forgot. I was just checking to see if you guys knew anything about us and our real lives."

"Remember, you volunteered for this?"

"Did I?"

"And we all see you with Dr. Rosen."

"What the hell does that mean?"

"All that time you spend."

The scientist I called "Doc" shook his head, realizing he shouldn't have answered me and revealed their depth of knowledge on the subject.

"You wanted this job. Remember?"

"Yeah, yeah. I remember. But there's been a change in the program. Listen, Doc, don't you worry. I don't think I'll be getting Stockholm syndrome any time soon. You're not that likeable of a guy. So, wipe the sweat off your brow before it drips down and fogs up those spectacles."
He listened to me and wiped his brow. I thought about what he said earlier about Dr. Rosen, I did think we had a kind of unexplainable connection. The thoughts passed quickly, and the urgency to get this experiment done and back to my life kicked in.

"Hey! I was about to be married. Does that count?"

"Does what count?" He looked at me and took another sample from just below the surface of my skin with a scraping motion.

"If I were married, then they couldn't keep me here, right?" I saw Elise. I could picture her, only her hair was much longer, her super-long blonde locks in a French braid. It was a perfect image to inspire me to distract me from this hellhole. She lowered her hair down to me and I took it and pulled myself out of this place.

"I heard you can get out of here for good behavior."

"All right, that's enough."

"I'll take double doses, man. I gotta get out of here. See, the love of my life is waiting for me right now."

"I'm sure she is."

And that was that, the most I was getting out of this square. I really wanted to know where the hell everyone had gone. It was never this quiet, and I'd gotten used to the constant prodding from the scientists. I was addicted to the shots; the one following the second blood taking of the day always gave me a rush. It also meant it was TV time.

They put me on another one of the underground trains through the tunnels. This ride was bumpier than usual. Felt like something was messed up mechanically. I figured it was magnetic, but that was probably too futuristic. It finally stopped. The air lock popped and the seat raised my back up. The arm restraints were the last to open. I was excited to go watch the tube. It wasn't the normal sitcoms I was acclimated to. There were all these caves that looked like catacombs. Next thing that happened, there were all these bees flying out of it. The bees flew right at me and started crawling into my nostrils. I could feel them crawling up my nose and into my mouth, the buzzing vibrating inside, humming and revving.

When the image stopped playing and returned to a vibrant star-filled sky, the bees stopped and there was nothing on me, or inside of me.

The images were still so real that I felt the bees' little toes tap dancing on my upper lip before entering my nostril. They were so thick, I constantly coughed and tried to heave them up. Nothing ever came out, but they made me watch the same video almost every other day. The other video didn't compare in the realism, but produced a similar claustrophobia. That was a whole 'nother story, but I did look forward to seeing images that resembled normal things from the outside world. I speculated that it was all prep work to get me ready for time travel in this portal, but the images didn't seem relevant at all for time travel.

The images looked more like Ireland or a pastoral landscape than a city. It was all plush green. It didn't look anything like the concrete of downtown LA. It was open and there was the sound of water. You didn't hear fresh water in LA unless your toilet was running. The closest you got to flowing water was the LA River, but that was a river of sludge and the waste of the residents of Los Angeles and neighboring cities. There was a lot of nasty shit that went floating down that body of water and out into the Pacific Ocean every day.

When the video stopped, I could see what looked like the portal. It looked just like the drawings Michael had on the wall of his office. There were huge gold rods with diamonds attached at the points. Inside was a swirling ball of light. It was like bright white DNA strands overlapping one another and spinning. I felt a sinking sensation in my stomach. Partly from excitement, but mostly it was a deep fear, and I started to sweat.

A couple scientists watched it closely and took pictures while writing notes. They seemed to be studying the patterns, or just trying to figure out what was on the other side—where this portal led.

Getting back into the tunnel, an eerie, flashing photographic strobe washed us with light. The capsule that hovered through the tunnel must have used magnets, I was now convinced, because it was dead-quiet. The capsule glass raised with hydraulics—it was automated and blew off the extra air from the internal compressor with an extended *whoosh* sound.

The blinking strobe light was nauseating. I just had to stare at it. I was sweating, still choking on imaginary bees and trying to track anything that resembled time. I just wanted to know what year I was in. How many days had I been preparing for this crazy leap of faith? Hopefully, I'd stacked up quite a fat paycheck. "Tell me... is it Sunday today?" I asked the blinking strobe. I didn't get any type of response. The chamber sealed and washed me with iodine and powder that smelled like bleach.

The bed was cold. Had I been gone that long? The fabric sheets felt like paper on my skin. I nodded to the scientist that I was ready for more testing. He didn't need my consent, but I felt better knowing I hadn't lost complete control. I just wanted real shit to happen—give me a bionic arm or something cool; don't force my mind to do all the heavy exercise. I was ready to go into this other dimension. All this prepping, all these tests seemed a little overkill. The expectation was so hyped up, now I was crossing my fingers that this wormhole or portal thing they'd found really worked. After seeing it, it was a little more believable.

Mind control got old when you were aware of it. I kept going, processing, reading the shit they told me to and not falling into the unconscious end—where I wanted to just quit and die. It would be so much easier to walk into the parallel world of death than face forward, take the injections, and keep my head on with none of the adventure

Michael had pitched me on. The other side. That was what I wanted to see.

The lab technician wheeled me down the hallway to the OR. The room was sealed behind five locked entrances, and by the time I got to the fifth my eyes were so heavy I could hardly remember where I was until I was back out with the rest of them. The right front wheel on my gurney was loose. It was squeaking and sounded terrible. The repetition made my whole body tense up in anticipation of the next turn.

"Doesn't anyone have a can of WD-40 around here? It would sure make this go a whole lot smoother." I never got an answer.

"OK, fine. Well, next time can I upgrade to first class? I know you got those extra-padded memory foam gurneys. You guys probably have races on them while we're all asleep."

I saw that we weren't going to the OR. We were on the other side of the portal from the video area. *Holy shit! It's finally the moment where I get to go time traveling.* I wondered if I was going to go into the past, to a certain date and time, or if it would send me into the future with other crazy new inventions. I was nervous-but-excited. I knew this would bring me closer to getting home to Elise. *I hope she's getting all my checks.* I knew she'd be so happy. I could finally take care of her like I'd always wanted to. That was important to me.

"Let's do it, Doc! I can't wait to get in there." He checked my wrist with the scope before wheeling me closer to the entrance to the portal. I could almost feel the energy pulsing from it.

"Shh!! What the hell is that?" the white-coated technician said.

"Holy shit, Doc! Are you talking to me? I thought you were a mute this whole time."

"No, shh!! Do you hear that?"

"Nope, quiet as fuck. I don't know. Wow! First time we get a chance to have a civil conversation and I run outta shit to say. Sorry, I'm a little excited."

"Wait here. I am going to seal you in and check it out."

"Don't do that—we can have good conversations. Talk about normal shit. How the Dodgers are doing or whatever."

"Be quiet. I'll be right back."

"Doc, don't leave me, damnit! At least unfasten these straps and push me into the portal thing."

"You're coming with me." He wheeled me quickly down the hallway and let go behind the second air lock. The scientist scurried out of the doors and ran to the middle of the room, where he joined the rest of the staff, who looked intently at the center of the roof.

He fucking left me there.

Right when I was only twenty feet away from finally completing this job. I could see the damn thing. The carrot dangled in front of my face and was pulled away at the last second.

I inched the gurney along by gyrating my torso up and down. I got a little momentum, and the gurney headed full-speed right at the portal. It crashed into the wall at first. It was hard to turn it. I had to push back against the wall with my feet. I kicked away and then I heard someone coming down the hallway screaming, "Go! Go! Get out of here!" I didn't see anyone, but gave one final full-body jerk toward the portal entrance. I closed my eyes and held my breath. My breathing cadence got slower, and I felt weightless from the excessive oxygen and nitrogen being pumped into my lungs.

I twisted and turned my body. I felt free, suspended in a different world with black-and-white dots around me. My surroundings looked like the pixilation on an old television set when there was no cable station. The sound of pulsing white noise was so loud I couldn't stand it.

I tried to make out any image in the static. The monochromatic pixels turned into a zigzag of crossing lines. There were no discernable images other than a face I didn't recognize swirling inside of the fragments. I heard trumpet sounds, muted and fuzzy.

The face felt eerily familiar, even though I couldn't figure out whose it was. My heart beat faster and I grabbed hold of the arms on the chair.

"I know you," I said aloud.

CHAPTER 7

I came flying back out of the portal. The zigzags and chrome pixels were gone. A cosmic mouth of metallic stars had regurgitated me back into the lab. I guess the other dimension didn't like my flavor and spat me out. A blaze of fire blasted through the roof of the lab, igniting the scientists into a cosmic inferno. A few of them in the direct line of fire were incinerated immediately, and their flesh melted off; I watched them crumple onto the floor behind the glass.

"Holy fucking hell! Here comes the goddamn Rapture." I held my breath and waited to feel the heat creep up my hospital gown and singe my face. I counted backwards from ten. "10, 9, 8, 7, 6, 5, 4, 3..." I opened one eye and peeked around. There was nothing around me. Nothing was moving, and there wasn't a soul in my immediate sight.

Everyone was dead or gone and I was basically free, which was cool, but I had no way of getting out of here. The smoke was billowing through the lab—it was getting sucked through the tunnels and trying to escape to find oxygen. I was so excited I could hardly breathe, but the smoke was going to kill me.

I was still strapped to the table. I shimmied my torso up and down, trying to get free, using my hips to pop the gurney into gear and get it rolling in any direction except a standstill. It was all I could do to get moving away from the fire. The over-gyration of my hips caused the gurney to move at an excessive rate toward the heat. I crashed near the epicenter and steered with all my weight to another desk. Crashing into it, I held still and felt the fire on my side, singeing my flesh.

I reached my hand into the flames, hoping it would ignite the cloth-and-leather restraint holding my wrist down. I lifted my head off the pillow and I could see the leather boiling. My flesh was melting with it, and I had an uncontrollable reaction to scream in agony, but I couldn't get any sound out. The time I'd spent here had made me feel nothing; I was numb. I let go of the pain until I felt my hand come free. I lifted it and put it under my back to extinguish the flame. I unstrapped the rest of the restraints using my teeth, and just like that, I was free.

What that meant, I had no fucking idea. I was willing to find out.
Heat from above continued to pour into the lab. I dropped to the ground and grabbed the concrete floor. It was cool. I crawled, scuttling, tracking the cold with my mouth. The cool air flowed in—it surrounded my tongue, coiling around it. I glanced up to look for a break in the thick clouds of smoke; there was nothing but gray billows. "The whole lab is fucking gone," I yelled out. I continued clawing along the floor, searching for one of the tunnels.

A loud beeping was continuous. It sounded like an alarm, but it wouldn't shut off. I was suddenly paralyzed, and started drooling from the high-pitched frequency. My mind kept trying to communicate to move my hands, but they were unresponsive.

Finally, one of them started moving in a spasm and I followed, doing a bear-crawl as fast as possible in the direction of the tunnel. Smaller explosions were occurring all around me; a fifty-gallon drum spilled chemicals in front of me, sizzling on the floor, turning a metallic blue. I crisscrossed around it and moved into the darkness. I could feel the cooler air coming from the tunnel. *Almost there.* Rolling forward into the tunnel, I landed hard on the pavement below the tracks of the transport cart.

The transport cart was in bad shape. The glass capsule on top was shattered, and there was safety glass all around me. "Fuck it. Let's see if this baby still has juice left in it." I searched the wall blindly, feeling for the box that engaged the cart. I'd watched them turn this on a million times, but I just had to find it. My eyes filled with particles of debris as I opened them for a split-second. I spotted the red-and-green push buttons on the silver panel only a few feet down. BOOM, engaged.

I pressed the green button and jumped down into the tracks. The cart knocked into the side of my shin, and I fell right into the dismantled capsule. I ducked down to avoid the layer of smoke that was filling the tunnel. My eyes were sealed; I rubbed them, trying to get the thicker pieces of dust and ash out to stop them from tearing. It only made it worse, and the stinging sensation returned to my eyes and the sides of my face. My hand was swelling, and the skin was bubbled up on my wrist. I wiped it on the gown, and the puffy scab layer peeled right off onto it.

"Aaaaah, fuck, that hurt." My own skin, stuck to the remains of my hospital gown, looked fake, like globules of burnt bacon. I glanced up to see if there was any end in sight. I'd never taken the transport to the end of the line, and since it was on magnets, it was hard to tell where you were on the track. I recognized the sign for the video conditioning center, because I knew it was right next to the wormhole portal. The train kept going.

Please, God, Jesus Christ, whoever is listening to this... get me the hell out of here. One piece, with my soul attached. I'll do anything. Hail Mary, Trinity, Brothers, Sisters.

My prayer kept repeating in my head until the train halted abruptly. There was nothing around me except darkness— pure, cold air. The thick, stale air filled my nose up, clogging it and making my breaths irregular.

I made it to the video center and jumped out of the transport vehicle. "AAAAAHhhhhh!" I couldn't help myself—I had to yell. I fell to my knees and kissed the ground. If I died in this cold dark tunnel, no one would care. I wouldn't ever be found until someone excavated this place in an archeological dig. I'd be a relic, an artifact. My bones would be put in a museum and shown as 'Time Traveler Volunteer' or a venue more scientific. I didn't really know or care at this point. I cared about surviving and doing whatever was humanly possible to get out of here.

I felt along the wall for any differentiation in texture, but nothing stood out. There was no way out of this chamber, and going back sounded worse. The smoke started heading my way, filling the tube of the train as far as I could see. The thickness of it was baffling, flooding, colluding, the thick chunks of particle mass forming gray fogginess. The moisture from the heat and the thick dust made my skin sweaty with ashy white-and-gray soiled mud. I wiped it off so I could still see the burned skin, the fleshy red exposed below the pinkish hue of my arm. I decided to count down again and searched for another prayer to say, but I was out of idols to worship. I knelt and pushed my face to the ground to suck in the last cool breath of oxygen before choking down another gulp of smoke.

As my lips kissed the silty ground in praise before I choked to death, I felt a metallic sensation against my upper lip. My lip was the first part of my body to contact, and it felt industrial, not organic. I shoved my hand on the spot that my lip was still touching and it was metal, an iron bar. My hands moved quickly, nails digging into the gravel to clear the ground. "It's a fucking grate!"

"Praise Jesus." I didn't know who else to thank at this point.

It was time to dig my teeth in. Not literally, but just get this thing up as soon as possible. I grabbed the grate, and slid my fingers inside the interlaced, thin steel bars. It was stuck to something; without hesitation, I scurried across the floor to find the train. I yanked free the clipped-on fire extinguisher and started blasting it everywhere. It cleared a path for me to walk back to the grate. Six paces straight back and one to the right. I started to smash the base of the extinguisher into the grate; it barely moved.

"Fuck this." I jumped on the grate.

I kicked as hard as a man who was fated to die could. My enthusiasm increased my breath, and my breathing was exacerbated by the faster pace of smoke pouring into my lungs.

"Damnit! Give me a fucking break," I pleaded, but it wasn't helping me get out of here. *What a way to go out.* It just didn't fit, though. *I need to get above ground. Suck in actual air and just take a look around.*

"Assess, access, and execute." The words were like a magnetic tape playing on a loop in my head. *Did they play this during the weird video conditioning?* I couldn't figure out when or where I'd heard this before, but it repeated and repeated. I tried to turn it off in my mind, but it wouldn't go away.

A noise started to rumble down the cavern. I knew it wasn't good. I ducked down, but before I could, I was thrown by a blast of concrete against my stomach. I felt the floor cracking below me, and suddenly I was tumbling down into the emptiness below the grate, along with thousands of pounds of debris and concrete.

It was freezing down there. I couldn't see a thing—my burns felt better, but my ankle was throbbing. I looked down and couldn't see it. I hoped the bone wasn't sticking out, and I ran my fingers down my leg. No liquid feeling— no blood, that meant—but the heat of my limb and the size of it meant it was busted. No telling how mashed the bone was in there. It didn't goddamn matter now because I was stuck right where I wanted to be. Below all the smoke and heat from the fire, and I was out of the lab, in the trenches of the earth. A place where I felt much saner than in that cage.

I rolled down the rocks, and then hobbled to a corner where a dim reflection came off a puddle of water. The sound of the water was so pure, freeing, and trickling; I could feel it inside me, making my blood move to the same rhythm. The drive to breathe fresh air, and above all to see Elise one more time, motivated me to keep going. It was easier to lie down and die, but my love kept me alive. There was another voice in my head that wouldn't let me. It just told me, "Survive. Survive. Survive."

There it went again—the looping. The endless white noise mixed with my own voice saying things repeatedly. It was like a bad chorus to a song that got stuck on a record and the needle wouldn't get past it. I pleaded inside my own mind to let the thought go. If it got me out of here and into the normal world again, then maybe it wasn't the worst voice to hear. I'd take it, if that meant I got to go back home.

The Instinct to live persisted. The thoughts were fragmented. They were lost and torn between the present horrible circumstances where I was spelunking through the earth, and the memories of Elise and me drinking and fucking.

I dragged my bum leg and walked down the dark cylinder, the water running over my feet. It was lukewarm, but felt so refreshing. I didn't know what kind of chemicals were mixed in with it, nor did I really care at this point. I needed to follow the one substance I knew would lead me to the outside: water. I bent down and cupped my hands and scooped the water to put into my mouth, until I saw an oily residue in the water and let it trickle out. I felt so dehydrated; the dehydration tightened my face into a smirk. I scooped up more water. I almost drank it.

"A little Gatorade would be nice right now." The word *electrolytes* sounded so foreign and luxurious at this point. I begged the world around me to let me know it again, and quench my thirst.

CHAPTER 8

For days I crawled. I crawled along with the rats and the smell of rank sewage through an underground cavern. It was only inhabited by the nocturnal. They survived where no one else could—their senses keen in the darkness, no reliance on their sight, just instinct. I tried to adapt, to learn their ways. They passed me quickly when I slept. I waited for them, counting the seconds and listening for their scurrying sound to hit the moist ventilation blowing through the chamber.

The thirst and hunger pains that grew inside my belly were wrenching. I bent over in a fetal position to try and stave off the pain of the hunger. The smell of rotten sewage made it worse. I wanted to cup the water in my hands that was flowing through the tunnel and drink it, but I could only imagine the deadly organisms swimming in it that would surely kill me, if dehydration didn't kill me first.

I heard the rats again. I tracked their sounds in the tunnel, the scurrying noise that predicted their presence. I heard them; they were moving swiftly in the pitch-black. With the echoes, I could hardly make out if they were heading toward me or away from me. I suddenly lunged out with my hands and snagged one. It bit my hand incessantly in small, miraculously painful bites that cut to my bone.

Its squirming made it hard for me to get a hold of its body, then I slammed the creature against the tunnel. It stopped squirming and twitched a couple more times. I grabbed its head and twisted it off. I felt the warm blood leaking and running over the burns on my hand. It felt good. I knew I might catch something from the parasites in its blood, but it didn't matter. I was planning to eat it raw, so it was my stomach that I was worried about, not the diseases lurking in my blood from encountering the gooey critter.

The fur was thick and got caught in my teeth, but soaked up a lot of the sour taste of the flesh. There was hardly any meat on its feeble body.

"This tastes like shit. And my luck, I grabbed the only skinny one." There must have been plenty of trash to eat down here; I wondered why he hadn't been fattened up. *Is he more like me? Deprived and then sent out into the darkness?* I thought about his purpose and compared it to mine. Down here, it was kill or be killed.

The carcass was nearly picked clean except the bones and the face and tail. I figured the amount of meat and organs I had ingested should at least tide me over and fill a space in my stomach. Next time I would have to differentiate the sounds to hear one of the big, juicy ones thumping by.

The energy from the morsel was enough to get me through another long stint down the tunnel. The tunnel seemed like it was never-ending. It must have run under the whole goddamn city. From utter exhaustion and lack of nourishment, I gave in and curled up in a ball and shut my eyes.

My dreams were more like I was awake and sleepwalking in a nightmare. I watched these demonic creatures wrap themselves around me. I saw flashbacks from my life, my childhood where my mom was bringing meatloaf and steamed carrots to the table. Only in the image, all my old friends were there at the table, holding their knives and drooling—they were filled with rage and had reddened beady eyes, their bodies mutating and contorting into vicious, wild beasts. Their teeth were sharp, and they continued to invade my space until they had been absorbed into me.

"Holy shit!" I reached around to grab something, but nothing was there.
When I woke, it was cold and my skin was covered in goosebumps. *If I don't get out of here soon, I'm dead.* I tried to get my body repositioned to continue to crawl. I didn't know how many days I'd been crawling through the underbelly of the city, but I was praying that mercy would find me.

I heard the scurrying; it sounded like they were close. I had better grab another one. I turned to grab, and a force unlike any other surrounded me. It was water flowing through the tunnel, and it sucked me into its ball of liquid like amniotic fluid. It took me and my lungs filled up with water. My eyes closed and my mind stopped thinking.

I opened my eyes and there was trash and broken industrial machines all around me. I was at the base of a sewer outlet. The world had changed.

I had been flushed out to freedom, "Thank the heavenly merciful. I'm back, holy shit." *Damn, it feels good to be alive.* It all felt different; the air was humid but still felt fresh on my skin. It was like being born again. But everything was different. There was a certain luster that was gone from all of it. The colors were softer, more dismal and grayish. It felt deadlier and much grimmer. As weak and delusional as I felt, I knew I needed to keep my wits and be ready for anything.

I wanted to reintegrate, go grab a beer with my girl, and celebrate the freedom of the simplicity of being, just existing. But something told me that wasn't going to happen.

I sifted through the crap around me to find something of use. There wasn't much but rusted computer parts, and then I found a real beauty. There was an axe. An emergency break-in-case-of-fire axe in decent, rusted condition. "Where in the hell did this come from? I mean, who would throw out such a perfectly good axe?" I grabbed it and tried to tuck it into my soaked hospital gown. That wasn't going to work. I took off the soggy gown and tied it around like a belt. I slid the axe in it and was ready to get on with it.

"Elise, baby. I'm coming home for ya." I paused and looked around at everything.

The place didn't look like I remembered. It was a whole other dimension.

"No, this place isn't right."

I climbed up a concrete embankment. It had been partially destroyed, the loose rocks falling past me as I climbed farther up. The horizon line was starting to show. The tops of the buildings vanished. A few of the skyscrapers

remained   downtown
—the rest destroyed, a few of them still burning. The smoke had formed its own layer of atmosphere around the dilapidated city rubble.

Los Angeles was nothing more than a wasteland.

The weirdest damn thing wasn't the utter devastation, but the lack of movement. I couldn't see any people. Nothing, not even a car intact, motoring through the debris. The only things still moving were the corners of orange flames tucked away behind the remnants. This wasn't how I'd left this place.

I'd convinced myself while I was in the lab that everything up here was fine. I'd convinced myself that nothing had changed. Over and over, I'd said to myself, "When I get out..." and I would finish the phrase with a million things I wanted to do. Even something simpler and more basic, like getting a burger from the new place down the street, to telling Elise I loved her more. I had a problem doing that. I always felt too vulnerable. Now I wanted to scream it at the top of my lungs and let everyone know.

"Elise. I love you, baby!" I let it out. The tears started to flow. It felt good, freeing, but harder to feel any true meaning behind it anymore. Would the words be lost now, or would I ever get to use them on her again? *Use them on her.* Like they were an incantation to bring her back closer to me.

I remembered the shower glass breaking. A shooting pain from the sound went off in my head like a high-pitched concussion grenade. It hurt throughout every inch of my body.

"What in the hell is that?" I looked around. I couldn't determine if the sound inside my head was real or caused by the memory of the breaking glass and Elise in the hospital.

I thought about the way Elise cupped her hand under the faucet to get water whenever she was thirsty instead of using a bottle, her coy smile from behind her sunglasses, and the way she kissed me. I thought about the way her tongue teased mine to get into her mouth and latch on so we couldn't let go of each other. I wanted to crawl into her spirit again and kiss her all night, reassure her that I'd never go anywhere and that we could be together forever. This fantasy was so good that I knew it wasn't real.

I let go for a second, and the repetition of words came back.

"Go and find her. You must find her." I nodded and looked around for anything else I could use in the mountain of waste I was traversing across.

My body ached. I could feel a numbness traveling up my left leg and noticed a large piece of glass stuck in it. I pried it loose. A stream of blood spurted up onto my face. I licked it. Then I leaned over and ripped off the bottom of my hospital gown that was already in tatters. I tied a makeshift tourniquet. My hand was shaky from the burns.

I walked with a limp. My hand was throbbing, but I was alive. I could heal.

The only thing to do now was track down my life that I'd left behind. I didn't know if anything or anyone remained. My girl, my love, still emerged as a priority above anything else. I wanted to see her, Elise. I made my way down the rest of the sliding concrete and began the walk into the center of this diabolical frontier.

I started thinking. *Maybe when I went through the portal, I went into another dimension. This has to be the future. How many years later?*

CHAPTER 9

My old street in downtown was ravaged. The signs were gone. I only recognized the remains of the corner building. The lot was still there, but the building was melted. The steel protruded like bones and the exterior scattered all over in clusters of rocky debris.

The oil fields down from my place next to the First Street Bridge were still standing.

"They must be made from heavy metal, man."

I saw something moving. I jumped and pulled out my axe that was still being held up by the tied and tattered hospital gown, which fell to the ground. I was naked, holding my only tool for survival. I waited, looking for any sign of impending doom. I prayed that I'd see Elise—her face familiar and beautiful like it used to be—but I knew this wasn't the same place it had been before. I couldn't discern if any of this was real.

I approached carefully, like a hunter. I didn't want to disturb my potential prey, but if anything, I hoped for another human being. I still felt the need to know I was not alone. That felt more necessary than food.

"You, stop, come back here!" I saw a man, covered in grey ash with a long beard. He scurried away under the bridge and out of sight. There was no way I could catch him.

"Looks like I'm not the only one left in this fuckin' place."

My head didn't feel right. I kept getting these weird pulsing images. The visions were biblical images of the Rapture, burning buildings crumbled to the ground, and trash scattered all over the streets.

Human civilization had gone into hiding. Then, from behind one of the oil derricks, came a horse engulfed in flames, burning and running disjointedly down the asphalt, trying to put out the fire. The more he moved, the more the fire burned. He slowed down. I quickly picked up the remains of my hospital gown—it was still moist—and threw it over the horse as he got close to me. He lowered to the ground, and my touch calmed him as the fire went out. The charred gown slid off of him, and he was burned pretty badly. We both had similar burns on our skin.

He leaned his head over to me, my vision still blurry, and licked my face. He then got up and ran off clonking down the street, wounded but alive. He staggered before turning and heading away from the oil field. I didn't know if the image was real, or one of the white horses they said you'd see when the Rapture came. I suspected they had discovered the key at the lab and had somehow known this was what the world was going to become. Whether the horse was real or a prophesized symbol, it all felt so real to me.

I could see the Los Angeles River from the other side of the bridge. I figured it must be where all the life that was left wandering around the city had camped out. It was a source of water, even if it was contaminated.

I continued to my building. It was the only one on the block that seemed intact. The exterior was covered with streaks of char, but the structure looked solid. I crept up the fire escape. I got to the third floor and looked inside for squatters that could put up a fight. No sign of anything alive inside. I used the end of the axe and scraped away the remaining glass edges from the window into my place. I flipped the lock and slid the window open. Then I went in, scraping my leg on the glass fragments—minor cuts compared to the rest of my body.
"Saving that horse almost cost me my family jewels."

My apartment was covered in asbestos soot, yellowish and chalky. It was hard to discern the dimensions of the different rooms with the unicolor layer. I went into the bedroom and found stuff packed in boxes.

Elise must have known about the disaster, and I guess she'd figured I wasn't coming home. I started to open the boxes, and halfway into the first one, I realized that these weren't any of my possessions. "What the fuck is going on here! Where's my shit?" I couldn't believe it. She must have moved out. This was another poor dude's place. He was gone now. *How long was I in there?* I couldn't get the thought out of my head. During the time that had passed while I'd been in that lab, being conditioned and treated like a specimen, I'd lost my whole identity on the outside.

I dug through more of the boxes and found old clothes. I sifted through a few shirts and found a clean flannel. It was red and black and seemed warm. I threw it on, and then I found a pair of jeans. "Yeah, these will do just fine." They were a little tight, but better than nothing. Felt good to look like a civilian again. I slid open the closet and there was a pair of old-school paratrooper boots. "Perrrfect." I threw them on. They were beat-up and worn, but they'd work. I zipped up the long side and it locked my feet in place.

I hoped that under the shoes I'd find my buried treasure. Sure enough, right there under the shoes right where I'd left it—it was my safe! It was still there beneath the laminate wood floorboard covering. It was untouched and sealed shut. I spun the dial and remembered my combination perfectly, ingrained in my mind, the numbers 8-8-33. It clicked and folded open. There was my .45 Glock, ammo, and a box with all my private shit in it and a Zippo lighter. I smelled the lighter and the fluid had all evaporated out of it.

"Fuck yes. This'll do serious damage when needed."

The gun and little torch might come in handy in this spot. I opened the shoebox and inside were all the letters from Elise.

Her picture was on top of it, blowing me a kiss. It was from the day we'd gone and had a picnic in Echo Park after going to the Grand Central Market. We'd grabbed so many different types of food. It was amazing. I remembered the day so well.
We were in Echo Park on a date. We had so much fun day-drinking and vintage-shopping. It was the day I'd asked her to marry me on the pedal boats. It had just felt right in the moment. She'd laughed and thought I was kidding. I meant it. I meant it more in the way you believe you're connected spiritually deeper than any contract. We had this bond that felt sacred. We were soulmates. She knew I didn't have a

ring in my pocket. The spontaneity of it and honesty was still such a beautiful moment I wouldn't change for anything. We didn't believe in government contracts or formalities. We celebrated tradition and shunned the bullshit of social pressures.

We knew our love was eternal because the connection was so sincere, we glowed from it.

We were bound to be together in this life and the next.

My heart felt different from the testing, the drugs; it beat in a different rhythm. *Maybe it was passing through that fucking portal that messed all my organs up.* My love was the same. I folded the picture and tucked it into my shirt pocket on the flannel. It fit snugly against my chest. I liked having her close to me again. "I'll find you, angel." I touched my chest, rubbed the picture over the fabric. It was my own personal talisman.

I put the gun in my waistband. It fit securely in the tight pants. I heard my stomach growling. I went into the kitchen. The cabinets were knocked off the wall. I checked below the counter and behind the lazy Susan. Elise used to love that thing. She'd said it was the best invention from the 1950s. "It sure beats the atom bomb," I would respond. She would laugh.

"Fuck, I miss your laugh, baby."

I was dying of thirst. I turned the faucet and rusty water followed by sludge poured out until it sputtered and stopped to barely a trickle. I searched the cabinets and

116

found a couple of plastic bottles of water. I drank one and it tasted like heaven. I stashed the other one in my bag.

I dug around and sure enough, in the far back was a stash of canned food. The cans were untouched. "Bingo!" I grabbed them and flung them out onto the floor.

"There's gotta be something to pop these babies open?" I checked the drawers... nothing. Not a single fucking thing. I guess I was lucky to find the cans of expired pinto beans and garbanzos. They would stave off the wrenching pain in my stomach and prolong the time before I had to resort back to eating sewer-dwelling rodents.
The thought was comforting. I grabbed my axe, lined up the edge, and *thwack!* I knocked the end of the can right off. The beans spilled out onto the floor. I spooned them up with my hand back into the can. I brought my meal into the bedroom and looked around for any other useful items.

I found a backpack and checked the contents. Inside was a homemade first aid kit with supplies: Band-Aids, bactine spray, matches, and a hand-crank radio. I sprayed all my wounds with the stuff, even my face, wiping it with gauze to get the crust from all the smoke off it. I used almost everything up. My face felt weird—I hadn't shaved in days, and I had a beard. The hair felt foreign. The alcohol in the spray stung on the pus from my hands. It numbed them, though, and that felt good. The Band-Aids were too small and made for tiny scrapes and cuts, not severe burns. So, nothing worked to patch them up.

I hesitated to crank the radio for fear of what lay outside. "I'm not sure I want to know. What the hell?" I cranked the handle against the friction. I wound it for a minute or two and pressed the button: nothing. I tried to fiddle with the knob on top to change frequency. Still nothing, "Eh, fuck it." I tossed the busted radio and slung the pack over my shoulder.

I heard a noise. It sounded like a rat scurrying down the hallway. I grabbed the axe in case I needed to take a swipe at it. The scurrying stopped right outside the door of the apartment. I heard sniffing from an animal. *Probably a hound of Hell*? I slid behind the door and waited for the creature to enter. *It probably smells the damn beans I spilled.* I saw the bean mess on the floor and figured it'd go straight for the food remnants.

It was clawing at the door. I reached over with my left hand and turned the handle, opening the door a crack. In came a little mutt with scraggly hair. The dog looked mangy and had a mohawk. I let him walk over to the beans on the ground and lick them up. "Hey, buddy," I called out. It spun and opened its mouth full of nasty teeth. "Be cool, pup. Those are my beans." The dog just looked at me and continued to lick up the beans until he was basically polishing the floorboards. I slipped around the side of him. His focus was purely on consuming every morsel. "I know how ya feel." I was sympathetic to the dog's cause. I grabbed another can of beans and used my improvised opener, the axe. The beans slid out, and I poured them in a pile and gave the pooch a whistle.

He turned and started to open his mouth again to show his teeth. He saw the pile of beans and tucked his teeth behind his gums. "C'mon, fella. Get over here and have the fresh ones." The dog was still reluctant. It was probably because I was standing over a can of beans holding an axe behind my back. I took a step back and put the weapon down. The dog came over and took a sniff, then went to work on the refried beans, devouring them like he hadn't eaten in weeks.

I could feel my own food starting to digest and for the first time in months, or at least if my memory served me, I was genuinely tired, exhausted. I went into the bedroom and ripped open a few of the boxes. I took the newspaper and stacked it underneath the cardboard as a mattress. There were a few towels in a box marked "Bathroom." They were small, but would work to cover me up and give me warmth through the night. I tried to turn on the sink. Sludge came out and then trickles of brown water. It was no good for drinking, as I figured it was contaminated from whatever had happened, but it felt good to wash the dirt and burned skin from my hands.

I went to check on the pup before crashing out. He'd devoured all the beans and had a shit-eating grin on his face. He wandered over to me, licked my hand, and went and lied down in the corner of the living room. There was trash and debris and that was a good enough bed for him. I locked the front door just in case the next scurry wasn't a pup, but a beast or street-wanderer looking to steal from me.

Lying down, the cardboard felt soft. It beat the mattress on the gurney in the laboratory without question. I shut my eyes.

CHAPTER 10

I woke up sweating. My face was covered in perspiration. I couldn't really remember my dream. The pup was curled up on my feet. He must have gotten cold in the night. There was no sun shining. Just a dismal glow that was giving off warmth through the remaining shards of glass in the window.

I rolled over and tried to go back to sleep, but there was a loud banging outside. It sounded like crackling. Even with nobody around, there was still no peace and quiet.

I got up. The dog stayed sleeping. I went over to the broken window and looked out. The partial building across the street started to crumble to the ground. The debris spewed all over the street. "I have to get the fuck out of here." My old place might be a haven for the nights if I needed it, but it also might just collapse into dust. I had made it this far. "I'm not gonna go out like that."

My mind ached and now I remembered my dreams from the night before. I had been here in this apartment, before the explosion. Everything had been normal, except there'd been this man trying to kill me. When I looked in the mirror it was me, trying to kill me. It was a different version of myself. The guy had this feverish grin on his face and was drooling. He was coming at me with different objects in the room, like a lamp, trying to attack me. I found a wine bottle and hit him over the head. He fell back and I shoved him through the window. He tumbled off the fire escape and was holding on tight to the railing. I turned the bottle upside-down and clonked him on top of the head. He smiled at me weird, then let go and fell to the pavement below, the red wine pouring all over. It was hard to distinguish between the wine and the blood coming from my doppelganger's head.

I'd woken up after that traumatic dream and it was like I'd been sleep walking, because I was looking out of the window to check and see if the body was still there, but instead at the base of the fire escape was this woman, a woman I'd never seen before. She had long black hair and was holding a book.

"Hey! You. What are you doing there?" She turned and ran off. It was good to see someone. I wished she'd stuck around.

The kitchen was filthy, but I still went in there for a bite before I explored outside again. I cracked a can of corn. I ate it and whistled to the dog. He came in slowly until he saw the food and his eyes got bigger.

"I have to give you a name, pooch. Chico. How about it, Chico?" He came over and chowed on the corn. I gathered up my shit from around the place in case I never came back.

I checked my flannel and took out the picture of Elise. I gave her a kiss and put the photo back in my pocket. I was ready. "Let's go see what's on the other side, Chico." He was done eating and followed me down the hallway. He knew his way better than I did around the building after it had been partially destroyed by fire.

The stairs were totally unusable. I walked to the end of the hall to the old-school freight elevator that worked off a manual crank. I checked it out to make sure the cables were attached to the top of it. It looked safe enough.

I slid the wooden slat doors open and stepped inside with one foot, putting my weight slightly on it to double-check its stability. I jumped in, and Chico followed me. The crank was tough to budge. There was no light in there, so I used my hands to guide me. I was used to surviving in the darkness now.

I felt another latch—it was the lock. I undid it and we plunged down a few feet. "At least this thing works, Chico." I undid the latch and held on to the crank. I lowered us down a few floors until we bottomed out on the basement. The abrupt landing jolted my knees, and I almost fell.

I took the Glock out and cocked it, loading a round into the chamber. Lifting the wooden gates, I listened closely. I couldn't hear a damn thing, but I was prepared for the worst—zombies, anything. All the apocalypse-talk over the Mayan calendar made me think we were going to see corpses rise from their graves and the earth split in two. So far, all the schools of thought about the future had been dead fucking wrong. Then I heard something that sounded like running in the darkness. It was coming straight at us. Chico was growling. I aimed the Glock and fired relentlessly.

"Bam! Bam! Bam!" I couldn't stop blasting in the direction of the sound.

The flashes from the muzzle lit up the hallway. I didn't see anything. There was no blood on the wall, nothing. And even weirder; there was no body. I could've sworn there was someone there. I checked the clip in the Glock and realized I'd unloaded the whole thing on it.

"Shit." And with nothing to show for it.

I kept the Glock if needed, but the axe would now be my primary weapon.

I looked around again. There still wasn't any movement, and I could barely see a damn thing. I got on all-fours next to Chico. We went in together; I crawled. I felt around on the floor and realized it was covered in trash. I gathered up a few pieces, anything I could get my hands on: newspaper, Styrofoam, and a roll of toilet paper. I crunched it up and dug in my pack for the matches. "I hope these little babies still work." I struck one and it illuminated the room for a split-second and went out.

The peek I got of the garage revealed a few cars and nothing else. I struck another match, and it stayed lit long enough for me to make out the dimensions of the garage and ignite my paper stack. The stack was engulfed in flames and started to burn quickly. I could see the door and ran over to it. The iron gate was jammed. I took the axe and wedged it in between the lock; it clicked open as the light went out. I pushed and the door screeched. I continued to roll it back into the wall. Light came pouring in. It wasn't daylight, but it illuminated the whole garage.

There were a couple cars still in there. A minivan and an old Jeep Cherokee with the wood paneling on it. *Not the most reliable.* I tried the handle on the minivan first, but it was locked. I grabbed the axe and used the end and busted out the window. I checked the inside for keys, no luck.

I headed to the Cherokee to see if it had hidden keys before I started the hotwire job on the van. As I was walking over to the car, I spotted some tarps in the corner. I flipped them up and there were a few motorcycles.

"Sweet." None of them were mine, but there were a couple of Harley-Davidson choppers half-finished, and a gem: a 1976 Triumph in fully restored condition. "What a beauty." It was much nicer than my old bike. This would be a shitload easier to wire. I checked the tank to see if there was any gas. The tank was half-full. "Not bad at all." I looked around and found a garden hose attached to a valve. I twisted it just in case any water came out. No luck. I took the hose and cut the metal end off of it. I sat on the bike and pulled the clutch and pushed my left toes down a few times and up once to make sure it was in neutral. Then I kicked the stand up and rolled it over to the minivan, opened the gas tank, and shoved the hose down deep. It ate up a few feet of hose before it hit the tank. I started to suck. I managed to siphon a few gallons of gas. The fumes almost made me puke, and I got lightheaded after I accidentally swallowed a gulp.

I jammed a piece of metal shrapnel into the ignition switch on the Triumph and turned it like a key. No light. I flipped the sit cover open. "What a smart son of a bitch." The previous owner had disconnected the battery so it didn't drain out. I reconnected the terminals. The light was green. I pumped the throttle a few times and jumped with all my weight on the kick-starter: nothing. I pumped the handle again, trying to feed it more gas. "It's probably dry as shit in there." I jumped down, and a beautiful sound spat out of the exhaust. It wasn't tuned right, so there were a few misfires. I tightened the screw on the carburetor and it increased the idle. It sounded better now.

Chico was in the corner ripping up a carcass of an animal. It could've been a cat, but I had no idea. "Chico, you stay here until I get back, pup." He looked at me, turned his head sideways and continued to ravage his meal. I would have loved to have my companion, but he'd be better off here until I got back. And I didn't want to disturb him from his meal.

I engaged first gear and ripped out of the garage onto the street. There were still fires burning on a few rusted cars. The dust in the air made it hard to breathe. I pulled my shirt up over my nose. It caught the tears from my eyes; even squinting, it was still hard to see. I didn't know what I was looking for, but intelligent life would do just fine. There was no sign of movement until I reached Palms.

There was a hand-painted sign made from red paint on a large piece of sheet metal that read, "Bohemian Grove." It was right beneath a line of palm trees still standing. I didn't remember seeing the sign before—it must have been added after the city fell into chaos.

Each of the buildings was still partially intact, and I saw gangs of kids in rags scatter into the shelter of debris as I rode by. They looked ravenous; it wasn't the best place to stop. "These street kids could be cannibals."

At the end of the grove of half-dead palm trees was a flickering, red neon sign. The dust in the air made it hard to read. The closer I got, the more I could make out the words "Café Revelation."

Thank god. This was one of the benefits of being part of the human race. Even at the end of the world, we still found a way to make alcohol, congregate, and get wasted together.

"Perfect." The sign was affixed atop a large set of multiple Airstreams and fifth wheels soldered together with big metal stitching to make a complete building. The front entrance was the nicest of the Airstreams. It had streaks of polished silver, but its luster was still lost behind a layer of grime. It looked completely out-of-place amidst the rubble, like it had come down from outer space and just plopped down in the middle of this shithole.

"I sure could use a real fucking drink."

I circled around the Airstream to look for a safe place to park the bike. *With all these savages creeping around, my bike would be a damn trophy.* I found a spot for the bike right behind the Airstream. The back of it was part of a larger building, enclosed mezzanine, purely a façade for us lowlifes still looking to booze it up during the end of humanity.

I turned the bike off and left it in the start position because I had no key to shut her down. I removed the negative wire from the battery, in case one of these scavengers tried anything stupid, and kept the change in it.

I wasn't sure what I'd find inside. I slid open the heavy steel door. The smell of ethanol and hashish hit me. *My kind of place.* The essence was liberating—the stench of people having a good, old-fashioned time. A Genesis song came on. *I fuckin' hate that song.* The people in the bar barely moved when I walked in. They were either completely shitfaced or dehydrated. The bartender looked in good spirits.

"Howdy, friend, you looking for something?"

"I sure am. How about a pint of that moonshine I smell?"

I was ready for something strong. I sat down at one of the empty bar seats. The guy brought me a small jar instead, filled to the brim with a yellowish alcohol. There was debris floating around in it, but I didn't bother to investigate.

"Whaddya want for it?" He looked at me, surprised. Had I said something wrong?

"We don't take anything from Riders. You guys drink for free at this café." I figured he was referring to my motorcycle like it was a special sign, or they really liked bikers at this place. Either way, I didn't object to drinking for free.

I took a sip. "Oooh. That's good." The alcohol was so potent it burned all the way to my heart. My veins started to pump and dilate in my arm from the warmth that pulsed through me.

"You want to see the light scope?" the bartender said. I didn't know what he meant; I thought there was something lost in the translation.

"Yeah, show me the scope, man."

"The name's Ezra."

"OK, Ezra. Thanks."

He took the light with the scope and shone it on my wrist. I turned my hand over and the implant under the incision started to project the symbolic light language. It looked like a radar pulse, and the symbols of green light were similar to abstract Chinese characters. It wasn't my DNA strand anymore. It had morphed into a specific type of coordinates.

"You got it, or you want to write it down?" I swallowed deeply and looked at the symbols. They were changing form before my eyes. I was fascinated by it. I kept my cool so as not to upset the balance here.

"I... I got it." I didn't know the significance, and I didn't know if I wanted to right now.

I drank down half of the jar of alcohol and started to feel buzzed, but not too drunk. I was still clearheaded.

"You Riders are all the same. Look at me like we've never met before. Suits me fine. I'm just another one of the sheep. Baaah!" he said and walked away.

A hand touched my shoulder. The touch was soft. I looked at the pale hand. I turned and there was this woman standing there. She was entrancing, like a doll that looked like it had a soul, staring into my eyes, reading my mind. "Come with me. I need to tell you a secret."

I hadn't been with a woman since Elise. It felt weird. It was wrong, I could feel it inside, but I needed information. Anyone willing to talk logically to me at this point was worth the risk. I didn't want to break my sanctity, my bond with Elise. She never liked when I talked to other girls. But I was not sure this was just some girl. Something inside me compelled me to walk blindly and follow her.

This girl was bizarre; she walked aggressively, like she knew each step before she took it. "Good luck to you," Ezra said and nodded at me. I nodded back to him and turned my attention back to the girl.

I could swear I recognized the girl, too. Her long black hair—she seemed so familiar. It was like I'd known her in a past life. A life we'd shared together. Maybe we were lovers, or maybe enemies.

"You want to talk?" She agreed with her eyes.

I grabbed the rest of my moonshine and walked to the back of the café with her. I started to notice how toned her body was. She was athletic and her hair was so black and straight it ran down past her waist. She was pretty, but tough. She'd been battle hardened. We sat down at a table in the corner. She faced me.

"Let me see your hand."

"You going to read my fortune?" I said sarcastically.

"No, I'm going to show you it." I was curious, so I gave her my hand. She flipped it over. The symbols were still there but fading fast.

"Cybernetics."

"I've seen that shit before, but not like this?"

"It's their language. That's how they communicate and how you get your orders."

"But I don't speak that code."

"You're not a Rider yet. I know that, but they don't. We need to go somewhere private."

"What's your name?"

"Epiphany." I paused.

"I got a bike out back." We got up and headed outside. She took my hand in hers; it was coarse and felt like sandpaper. Callouses lined the base of each of her fingers.

We walked up to the bike and a scumbag was trying to start it. He was trying to kick-start it with no luck. I tossed the remaining mug of moonshine to the ground. The guy saw me and shifted the bike in neutral to get it rolling.

I didn't hesitate. It was like I'd had years of military hand-to-hand combat training. I slid my axe out from my belt;

spinning with all my force, I slammed the blade into his stomach. I hit him so hard he went hurtling off the back of the bike onto the ground. He fidgeted around trying to get up for a few minutes before becoming almost motionless in a pool of blood. It was hard to watch him lying there, still moving.

"End it," she said. So I did. I took another big swing and hit into his heart.

I was nauseous. I stopped and stared at the body. It felt too easy to take someone's life out of necessity. It was all-too-easy to execute another man, but I felt a disgust and gut-wrenching sensation inside of me that was pure. I was more fascinated than remorseful as he took his last breath on the cement.

After my adrenaline slowed, I couldn't help but feel the guilt. It hurt me, twisting up inside of me. I felt sick to my stomach, and I threw up some bile in my mouth. I could taste the alcohol mixed with stomach acid. The sour taste made me feel worse about what I'd done.
The world was primal in this future, and I'd acted like a savage. The rules seemed simple: kill or be killed. But the more I looked, the guy trying to steal my bike was just a boy. He couldn't have been older than sixteen. The smeared dirt on his face made him look aged. Underneath the grime was just an innocent boy. A tear leaked out of the corner of my left eye. I felt for this kid. I created a story for him, a normal life, and I thought that his family must be missing him. He'd grown up in the San Fernando Valley and had had a good mom and a hardworking dad. When the

explosion hit, he'd lost them, and now he was fighting for survival, and worse, now he was dead.

I would never be the same now. It was like going through puberty into a fucked-up, merciless adulthood.

"He would have done the same to you," Epiphany said.

I looked at her and then at the ground where my motorcycle was lying. My bike was scratched, but nothing major was broken. I lifted it up onto its kickstand. I connected the battery cable, screwed down the bolt on the clamp, and got it started after a few kicks. Epiphany jumped on the back. We tore off.

She pointed and held my waist tightly. Her grip felt good on my stomach. I followed her lead. "Where are we going?" I asked.

"You'll see," she whispered in my ear. Her breath was warm and felt nice on my skin. I hadn't felt human contact that wasn't for the purpose of experimentation in a while. It sparked something in my core.

Her pointing guided us through the empty streets. I pulled back on the throttle and we took off down the remnants of the 10 West Freeway. The left-side carpool lanes were destroyed, caving down into the sewer tunnels below. We flew past the mounds of dirt that used to be the California Incline. The concrete columns were scattered in heaps of ash.

We reached Malibu. It was different there. There weren't any of the wandering scavengers—it was quiet. It looked nearly untouched, like nothing had ever lived here. All the homes washed into the Pacific Ocean. The water was so dark and saturated their roofs.

"There, over there," she said. We jumped off the bike and walked down the sand to a large enclave of red-and-brown-colored boulders.

"This looks like Mars," I said.

She shuddered. "Are you cold?" I wrapped my arm around her to keep her warm.

"These are the moon rocks," she said, and we climbed up them. We sat in between two large boulders sheltered from the wind.

She was gorgeous, but strange. I just wanted to get answers from her, so I played along.

She climbed up on top of me, her face directly in front of mine. "You know what you have to do, don't you?" I wasn't sure if she meant have sex with her, or some other meaning. I believed more and more in my new reality, becoming aware that this really might be the end, and she and I were here to save the world.

"I can't tell you. It's fate, you know." She looked at me, paused, and then wrapped her legs tighter around my back like a clinch knot. I could feel every crevice of her body against mine. I was turned on, but I kept thinking about Elise. Before my loyal thought finished, her tongue was inside of my mouth. It felt cold, almost mentholated, and she used it well. I tried to resist, but it was no use—my

134

body was acting independently of my mind. It felt so good to connect with another human. To feel some type of physical affection, but she pulled away from my lips. Then she turned around and looked at the sea; amidst the debris, something was moving.

"What the hell is that?" She looked at me.

She kissed my eyes. "A timekeeper." I was confused until it started to spout water.

"It's a whale," I blurted out, shocked to discover sea life still existed in the toxic ocean.

Epiphany nodded. "They follow the meridians of the earth. It's the only way we can track time anymore. I come here to see them to determine the month based on where he is."

"I don't know what you mean, but I believe you."

"It's getting cold. We're going to need a fire." I was intrigued by her knowledge of this new reality. She knew how to create some consistency, some reference to the old structure of society. Something as simple as time and how to survive in it. My instinct was to protect her. To keep us both alive.

"Now, I'm freezing," she said.

I looked at her. Her face had turned a shade of purple.

"I'll be right back."

"Please don't be long. It's not safe here," she said.

I grabbed my matches out of the pack and went down to the bottom of the rocks. I looked around, and there didn't seem to be life for miles. I could see the line of the horizon, and it was naked, only blocked by the plumes of smoke wafting back and forth under the rays of the retreating sun.

There were pieces of wooden siding and busted doors from houses scattered about. I grabbed my axe and went to work on the wood. It shattered all over the sand. I collected the pieces and put them in a pyramid shape near the base of the rocks. I headed back to the bike to get a little gasoline. I stuck a piece of old newspaper trash into the tank and soaked it. Then I walked back over to find Epiphany standing on the top of the rocks, chanting something.

"And God allowed us to see, let there be light in our dreams." She looked at me and nodded.

I lit up the wooden scraps with my Zippo. I'd gathered with the gas-soaked paper. The wood was engulfed in flames in seconds. Epiphany came down closer to the fire. Her face was half-lit by the flickering light. It was just us on the beach, no movement for miles. She came over to me and stared into my eyes. She slipped the straps of her leather body suit over her shoulders and peeled it off. She was standing completely naked. Her body was flawless, muscular, each abdominal muscle defined, her arms covered in tattoos that I hadn't noticed before. Her fake breasts were perfect and disproportionate to her small frame. She took my hand and pulled it close to her chest.

"Touch me." I hesitated. Something stopped me from reaching out in response to her invitation. It was the guilt inside. It was eating me. The guilt from being disloyal. The guilt from taking another life. I felt the fire of fear flowing through me, but was driven by a savage desire.

I couldn't control myself. My inhibition started to deteriorate. I grabbed her body, pulled it close to mine. She felt hard, her skin tight with no softness to it. But the sexuality in her blood fed my hunger.

"I want to feel you, Kyle." My body responded to hers intrinsically.

We kissed aggressively all over each other. I threw her on the sand and licked every inch of her, until she yanked me closer and ripped my pants off. She grabbed my cock and put it inside of her. I'd never felt anything like it. She was tight and dripping, her pussy pulled on my cock from every direction. She felt like perfection. I dove into her body until she pulled away after a few deep penetrations. She turned over and got on her knees, and I went even deeper inside of her than I'd imagined possible. She folded her arms on the sand. The sand was getting all over our bodies. It was like a carnal tribal ritual on the beach.

"Give it to me," she repeated.

"I'm going to—so fucking hard."

"Yessss! Harder," she shrieked.

"You feel so good. Oh, my god."

"Harder, daddy," she yelled again.

The warmth from the fire felt so good on our backs. One side of us so hot, the other gently cooled by the icy ocean air. "Bite into my skin!" she said. I could feel her starting to orgasm. I was so entranced, I bit into her back. The skin broke and blood leaked into my mouth. It was warm, and her taste turned me on so much that I started to cum inside of her. I felt a shock. It was like some high-frequency wave pulsed through us right where our bodies connected. I exploded even more into her.

Epiphany continued to jerk back and forth until she was sure I was done. She jumped on top of me, pinning me to the ground. "Spit it into my mouth." I stopped thinking; she was kissing me, her blood left in my mouth mixing between our tongues, sandy grit in our teeth, and my seed inside of her.

She rolled over and onto her back. Sand got in her wound. She rested her hand on my chest. I saw the tattoos more clearly; the entire top of her hand was a lion face with the large initials *K.W.* in script on a red banner underneath. It looked like Latin. She pulled away and fell asleep. I covered her sweaty, sandy body with my flannel and her bodysuit as a blanket. I got up to go get some more fragments of firewood. I heard something in the darkness. It was getting closer. I couldn't discern what it was, and my vision was blurry from such an intense exertion of energy.

I passed out next to her. The fire was burning out, so I'd added some more big pieces of driftwood.

When I woke up, it was early morning. The fog was still hovering over the beach. I saw something—a figure in the distance. I started to walk away from our firepit. I looked closely as I walked, squinting, trying to see into the mist. Then, I saw her, my girl, Elise. She was embalmed in a white glow. She was covered in strands of silk, and looked like an angel coming toward me. I fell to my knees and held my arms out. Tears started to fall from my eyes. I could even smell her, the loft, and our bed. The nostalgic longing seemed real.

"Elise. My love, I'm so sorry. I thought you were gone. I've been looking everywhere for you." Her face looked different. She didn't respond to me. Her lips contorted slightly, but it was an expression I'd never seen her make before.

I suddenly felt fingernails in my shoulder. "Get up! Leave her." Epiphany pulled me out of my delusional state.

"Hey, get off of me," I said.

"She isn't real. She's dead, Kyle. Everyone is!" Epiphany said.

"What are you talking about? What in the hell are you talking about? She's alive." I was confused and kept looking back at Elise.

"Listen to me. Listen to me." She put her hands on my face, trying to get me to focus in on her eyes, "It's a wraith pretending."

The ghostly image faded out, and the expression on Elise's face changed again: she sneered at me. It wasn't her. It couldn't be. That wasn't my Elise. *Is she dead? What the fuck happened?* I went back to thinking about the moment on the bridge. *Did I make everything up? Did I make it to her and save her in time?*

The sand embankment started to slide out from underneath us.

"Let's get the fuck outta here now."

We ran back to the fire area and climbed onto the rocks.

"What did you say that was?" I asked Epiphany about the ghostly image.

"A wraith from inside the Gate of the Beast."

"What in the fuck?"

"Another dimension—they imitate the lovers, mock the human emotion in another plane of existence. The astral plane."

"Why are they here?"

"That's what you are going to find out for us." Epiphany rested her hand on my forehead; my breathing slowed and returned to normal.

"We have to get back into town. I will help you get the answers you want."

"Yeah, I guess I'm down for it. Let's go."

I was confused by the whole thing. The aftermath of the sex, the intoxicants in the air had blurred my understanding of

140

what was real. I started having flashbacks about the loft, my life before; the pain of the memories caused tears to pour out of me, and it hurt my temples. I massaged my temples with one hand until I spiraled and fell against one of the rocks and onto the sand.

"I can't remember. I can't remember," I said.

My thoughts faded as I felt Epiphany's lips pressed against mine. She was forcing air into my lungs. Her breath tasted like rye bread from being so dehydrated and unable to brush her teeth. It worked to resuscitate me, though, and I was breathing again.

"Thank you," I said.

"We need to get going, though. Now."

"All right. Give me a second. I can still hardly breathe." I touched my chest.

"Drink this." She pulled out a glass vial.

"What is it?"

"It will make you feel better, I promise." I didn't resist. The vial was already open and she was spilling it over my lips. I choked it down.

"That's disgusting!" The taste lingered like patchouli and salty parsley on my lips.

"Just wait a second." She kept her hand over my lips. Probably holding in the serum in case I chose to regurgitate and spit it out.

"Holy fuck. I feel good." My head was clear, but my body was still achy. I could feel the weird concoction flowing through me.

My back was pinned against the rocks. They were jagged and felt volcanic. Like they had tumbled out from some huge flaming mountain with lava. But I knew better. Their shape came from the power of water. The fresh, clean blue ocean that had pounded against it for thousands of years and worn it down to fragments. It was just hard to picture anything serene now. Even the color blue seemed foreign.

The old ways of the cycle of life didn't seem like the law governing this wasteland. There was no erosion and evolution; this was cosmic destruction. It was a crude experiment.

CHAPTER 11

We jumped back on the bike and tore off down the Pacific Coast Highway back to town. There was no telling what time it was, but the air felt like morning—it was cleaner and not as thick. The harsh wind blurred my view of the road ahead.

The sand was sliding into the ocean. The chunks supporting some of the road fell, and with them, the asphalt in fragments. I gunned the throttle and blazed past the falling debris and back into the city limits.

"Go to my place," Epiphany shouted into my ear.

The Malibu sign was scorched and sat bent on the side of the road. I noticed it only because we had to swerve around a tire sitting in the middle of the road. The car that was attached to it was nowhere to be found. I replayed different scenarios in my head of what must have happened to the people inside that car. The tire was the only remnant; it stored the screams of a driver who'd met with a grisly end. *I wonder if he saw it coming?* I had to ask myself if a person really knew the moment before they died. I thought I'd seen as close to that moment as a person could get when I had gone through the portal.

If this was Heaven or the afterlife, it was even more miserable than the religious fanatics had predicted. Less people than I'd imagined. The Pearly Gates were nothing more than piles of trash on the side of the highway.

Even with the wind in our faces, I could feel her warm breath on my neck. Her cheek pressed close against me. Our faces melded together. I couldn't tell for a minute where mine ended and hers began. Even our breathing colluded in a rhythmic synchronicity. It was a kind of music between two lonely riders that I hadn't felt in a long time.

I followed the pointing of her finger, until we reached what used to be Echo Park. She navigated as precisely as a ship's captain, jutting out her hand at every turn through the hills of Elysium Park.

The small community was in shambles. Even Dodger Stadium was reduced to rubble, a circular stack of melted plastic chairs, and protruding glass. It was a fucked-up version of modern art. We tore past Rowena and turned up a hill to a four-story apartment building overlooking the I-5 Freeway. It had a façade of glass and angular plaster that was made to look like cement. The stucco was polished and the overlapping paint layers were endless.

"Who else lives here?"

"Just a few other Telepaths," she said, squeezing my side again.

I was hesitant to trust her, but she hadn't done me wrong yet. She had done me really fucking good so far and gotten me out of a huge fucking mess. I was beginning to trust what she was saying. I realized I didn't have many other alternatives, so I was defeated, but I believed her.

144

We turned into the driveway and there was a feeling of slime on my face, like the air was sweating. It wasn't humid outside, so I couldn't figure out if a mist was coming in again from the dark clouds swirling overhead, or if this was some force field around her building. It seemed like a shower of polluted rain by the time we made it through. It stained our clothes from the residual moisture.

"This way." We parked behind one of the buildings, out of sight.

"If any of those street-walkers come, I want to make sure the bike is secure."
"They don't come here."

We walked up a flight of stairs. Epiphany used a big blue-and-silver-looking key that was hanging around her neck to open the door. We went inside. It smelled like incense and musty orange peels. I looked around and tried to discern something familiar in all the relics and artifacts she had collected in the room.

I didn't recognize anything; even the silks and tapestries looked foreign. Epiphany motioned me over to a beanbag chair in the corner below the silks draped from the ceiling. She was busy lighting candles. I saw her take out a silver spoon with tarnished patina edges and pour some liquid out of an amber tincture bottle. She put a piece of cotton on the spoon and then filled a syringe. She came over to me and tied me off. I wanted to push her away. Out of instinct from the scientists' tests, I grabbed her by the neck and spun her around into my chest, choking her. The killer instinct started to pass. I began to slowly release my grip.

"I won't hurt you, Kyle. I know who you are." Her voice was calm, muffled by my arm around her neck. She was turning bluish and released the syringe. I snapped out of it and let her go. She gasped for air.

"This is to counteract what they did to you. Don't you remember?"

A cycle of images surged through my memory. I saw them, the white coats congregating in fast-forward motion around the lab, sticking me in the arm, monitoring the data. The tube—I remembered the tube going into the darkness to watch the projection of engineered videos on the wall. I remembered the portal and going through it to the other side, this side.

"Give it to me," I said. Epiphany picked up the needle and tied me off again. She held my arm with the main vein protruding, thumping. I could almost hear the vibrations.

She injected it; the warm liquid was sucked up into my vein, the rubber tie came off my vein filled and then my stomach with warmth. It felt so good. I doubled over and almost fell forward. She caught me before I fell. The blurry image of her pushed me back onto the pillows.

My eyes closed. There was an empty street, a street I had seen before on the outskirts of LA. I was moving fast, hovering over the ground as I was carried by a miraculous force, and at the end of the road the space around me stretched like it was made from latex, and I pierced through it. A loud suckling sound bubbled around me.

Inside there was darkness, and a matrix of interconnecting webs of light. And just as it flashed to the dark, it was back to the light and looked like the same highway. The empty desert around me was filled with lush pockets of orchards, with chickens, cows, and other familiar farm animals. I saw a fire in the distance and there was laughing, gruff laughing. I turned my head and my body followed, still hovering above the ground. Before I could get close enough to see who was laughing, their faces vanished and I returned to Epiphany's apartment, the pillows around me, and she was blowing some smoke onto my face.

"What the hell was that? Who were those people?"

"The Riders."

I felt a shock go through my body. Like the pulse I'd felt when I was in the middle of cumming inside of Epiphany. It was a shockwave, a high-level frequency. She grabbed my wrist.

"See, they are calling you. When the portal is open."

"That's what I saw. Another portal, the space, it..."
"Stretched and sucked you in. It looked the same, but it wasn't."

"No, there were all types of plants, and animals walking around."

"Like how it was here before, you know, before the explosion."

"Yeah, better than I remember."

"Now drink this." She gave me a milky-white serum with oil floating in it.

"This is the protein mixture—we figured out how to survive on it. The Riders bring in food from the other side, but they only trade it for information."

My head hurt, trying to understand the rules of this new world. I tried to remember again what my life was like before, but I couldn't. I couldn't remember anymore.

That world was gone—only the faint memory of Elise, her ghostly image on the beach, remained. *Would it be the last time?* I didn't want to believe that. I tried to reach up to my chest pocket and feel the picture of her, but it was nowhere to be found.

I knew she was still alive somewhere, maybe in another dimension where I could see her spirit, her energy in some other form. Whatever shape she was in, I still craved her.

My body tried to simulate the sensation of love, but I started to feel nauseous. The thought of her skin against mine made me sick. Something was wrong. I couldn't feel her love. It was gone.

I was propelled back into the present, staring deeply into the eyes of Epiphany. They went on and on for miles into nothingness. I stared at my reflection in them. She didn't blink. Her breath flowed into me; our bodies shared the same air. Her mouth was locked to mine. Not kissing me, just breathing hot air in and out of my lungs.

I grew lightheaded and threw up on the floor beside me. It broke the trance, but she lifted my head again and wiped my face with a warm rag. She was blinking rapidly, and picked up a journal with a large Bodhi tree on it. It was locked by a gold clasp, and she opened it with a key. She began scribbling wildly into it, drawing all types of symbols and stars that she circled with so much intensity. I was sure the paper would bleed out if it were alive.

I drank the rest of the milky serum she gave me and started to doze off.

"You need to wake up. You are going to see the Riders in the other dimension."

"What? Me? No! I need to rest." She took out a box that had a paisley pattern on it. From inside, she pulled out a slimy object that looked like biological matter that had once been alive. It had discolorations on it and appeared to be a piece of squid.

"Bite this." She put it near my mouth.

"No more, Epiphany. I gotta rest. I'm fucking exhausted. The beach, the ride, this whole trip is a total mind fuck." Next thing I knew, I was biting down on the slimy piece of skin.

"Chew on it."

I did. Suddenly, I had so much energy, but my vision changed color. The world around me was yellow. Even Epiphany was now yellowish and looked like she was glowing. The light was so strong, it was blinding. Spectral rays emanated from behind her, like staring at the sun.

"Now go and ride south on the 5 Freeway until you go under the bridge, and you will see them. Come back to me." I did as she said, gathered up my bag and my axe and went out to the bike.

My vision was starting to clear up. It was crystal-clear again by the time I started the bike.

The freeway was empty, and I gunned it. Debris flew away from the bike's path and the particles of shit in the air hit me in the face. I coughed and pulled my shirt up over my mouth. I could see the bridge. I was approaching fast, and there was a bus broken in half below the bridge. Just a thin separation, but large enough to fit me and the motorcycle. I accelerated at the last second before piercing through to the other side.

The passage through the wormhole felt like gelatin, different than the first portal I'd gone through in the lab. It surrounded me and the moist wind blew by my ear canal, making a scrunching sound like paper being crumpled all around me in hyperspeed.

The other side was calm, the air was clear, and it felt the same, but I knew it was different. The way the trees moved was independent of any outside force. They had their own energy, no wind needed to move them. I could feel the jacaranda flowers growing, changing, and producing vibrations. The purple hue looked synthetic; it was too perfect.

I was still on the bike, moving fast. I hadn't changed gears, and yet I was moving more rapidly over what seemed to be the same road I was on before, the I-5 Freeway. The scenery of crumbled buildings and devastation was gone. It was replaced by a clean desert landscape, Joshua trees, cacti, meadows, and rows of fruit trees. It was a miniature biosphere contained in the limit of my periphery, all the types of desert ecosystems in the most perfect shapes I'd seen. Birds flew in and out from between the oversized prickly pears on the cacti.

I'd seen this before in my mind's eye when I had been in Epiphany's apartment. I could hear the laughing again. The bike edged off the road without my doing. I was heading off road into the desertscape. The laughing ceased. I could only smell the fire. The fading light bounced around the shadows as the sun set, and I spotted a figure near a campfire. There was a man sitting there.

I reached to feel for my axe, but it was gone. I eyed him and downshifted to slow down and checked him out to make sure he was not armed with anything. He didn't look up from the log he was sitting on. He poked at the fire, carving in the ground underneath the mound of sticks and brush burning. I killed the engine and coasted up the dirt path beside the fire.

"Got room for one more?" I asked him.

He didn't respond. The pause was uncomfortable, "Listen, man, I can start my own fire..." I got off the bike.

"Sure, mate. Join me, fellow Rider," he said in an Australian accent.

He looked up. Half his face was burned with a strange symbol, like an ohm. I couldn't make it out because he turned back to the fire. The other side of his face was worn and chapped from years on the road. I couldn't place his age, but his eyes told me he was in his forties, at least. I sat down on another log.

"What's your name?" I asked.

"The name's Reamus, you?"

"They call me Kyle."

"Oh, yeah, who's they?"

"Doesn't matter."

"Well, it does if you want to join me at my fire, Kyle. Just because you're a Rider doesn't give you any rights with me."

"OK, man. They, the fucking Beast and everything, you know?"

"That's what I thought you meant. I'm just fucking with you, mate." He laughed to himself.

"It's cool. Thanks for the wit. Dying artform."

"Sure is. What kind of name is Kyle, anyway? Most of us have weird names."

"That's my given name. You know, Mom and Dad and the book of a thousand names. They threw a dart at it and bam! Guess that solved the confusion and saved the arguments. I think it means 'survivor' or something in Gaelic."

"You survived. That's a start. So that's your real name. What did the Beast give you when you passed through? Never mind, mate, you're good with me."

I knew he was alluding to some strange code or assignment that I guessed the other Riders received as a rite of passage or something. I didn't want to get into it and reveal any more about who I was before finding out his motives. So far, he had been cool, shared his fire and he had some food nearby, a pile of it. I turned the questioning back to him.

"Reamus."

"Yeah, that's me. Pretty true to form. My parents were like bloody wolves eating their own."

We continued to talk about our past lives. The memories he described were distorted and didn't make much sense. Still, we went along and humored each other.

The food tasted like it just came out of the oven—fresh turkey legs, cranberry sauce. It could've been Thanksgiving, if it wasn't charred and covered in a layer of dirt.

We ate with our hands, scooping piles of food into our mouths, and talked in superficialities, avoiding any real confrontation. I was still unsure as to whether his motivation was to befriend me or kill me. The frontier seemed like paradise compared to the wasteland of Los

Angeles I'd come from. In this moment, I had no desire to go back. I wanted to stay and ride my motorcycle through the desert and build fires, eat well, and make abstract conversation with other Riders.

It sounded good, but I pictured Epiphany, and it wasn't her that I sympathized with. It was just her face, her memory, the inescapable feeling inside of my loins that seemed to pulse with the same blood as her. I couldn't leave her. It was too easy to forget your past in this place. It was like you'd been brainwashed, but you could be whoever you wanted to be. I'd been following the signs. This was my destiny.

"I'll be right back."

"Where you going, mate?"

"Take a piss."

I walked off about twenty feet into the desert. My vision started to blur with fatigue, and I saw Elise again. This time, she was no phantom or wraith. She looked clear as day in the desert. I walked off into the Joshua trees. In the middle of a grouping of trees was Elise; she turned and spoke to me, "Have you forgotten me?"

"Of course not. That's why I did this. That's why I was willing to go through that portal. For the money. For you."

"Don't lose yourself, and don't be so easily seduced by this place. Don't forget me. Come find me."

154

"But you're right here." I couldn't look directly in her eyes because I had so much guilt inside of me.

I reached out to grab her, but my hand passed through her skin like a thick vapor.

"You will touch me in the flesh soon enough. I came to warn you about him." She disappeared.

"Hey, mate, you get lost? You'll freeze out there." Reamus interrupted my first real conversation with Elise in what felt like forever.

"I just wanted to get some air, walk around. Get the blood flowing."

"Plenty of air by the fire. I nodded out for a quick minute, woke up, and you were gone. Thought maybe you smoked toad venom and spaced out. Went all trippy hippie on me. Started seeing the monsters out here."

"No, no monsters out here. Just a beautiful woman." I laughed to play along with his story.

"Yeah, right. Your hand don't count, mate. All right, let's get some rest. We got a long ride tomorrow."

"Sure. Be right there." I sensed something sinister in his tone. I followed him back to the fire carefully, watching my every step.

"Night, Reamus."

I turned over against one of his saddlebags on the ground. The fire was blazing and I watched his reflection in my chrome tailpipe. It was the perfect mirror to keep an eye on him. I drifted in and out of sleep.

Seeing the flames dance soothed me and my eyes grew tired trying to track each orange tentacle's next move. And then it came. I felt it first. Then I saw a figure in the darkness. It leaked a silty substance behind it. The shadow was effervescent against the desert, flashing and moving synthetically. It came over to Reamus—his body was motionless. It seeped into him like smoke going in reverse, sucking into his static body, which inhaled the venom into his lungs. Within moments I saw him stretching in his skin. His silhouette's reflection now completely filled the tailpipe, and I knew he was getting up, contorting like something was ripping his ribs open from the inside of his chest.

I had no weapons, nothing to protect me but the fire. Fire was always powerful against the darkness. I rolled and in one sweeping motion reached into the blazing coals and grabbed the last stick covered in flames. Reamus jumped on top of me and pinned me to the ground. I freed my hand and struck with precision into the air, jamming the stick into Reamus's eye. His other eye was filled with emptiness and beamed into me. His stare was deadly before he fell back and onto the ground.

He lay there, unmoving. Then there was a screeching sound that came out from inside of his body as he tossed on the ground, convulsing, and trying to yank the burning stick out of his head. The sound was heart-wrenching as he wailed to his death.

156

He yanked the stick out with his hands, flesh melting from the sides of his face as dark ash scattered all around him. The strange figure emerged again out from the burn-hole where his eye had been. The shadowy figure combined itself with the darkness of the night and slithered away.

I rolled on the ground and lifted my body to look at Reamus as he took a few final breaths.

Whatever had possessed him had taken the remainder of his soul with it. His good eye was back to the light blue it had been before. His breathing was slow and deep. I looked at him.

"What was that?"

"That was the Beast." He choked and blood came from his mouth, soiling his lips.

"He's coming for you." Reamus said his final words. He closed his good eye forever. The wound on his face boiled and glowed orange. The fire had gone out. Reamus was dead. The thing that possessed him was also gone.

I felt bad for Reamus. He was kind of a cool dude. He'd let me share his fire and had told me more than I'd expected. It was one of the first normal conversations I'd had since I crossed over into this dimension. Sitting out in the desert with a fellow man and sharing a fire. It was like the beginning of human beings. When we'd evolved and found fire, only now his fire was extinguished. And it was at the end of my own hands.

I wished I could wash the death off me, but that wasn't possible. It lingered, and the smell of flesh was still in the air. It smelled rancid, like spoiled milk and burning hair. I plugged my nose up with a piece of my shirt, but the smell was too piercing to avoid.

I tried to sleep again, but I couldn't turn off my adrenaline. It was in my veins and it was making my insides churn and ache. I used the wild force from the pain inside and I rolled over and got up, dusting myself off.

I wasn't safe here anymore. They knew where to find me. I grabbed the food and threw it in his saddlebags, affixed them to mine, then got on the bike and rode out of there the same way I'd gone in. On the main road, the bike caught a hovering force and seemed to slide above the earth at an incredible speed again.

My face stretched back with the insane energy force as I pierced back into the portal. The other dimension was not the Eden I'd thought. It was grim and seeped into this reality to take its victims when it craved human blood.

CHAPTER 12

The 5 Freeway and busted cars were a nice welcome home for me after that nightmare. It had started off so interesting, like going to the Garden of Eden after being trapped in a more primal existence.

Heading back to Epiphany's, I hoped she'd be there. She was the only other person I could connect with, and the only person who could tell me what the hell was going on. I drove up to the complex perched on the hill. Her apartment was still protected by a gelatinous forcefield—a weaponized jellyfish conjured up there to sting anyone not welcome.

My thirst for information had become savage. It was boiling up in my stomach, causing knots to form. It ached, but I had a new drive. It was a drive to understand what purpose I served here. No matter how deranged or diabolical it became. I had to follow the signs. I knew that each person I encountered played a role in collecting the answers, and offered up tidbits of information in the puzzle.

I was almost to Epiphany's place when the analytical part of my brain turned off, and I went back to relying on my instinct.

Before I pulled in, I saw movement in the bushes. It was a young kid with long hair. I didn't trust anyone, after where I'd been. The shit I'd seen now made everything before seem so unimportant. The mundane reality of everyday life paled in comparison to living in the supernatural state I was in when hunting the Beast. I was filled with the lifeblood purpose to save others.

I gunned it into the complex, and the same sticky, humid feeling from the psychic shield surrounded me. I turned around and saw the kid running after me. Then he hit the field of energy. It rejected him. He was not permitted, and only got to the edge of the complex. He backed away like he'd run into an impenetrable force. He couldn't pierce through it. He fingered the air, prodding the molecules, eyeing me all the way up to the building. The sorcery behind the protection spell was working.

I couldn't forget the number of Epiphany's apartment: 88. I walked up the stairs to the third floor. Her door was open. I peered in, and she was sitting there in the same place I'd left her.

Only she was unconscious.

"Oh, fuck!"

Her eyes had rolled back in her head.

I grabbed her limp body and started shaking her.

"Epiphany!" There was no response.

"Wake up. Get up. I need you."

The whites of her eyes were all I could see, and she wasn't breathing normally. I felt the air passing in and out from her nose, but it was barely anything. She was still warm, too. I propped her body up and cupped water in my hands from the sink and splashed it on her face. She still wasn't waking up.

"Epiphany!"

I tried slapping her face. I felt bad hitting her, but I'd try anything to get her back conscious again. She didn't budge, then started to make a choking sound.

"Kk... I... I... I didn't make it."

"Fuck. I'm here. I came back. It's me."

I shook her again. I didn't have any way to jump-start her heart. I felt such a deep connection to save her life.

"Epiphany!"

I grabbed the lighter nearby. I flicked it and pressed the flame against her forearm; she started to shake and convulse and then opened her eyes. She fell with all of her weight onto me and I almost fell backwards. I lifted her up to her feet and held her in my arms. She started to breathe rapidly now, and her heartbeat was soaring. The pulsing of her heart opposed the fast pace of mine. Then our hearts synced—we were dialed back into each other's frequencies.

After a few minutes, she started to settle down, looking up at me with the sweetest eyes. Her pupils dilated and filled her eyes like saucers. She made a soft humming sound, a needy sound. A come-close-and-touch-me-with-love sound. I leaned down to kiss her lips. They were chapped and cracked, but felt good. Her skin was warm and balmy. She kissed me hard and put her tongue deep into my mouth.

She pushed me to the ground and started to pull my jeans off. Before she got them all the way past my knees, her lips were already gliding up and down on my hard dick. It felt so good, like she was drinking my soul. She stopped right in the middle of sucking it and looked up at me and smiled.

"I forgot… I have a surprise for you."

And just like that, we stopped messing around and she went to her bedroom—a part of the apartment I hadn't seen yet. I wondered what she had hidden back there. Probably crazy potions and spell books. It couldn't possibly be weirder than what I'd just seen in the other dimension with Reamus and that shadowy figure trying to fucking kill me.

"What is it?"

I pulled my jeans up over my still-hard body; it hurt to push it into my pants. I was walking toward the bedroom when I saw a silhouette come out of the hallway.

"Chico!! Holy shit."

The pooch I'd found from my apartment.

"How'd you get here, boy? I'm sure glad to see you." I kneeled to pet him. I looked up at Epiphany, who was staring at me with a smile on her face. She walked to the cabinets in the kitchen and pulled out a large bone. It was so big, it could have been the femur from a person, but it didn't matter even if it was. She brought it over to Chico, who was contentedly licking my face. This time he was happy to see me.

"He was sitting outside the apartment building when you left. Poor boy was starving, and I could tell you needed him, too. It's incredible no one ate him up for food," she said.

It made me happy to see a semblance of a normal life. Having Chico here in her apartment felt comforting. She was right. It felt good to have him by my side. His energy, dirty coat, and dog breath made me feel human again. His breath smelled like tuna fish and sewer water, but I still let him lick my face until he was done and moved on to the bone. I was just foreplay.

"Come with me. You need to pay the toll." A shudder ran through my body.

I walked with her, down the hallway to the bedroom. Chico, meanwhile, was chewing obnoxiously loud on the oversized femur bone. I could hear the sound bouncing off the hallway walls.

The bedroom was filled with candles, and there were glow-in-the-dark cloud stickers stuck all over the wall in rolling formations like imitation paisley wallpaper. It was disorienting, trying to follow all the cloud shapes, because of the handwritten notes on them that read like prayers.

In the corner was a big leather book with ties, opened to the middle page. Incense was flaking to ash all over it. It was nag champa incense, the real stuff from India with a distinct smell that never faded. It lingered forever, pungent and spiritual. It was what I pictured all those Buddhist Ashrams smelled like permanently.

The words in the book were written in felt-colored markers, and there were symbols of stars and circles all over it, large enough to see from where I was standing before she yanked me onto the bed. I was still distracted by all the images, the symbols; I was trying to decipher them, to catch every detail, looking for a clue. I knew they wouldn't do me any good. I was in way over my head.

"Why me?" I said, as she took my pants off again.

She didn't answer. She looked at me, disappointed that I was not still turned on. I couldn't seem to get into the mood. She reached under the bedframe and pulled out leather ties. She put them over my hands and started to bind me to the bed frame. I let her do it. It seemed kinky enough, and maybe it would get me back into the mood.

I kept thinking about what I'd just experienced in the other dimension. I thought of Elise and what she'd told me. It was hard to know what she was warning me about. I couldn't stop myself and said her name aloud. Epiphany looked back at me after tying my feet to the frame. Her eyes looked entranced and all blacked-out again, and all I could think was, *fuck me.*

Next to her book in the corner was a thin knife made of a semiprecious stone, or maybe onyx. It was jagged. She took it and squatted on top of me. She took off the rest of her clothes. And then she carefully started to carve a symbol over my heart. She wasn't cutting too deep, but I felt it.

"Damn! That hurts!" I said, but she was in a trance.

After she finished tattooing what felt like an infinity sign, she pressed her lips against my chest and started to suck the blood off of me. She felt like a leech, pulling and sucking on my skin. I writhed in pain, but it felt good, too.

When I thought she'd sucked me dry, she leaned over the side of the bed and spat the blood onto her book. She scribbled something with the knife in the book. Placing the knife back down, she turned.

An electric greenish color returned to her eyes, and she started to touch herself next to me. Within minutes, she started to orgasm, again and again, until she couldn't control herself. She put her pussy into my mouth and commanded, "Drink me." I did what she said. I drank her up. She tasted like the last girl in the world. I opened my mouth wider and started to move my tongue up and down her clit. She started to scream again and slid down my chest, over the amateur tattoo inscription, and then put me inside of her.

I shook my head from side to side, resisting, and started to pull on the leather ties. They were cutting into my wrists. As I pulled tighter, I could feel blood wrenching out of them, and I started to panic a little bit.

Epiphany put her finger over my mouth, "Look at me. Look into my soul." Her words were intense. It made me feel weird, but I liked it.

I avoided looking at her like she was Medusa, thinking I might turn to stone or never come back from inside her eyes. I shut my eyes tight. When I looked up and opened my eyes again, there was Elise.

"My love!" I blurted out and tried to pull her close to me. My arms were still affixed to the bedframe, but I could feel them wrapping around her body like my spirit coming out of my being and holding her in my hands, like ghost limbs.

"Cum for me. Cum for me, Kyle." Elise's body was so warm. I could smell her perfume—fresh vanilla and tobacco combined with the lilies I had gotten her that Valentine's Day. She was so intoxicating.

"I love you, Elise. I miss you." I almost started to cry. It was a familiarity I hadn't felt since I'd gone through the portal.

I started to climax and looked up to see Epiphany smiling and shutting her eyes. I jerked my hips, trying to free myself. It was too late; I barely had any fight left in me. I came so hard inside of her. She kept riding me until my body went slack and she'd gotten every last drop. She flipped onto her back and pulled her legs in close to her chest.

"What the fuck was that?" I asked.

"Shhhh... it's OK. We need a child to keep going."

"What are you talking about?"

"Don't worry. It's not what you think. We are going to have a savior, in case you don't complete the mission."

"I don't know what in the hell you're talking about."

"You will soon. Now close your eyes. You need your rest."

"Fuck. You can't do this shit." I could hardly stop myself from strangling her, but I knew I couldn't do it. I was too connected to her now. We were fatefully tied to each other, and I needed to accept it. I'd come back here because I knew I needed her. I cared for her, but now I'd been betrayed by her. She put a spell on me, used me for my seed.

My urge to take revenge on her for stealing my genetics subsided. I lay there in a momentary paralysis, feeling lost and alone. A tear fell from the corner of my eye. I felt guilty, and I was overloaded with the realization that I might never see Elise in the flesh again.

Before I could move my mouth to say anything, I fell into a deep sleep. It felt good to dream again.

The dreaming grew intense. My mental trauma blurred my memories until a triangle shape came swimming in the horizon. It was a shark with a huge dorsal fin. It swam by me in the dream. The sea was a clear blue, and everything was so vivid, right down to the shark's sandpapery skin. I grabbed the elongated dorsal fin and rode to the edge of an abandoned craft.

I sailed the ship farther into the island inside of my head. The island was covered in perfectly green grass. I looked

for a way to get onto land. I felt a tugging at my pants.
There was a small man. I had a conversation with him. He
was bald and had short toenails, with moss growing or
caught in between them. He looked like he was born out of
the earth.

"You have to trust the shark." He motioned.

"That shark will eat me."

"No, it only has two crooked teeth." A quick snapshot filled
my mind. The shark was smiling, with two corkscrews as
teeth. They were sharp, but crooked, and there were only
two. He was right. That was what he looked like.

"Where will he take me?"

"To the Gate of the Beast."

"Why in the hell would I want to go there?" I questioned
him, as he started to hop around. His face was rather
attractive and androgynous. His familiar voice was
comforting, and his words seemed true. He convinced me.

"You must go. Didn't she tell you?"

"Who?"

"You really are green. And not in a good way. Follow me."
I grabbed hold of the shark's dorsal fin, and the man rowed
the strange wooden craft rather effortlessly into the water.
We reached the island and I let go of the shark. A pond
secreted a substance like volcanic ash melting into the

water. The heat from the bubbling minerals was purifying and I breathed it gratefully into my lungs.

"What is your name?"

"I am Cabal."

"Yeah, alright."

"After the explosion, my life changed, too."

It was hard to picture Cabal as any other person than this ferryman of Hades who had taken me to a strange island. Picturing him with a wife, kid, and dog in a domestic setting, with a white picket fence in the suburbs of Los Angeles, was difficult.

No, I couldn't take him out of this context. I still seemed to be dreaming, but this had become my reality and was no longer imaginary. It was a world where I trusted Cabal to take me where I had never dreamed of. This was my purpose now, and I had to let go of my control and allow fate to take over.

We jumped over the crevices in the treacherous earth. The grass was so soft and moist on my bare feet, like it was made of tentacles. The dew clung to us. The cavernous shape of the land seemed to move quickly, like the erosion process had been sped up to a rapid rate.

When we reached the top of the hill, there was a glass prism. The structure looked like an architectural house with perfectly angular glass. The walls built on the cliffside fractured the space into varying beams in a spectrum of colored light.

"There it is," he said.

"That is the gate?" I questioned, still in a state of disbelief.

"You must ride through to the other side. He is waiting for you."

Cabal's voice faded as I walked up the final precipice into the beams of light emitting from the sides of the prism structure. The grass was effervescent, illuminated by the yellow shades of the dying tips of each blade of grass. They waved around in the air, moving to their own life force or controlled by the radiant energy.

A sharp pain was forming on the right side of my face. "WAKE UP!" I heard a voice I knew. *Why is this voice so familiar?* I had lost track of the past. The light was soft against my hand. "You are not ready!" My eyes fluttered open to Epiphany slapping my face repeatedly. My reflexes kicked in and I grabbed her hand before she could hit me again. She was trying to wake me up from this wild dream.

"What in the fuck are you doing?"

"You're not ready yet..." She trailed off and collapsed on her back next to me.
"You are the one who wants me to save the world, and all of this bullshit you've been filling my head with. You told me about the Beast."

"Yeah, well, you're not ready."

170

"I don't think you need to be ready, to meet the creator of all this. It's a goddamn mess, don't you think?"

"It's not about that." Epiphany always knew more than she told me. Her knowledge was beyond anything I could comprehend.

"It's pretty much just us here trying to battle weird-ass shit that I don't even know what the hell it is. You do. You're the one who has all the answers."

"Don't you remember when you were little?"

"Honestly, I don't really remember much after that lab— the explosion, the damn horse running after me. And Chico, my main man." The pooch was lying down in the corner, resting. His ears perked up and he gave me a look when I said his name.

"That was so close. You were almost gone."

"I'm right here, baby."
I stroked her long hair with the back of my hand. I decided to be cool even after being repeatedly slapped in the face. Epiphany had her reasons, and while I didn't really trust her, I believed her, since she seemed to know everything about me already.

"Remember what you saw in the other dimension?"

"Yeah, with that crazy guy by the fire."

"And then what happened..."

"He got possessed."

"Looked like a spirit, right?"

"It was hard to make out in the darkness."

I did remember the slithery snake that had formed out of the darkness into a metallic shape and had sucked right into Reamus.

"That was from inside the gate. He sent it to kill you if you were weak, or to test you if you were able to kill the vessel he possessed to attack you."

"Well, I passed the stupid test."

"Did you make any deals with him?"
"Deals? What sort of deals? You mean with Reamus?"

"The Rider."

"No, no deals. I just shot the shit with the guy. Wandered off for a minute into the desert." I interrupted myself, thinking about Elise again. I remembered her warning and continued, "You know, there's some crazy-ass shit over there in the other dimension."

"What else did you see?"

"Nothing really, just all the food. It seems like the fucking Garden of Eden."

"It's whatever you want it to be."

"Yeah, well, it didn't give me what I wanted. Guess I will save that for the Beast guy or whatever."

I was done talking with Epiphany about the other dimension. I was hungry again and needed a drink to quell my nerves and think all of this through. A nice period of reflection was exactly what I needed after I'd ridden a motorcycle into another dimension and stuck a hot poker into the eye of a demon spirit.

"You need to go back to the Café Revelation and see Ezra. He's the bartender there. He will tell you where to find the real Cabal."

"That's funny. I was just thinking how bad I needed a drink." I depended on alcohol to make it through this place.

"I know."

"OK, I'm leaving. Take care of Chico."

"Sure."

I started to walk out. I had grabbed my axe and my pack, when Epiphany laid another wet kiss on my ear and whispered, "Don't make any more deals with them. I can't protect you."

"I'll keep my head on. You stay, well, um—you, I guess."

I'd overstayed my time with my new lover and sorceress. Epiphany was real. She was a mystical being, and I was falling for her—her seduction, her knowledge, and her ability to show me what was going on in this place.

She hadn't replaced Elise and real love, but she was a companion in this dreary, future, replicated version of Los Angeles. I was going to take her advice and go see this Cabal, go back to the Café Revelation, and get more information.

I was unraveling a mystery that got even more fucked-up every step of the way. I was just not sure what I was uncovering. It really couldn't get much worse. I traced through what was left of my memory and remembered Michael and his drawings of the portal and weird artifacts. Maybe his religious cult wanted to be certain how the end of the world happened. It could be the way to substantiate their religion or cult as the real one amidst all the millions of different faiths out there across the universe. Maybe it was in order to be the one who saved everyone, the true savior, or at least to predict the end to civilization.

While I was leaving Epiphany's apartment, I started to think back to my normal life before the lab and going through the portal. I thought about my daily life, the sweet idiosyncrasies that used to make me feel human.

I got back on the bike and fired it up by kicking a few times pretty hard. I walked it backward in neutral and saw Chico come running out from the apartment. "You can't go with me, boy. It's a long haul to the café." He shrugged me off and licked my hand. My burns were almost healed. I shifted down into gear and cruised out of the driveway. The dog came running just past the end of the driveway, nipping at the back tire. I saw a person moving in the bushes.

"Is that fucking kid still following me?" I crossed through the protective Jell-O sphere and into the world again.

Before I reached the street, I felt a net made of thick braided sailors' knots cover my face like mesh.

"Let me go! I'm not a fucking fish!" It was the only thing that came to mind.

I downshifted and tried to slide the bike sideways to get free from the net. It didn't work the way I'd planned, and the bike went sliding in a shower of sparks. I was jerked back in the opposite direction.

I thought I heard Chico barking in the background; I saw another kid throw a net over him, too. "Leave him." I struggled, stripping the net from my body. I looked up and felt a blunt object hit me in the head. My vision went blurry and then faded to nothing.

PART III

CHAPTER 13

I woke up to the smell of mold and sulfuric minerals. My head hurt. The pounding sensation in the back of my skull reminded me of the lab. It was the same burning inside I'd felt after being injected with a concoction of drugs. I heard voices, but didn't recognize them. They barely sounded human in my condition. I didn't know exactly what my condition was, but it wasn't good.

I tried to roll over and shut my eyes again. I couldn't move. I was restrained. Staring up, my vision became clear again and I saw the ceiling was made from rocks. *I am inside of a cave.* I breathed deeply.

"He's awake," someone said.

"Where am I?" There was no response.

I heard feet moving rapidly away from me. Whoever it was, they were light on their feet and scurried down the corridor of the cave. I pictured the feet attached to the same longhaired, dirty kid I'd spotted in the bushes outside of Epiphany's. A similar breed to the idiot who had tried to steal my bike outside the café and signed their death warrant.

I heard more footsteps coming down the hallway. At least eight feet, all out of sync. It was a combination of different feet shuffling toward me.

"Why'd you take me prisoner?" I asked.

After a pause, "Shut the fuck up. We need to figure out who you are."

"I'll tell you who I am if you get these restraints off me. I'm sick of looking at shadows on the cave walls."

"You're not a Rider, but you look like one. You have the markings and can go into the other dimension, so tell us who you are, and we will let you live."

"You sure know a lot about me, but I don't know the first goddamn thing about you. I'm real big on getting to know each other first before sticking it in, ya know, a little foreplay." I felt a sharp object being pressed into my chest.

"This is your second chance. And it'll be your last chance to tell us."

I considered another witty retort, about having nine lives or another dumb metaphor, but I dropped the act. The sharp object was starting to cut into my chest. I felt my warm blood leaking out onto my shirt. I thought about what I should say—my name would be a start. Or maybe that I was a friend of Epiphany's, or about the experiment, and going into the portal. I made my decision.

"I'm the one sent to kill the Beast." There was silence. The sharp digging pressure against my chest lessened. The blade was pulled away from me.

"You really think so, don't you?" a strong male voice responded. There was a bunch of commotion in the background.

178

"Yeah, that's me. I'm the one," I answered affirmatively.

"And how do you plan on doing that? You can't even get away from us Washouts."

"I guess you're the Washouts?" I put two and two together.

"Yes. How are you going to do it?"

"I was trained. Trained to kill the Beast."
I thought back to the lab experiments. Had it been training for this purpose, or was the Beast a newly created figment of everyone's imagination that lived in the future as a kind of devil figure? Fuck it. Didn't matter because I was in this shit now, and I'd say just about anything to get the restraints off my wrists, and out of here.

"What were you doing with that witch?" he said.

"She just took me in when no one else would. It felt good to be with a woman again."

"Ah. Huh." He was unconvinced by my answer.

"Untie him." I felt fingers on every restraint, untying the knots used to keep me immobile.

"Now, this is a little more civilized."

I looked around, my head still throbbing. In front of me was a man with a white beard in ripped shards of cream clothing like an ancient Greek toga.

"You guys huddle up in the caves here to stay out of sight."

I stated the obvious because small talk was the way to go here. I didn't want to trip up over any more philosophical terms. I'd wait, listen, and then figure out the angle. Just let them do the talking and go from there.

"I'm Hiram. You are here because one of my kids followed you from out of the café and with that witch." He paused.

"We are the last of us humans in Los Angeles, about 13,000 of us in the hills stretching all the way to Malibu in the Santa Monica Mountains."

"Damn, that's it. And you are the leader now?"

"I am the king of the Washouts."

"Washouts, right." I nodded. "It's a cool name. Got anything to drink?"

"Plenty," he answered.

His smile was reassuring, but like everyone I'd met so far in the Wasteland and even in the other dimension, he wanted more—they all wanted something more. You could dig and dig and sometimes never find their true intentions.

They walked me down the caverns cut out of the bedrock in the side of the mountain. I figured we were near Hollywood, as they couldn't have taken me too far—I was a heavy load.

My feet were having trouble walking one step in front of the other; my equilibrium felt off. I couldn't wait to see if I got the spins after a few brews. I was teetering and still thinking about the taste of alcohol. It didn't get me drunk

180

anymore, but seemed to numb the confusion. The constant questioning in my brain, the repetition, would calm down for a moment of peace and beat faintly in the background.

At the end of the cave, light was pouring in through the rocks. I could hear a wave of voices and sounds so thick it felt like a wave crashing through the tunnel—pulsating with energy. When we got to the end, we stopped at the edge and there was a whole fucking city inside.

There were old street signs, neon illumination from advertisements, a huge Coca-Cola sign flickering, and structures made from rusted cars, parts of buildings, debris, and scraps. It was a very sophisticated gypsy encampment.

"Holy shit! You guys have been busy."

I stood staring out at the expanse of it all. It smelled like home: the people, the scent of meat cooking on fires, and human sweat. The noise was music to my ears. It filled me up with more than nostalgia, but a sense of belonging. I had forgotten what it felt like to have the energy swarming around you when you were in the presence of so many people, colliding stories with a purpose, a place to go, a community. The real connection to other human beings.

It made me think of Elise and remember our life together. It was the first time I could vividly remember the moments we'd shared, without the haze or the fragments. It was also real again. She was real again to me, but she wasn't here anymore.

Inside the encampment, kids ran by me. They played with makeshift toys constructed from wood and shredded wiring casings. They looked like savages carrying trash, but the glow of their smiles told a different story.

I walked on through the encampment, following Hiram and his crew of misfits. "You will be staying in here." Hiram lifted the flap made from bubble wrap, and inside was a large dome structure.

"These are pretty sweet digs, Hiram." He looked at me kind of funny.

"Get yourself cleaned up and then join me for a meal," he said.

"You got it, boss." He was already leaving. His back was barely out of the door when a young girl walked in carrying a bucket and folded fabric.

"Can I help you?" I said to her.

"I am here to clean you up for dinner with Hiram." I looked at her, a little confused.

"I'm a lot dirtier than that small bucket!"

"It will do for now. Please take your clothes off," she said.

I was intrigued. First, they pummeled me, chained me up, and now they had a beautiful girl hand-bathing me. I must have said something right for once. I did as she said and took my clothes off.

"OK, I'm in my birthday suit. Where do you want me?" She stood staring at me, looking at my body, examining every crevice, every line. It was a bit awkward, but I was comfortable in my own skin. Finally, she pointed to the left side of the tent.

"Please stand in the basin." It was a metal circle that reminded me of a dog wash. I walked over and put my feet in. I felt the cool metal on my feet and then the sponge on me. It was dry and rough on my skin. Her hand touched mine as she scrubbed my arm. It was a nice change from the rough texture of the sponge. The soap smelled minty. It cleared my sinuses and made my skin tingle. Her hands cleaned my genitals and she scrubbed me gently.

I wanted to grab her right then out of instinct, but I resisted the carnal urge. I relaxed and let her finish cleaning me. She patted me with the fabric to absorb the remaining moisture. I took the cloth from her and dried myself off more.

"Thank you. I mean really, it feels good to have the filth scrubbed off of me. And that was my first sponge bath. Thanks for taking my virginity."

"You're welcome." She smiled and started to leave.

"Hey, wait. You see me naked and I don't even know your name?"

She tried to pull away and exit, but she turned and her bluish-green eyes caught mine. It was like I could see her entire life's history in them: her childhood, the awkward teenage years, and now here she was in the city in the caves.

"I'm nobody now."

"That's not true. You are alive. I know that much. And I know you're a magical soul."

My compliment took her off guard. It seemed she was distracted—estranged, maybe, from the savagery that had happened after the explosion. I could only imagine what had happened to beautiful girls like her out there in the aftermath. I didn't want to think about it, but I also needed to acknowledge it.

"I'm sorry. I didn't mean to be so forward. Thank you again."

"I'm Carmella," she said in a near-whisper, and then left the tent. Her words remained there. I could hear her name at the edge of the room like the letters just hovered there and never made it all the way to my ears.

"Carmella."

I repeated the word. Her name tickled my tongue when I said it, and my mind could only draw on the smell and taste of caramel—the sweet sugary cream that I only wished to taste again one day.

"Are you ready?" The same boy who had been following me earlier with the long hair peeked in.

"Almost, soldier. Give me a second."

"Hiram is waiting," he added.

I threw on my old clothes. The jeans were tattered and the flannel was soiled, but I didn't care. I was still clean underneath the rags. I couldn't bring myself to throw on any toga or bullshit like that. I was going to indulge Hiram with my stories, but I was not going to be consecrated into this new civilization by putting on their ugly uniform.

I also had to get back to the Wasteland. I had unfinished business there.

We walked out from under the plastic bubble wrap door, back into the carnival of people. I could hear music being played live, and it sounded like a dulcimer over drumming. We walked up stone steps near the end of the city.

At the top was a throne carved out from the limestone rock. Hiram was sitting on it.
"Welcome again, friend." He motioned his hand to a collection of boulders draped in cloth as chairs. I sat on one of them.

"I don't want to waste any time with you. I know you will try and escape at the first chance you get. I assure you that is a mistake."

"I'm not leaving. You got a pretty good setup here, old man." He wasn't keen on my flattery.

"Do you know the story of Moses?" he asked me.

"I mean, yeah, bits and pieces of it. You know, Sunday school as a kid." I never had paid attention in class, and my folks had pretty much just dropped me at the back entrance, so it had been easy to avoid going. Now I had a growing sensation that maybe I shouldn't have skipped out on the Moses narrative.

"You wouldn't have learned it anyways. This is the real story of Moses—the one that starts with a murder."

"Yeah, this doesn't sound like the Sunday School version."

"Moses witnessed a murder of one of his fellow tribe. He came to the aid of his tribesman and killed the Egyptian. He had to run from the other Egyptians to escape his own death."

"Why are you telling me this?" I was growing weary of all the metaphors and symbols that Epiphany had first dropped on me, and now Hiram was flooding my mind with biblical subtext that clearly applied to my own existence, but I had no idea how.

"So... Moses. He ran and was taken in by tribes called the Midianites. It was there he was married and then became ready to go and face the god of the mountains."

"God of the mountains..." I was confused, but I continued to listen, feeling belligerently drunk even though I wasn't. "You mean Jesus, man?"

"No, I do not mean Jesus. According to the name they gave to Moses, or the one we know that has been passed on to us, it was YHWH who he met." Hiram wrote the consonants on the smooth section of stone next to him with the ash from a carved bowl inlaid in the rock surface.

"You see, the Hebrews had no vowels. We do not know if this was the real name of this god. Because you see, if you call a god by their name, you enslave them."

I started to think about calling all the people in my life by their names, even the casual relationships with women I'd had over the years.

"Shit! You're right—as soon as I knew their name, it was almost a guarantee they would be going home with me," I laughed.

"Not the same." He wasn't laughing at all.

"This was all before Elise—I was loyal to her."

I thought about how, if anything, she had enslaved me in the best of ways. I wanted her to capture me again, in her arms. My daydreaming fantasy stopped when Hiram hammered his fist against the table to get my attention.

"When Moses came back after learning from the god YHWH, he freed over 600,000 Israelites from Egyptian enslavement." Hiram smiled contentedly.

"Well, how in the hell did he do that? With a huge ghost army, or what?" I said sarcastically, but half-believing.

"He did it with a new form of magick that the god gave to him. His powers caused misery and death to the Egyptians." He nodded at me.
"Right, OK, Hiram, so this is all about me going to the Beast?" I questioned his reasoning.

"If you really are our Moses, then you will return from inside the gate to lead us. If not, then I'm sure you won't make it very far, and will fall like the rest of the Riders who have tried to destroy the Beast and take power into their own hands. Right now, you, like us, are just a slave to the Beast. You might not understand, but you have to trust your instinct. It's much deeper than what they tried to do to your mind in the lab."

"OK." I tried to understand what he was saying, I really digested his words.

"I just went straight to the point, but are you feeling better? A little cleaner, fresher, and revitalized, I hope?" He retreated into simple conversation.

"Yes, thanks. A bath was just what I needed."

Hiram started to take ash from the carved bowl. He made a crucifix motif on his forehead and on two younger boys next to him. They went to fetch a plate of food. It was fresh meats, poultry, and an animal lathered up Peking-style, with that orange glaze over it.

"Are you hungry?"

"Sure am. If I'm being honest, I could really use a stiff drink." The food looked good, but I was parched. The only thing to settle my nerves was alcohol.

"My daughter, Carmella, will pour you some. It's like moonshine, but we sweeten it with herbs to make the bite a little less than the hillbilly stills we get it from. Make it a civilized drink."

"Holy shit! She's your daughter?"

"Yes."

I learned that Hiram had the respect of everyone in this community. It didn't seem like he was elected through a democratic process or chosen, but more like he was the only one who had stepped up to organize and inspire everyone. It was a merit-based thing, and he'd won over the hearts of the survivors.

He didn't lead because of his wisdom, or material objects, but because of his will to keep the human spirit alive. As we talked more, he expressed his belief that humans' pure will to survive, and love for one another, would get us out of these dark days.

"We have a drive, a force unexplainable, that connects us all. We think it's inside of us, but it's through all of our collective consciousness that gives us power."

The more he talked, the more I believed in what he was saying. He was able to make sense of all of this, which was more than I could say for anyone else.

Maybe he was just a normal person on the outside, a hard worker in construction or in a nine-to-five, or even one of the homeless people who used to dig through Elise's and my trash looking for recyclables downtown. We'd always thought they were saying crazy shit, but maybe those random irascible phrases and spontaneous outbursts had been not only relevant, but the truth.

Carmella poured me the alcohol. The smell burned my nasal cavity, and it felt good, like fiery cinnamon. I held up my mug, a mug that read "I heart Dinosaurs."

"Cheers," I said to Hiram, who was not indulging. The first sip went down like lava inside of my organs; my whole body was awakened with life. Every follicle on my skin perked up, and the air around me suddenly felt cooler.

"Now remember," Hiram said. My vision was going blurry from the potency of the drink. I reached out to grab a leg of the Peking-style animal breast, but I couldn't seem to reach it.

"Damn, this shit is strong." I pointed at the coffee mug.

"Where did you come from?" he said to me.

"Los Angeles. I was born and bred here."

"How did you survive the blast?" I started to recall the memories of the lab and the portal. I didn't know if I should even talk about it. My words flowed from my mouth in an unorthodox way.

"I was in this lab, man. I volunteered for a job with these religious scientists. The pay sounded amazing. I knew the job was weird—other dimensions and crazy ideas. I just didn't think they were real."

"Oh, they are real, my friend. I know about the lab."

"You do! Oh, damn, of course you do. Yeah, I was getting all these tests done on me when bam! The blast hit, you know, scientists in their white coats spread out everywhere, bleeding and grasping at any remaining sense of life. I got out of the gurney and headed underground.

190

"Do you remember making it into the wormhole?"

"That's right! I went through the portal. Wait! Fuck, man. I went through the portal and then the explosion hit. Or was it the other way around? I don't remember."

"Yes, and do you remember the projection from your wrist before you went through to this dimension?"

"No, sorry. Can I get more to drink?"

He wasn't amused by my need for booze. His questions seemed important, but I honestly didn't remember. Besides, I wasn't sure those complex numbers below my DNA would help him in any way. I looked down at my wrist. The implant was raised, and the scar was pulsing pink.

"We are trying to figure out what year this is in the future," he finally said.

"What about this?" I lifted my wrist and showed him the microchip that was projecting a morphed image.

"Yes, yes. Let me see it." Hiram looked intently at the hologram.

"Get me the scope," he commanded. One of his cronies went and grabbed a metal, handheld light with a scope made from a multitude of lenses. He held it over the implanted microchip in my wrist to see the inscriptions.

"The year is 2033. This is incredible."

"Fuck, man. This is the future? Not much to look forward to."

"Do you remember how you got to the laboratory?"

I took another huge sip from the mug. It was empty now. I shook it in the air, requesting more.

"They said it was an image of my DNA. And said six, three, nine, I think."

"That doesn't really matter now. The projections will change based on your reality."

"Whatever you say."

"Will you go and kill the Beast?" Hiram cut straight to the point finally. He must have had enough of the small talk and finally asked me what he wanted to ask me.

"I'll do it, Hiram!" I said it with confidence, but inside I felt the fear. I wasn't sure this was something I could do. I might die. The thought didn't sit well with me.

"My boy!" Hiram raised his fist to me.

"I killed him off once. He took my buddy Reamus with him, but fuck it. I saw him. I'll get his name and take it from him."

"The sphinxes will get you! They will," one of the young boys shouted at me, almost excited about the possibility that a winged lion with a human head would tear me apart.

"You'd like that, wouldn't you. Me shredded by mythical creatures. Listen, kid, I got this. Let me loose. I'm ready."

"No, they will help you enter the gate. You will stay tonight and learn the strategy before you go back into the Wasteland."

"OK, I can dig that. This is a breath of fresh air compared to that place."

I did miss my old life, but the new one I was making in the Wasteland distracted me from the painful memories of the past. It was a seductive reality alongside Epiphany and her rituals and my strange fucking dreams.

I ate the food, and I felt better. The buzzing sound inside my head started to go away. It was like trying to swat a fly inside my head. It was impossible.

I sat and pictured going back to the Wasteland. There wasn't much for me there, but I knew I had to get back into the streets. I could go any time I wanted. I'd amuse them and stick around and share their food. I was their guest of honor, after all. Even though they'd ransacked me and kidnapped me. I wouldn't have gone with them otherwise. They hadn't wanted to put up with a fight, and I didn't blame them.

They made a sculpture from stone and spraypainted it gold. It looked like a sheep, but they assured me it was a calf. It didn't matter much to me. The symbology was wasted on my brain. I used it as a sign of freedom, to inspire me to get out of this cave to go see this Beast. Even if I was the sheep to the slaughter.

Before I went there, I had two more stops to make: first, the Café Revelation to see Ezra. My intuition told me that

Epiphany wasn't lying to me. She knew more than these false prophets, and she had helped me ward off the Beast in my first encounter with him in the other dimension.

The other stop I had to make was the First Street Bridge near our old apartment. Elise and I had exchanged our vows there, our life vows. The ones that bound us eternally. After that, the Beast could do whatever he wanted with me.

Hiram motioned for something from one of the younger boys. He came over with an object wrapped up in a stained cloth. He pulled back the layers of thick fabric, and inside was a knife. It was made of stone that looked like serrated onyx attached to bone.

"You will need this to kill the Beast."

"I got an axe, man. You want me to stick that tiny toothpick in a mystical fucking creature?"

"Yes. You will if you want to survive."

"OK, man. I'll take it." I reached for it, and he pulled back.

"Don't fuck this up." He looked at me in my eyes. It was the first time he'd been totally and completely direct with me. I listened like a juvenile delinquent who finally listened to his father.

"What's it made of?"

"Human bones and carbon."

"All right." I didn't really know how to answer that. "Like diamond?"

194

"Just use it. Don't forget."

I got up and shook his hand. He looked at me, recoiling from the formality.

We talked a little longer. I felt my eyes rolling back in my head and nodded off.

I woke up and I was back in the tent and felt weird. I didn't remember walking back there. I felt a stronger connection to humanity, my faith restored that there was an end, a means to fulfill this prophecy that I was a key player of. I couldn't remember being a part of anything bigger than myself before, and it felt good.

I smiled. It was a crooked smile, but I felt a light starting to return to me. The desperation was gone, replaced with the idea that the Wasteland wasn't the only place left, that beyond the borders there was a sense of normalcy. And most of all, my Elise lay just beyond the outskirts, waiting for me in this dimension or the next.

Anything was possible.

"Can I come in?" I heard a female voice.

"Sure. I'm just getting ready to leave." Carmella came in.

"Another bath?" I asked. She laughed a little.

"No, I wanted to tell you that I respect you. You are the first man who has not tried to touch me, you know, or come on to me."

"That took a lot of restraint—you are a beautiful girl. But you already know that." She looked down.

"It was very bad after the explosion. Men turned into animals, ravaging anything they could get their hands on."

I tried to feel her pain, but I couldn't. I couldn't possibly know what that was like. Having your body, your soul, taken from you against your will. I just knew it probably felt like having the love of your life taken away from you, but even that couldn't compare to the pain I saw inside her. She had been stripped of that sanctity of feeling safe. It was replaced with a certain hardness, and strength.

"I wish I could take your pain from you."

"Me, too. You would have to wipe my memory clean."

"I'm sorry."

They were the only stupid words I could get out of my mouth. I needed to get going, and this conversation was bringing me into a worse place than when I'd gotten into back in the tent. I wanted to listen to her forever, but I had to go. I leaned in to kiss her on the cheek and say "Goodbye," and she turned her lips and kissed my mouth. We fit together so softly. It felt perfect. But it made me think of Elise. "I'm... I don't know what to say." She placed her finger over my mouth. "No, you don't understand. The only reason I'm doing all of this is for my girl, my love. She's the one." Carmella shook her head.

"You really don't understand."

"Understand?"

"We are going to be married after you kill the Beast."

"Hold on there. I don't know what kind of stories good old Hiram is telling you, but I don't think so."

"That is the prophecy. Our union is fate."

"Fate seems like a mixed-up word here."

"Destiny. You prefer that?"

"I think I have a different destiny."

"This is it."

"When I find Elise, we will be together forever. You know, we're soulmates. You believe in that kind of thing, right?"

"I do. But she, she is gone now." Her words penetrated me. Not enough to cause me to tear up, but I knew the furrowing of my brow and my watery eyes let her know she needed to stop pushing me.

"I'll see you when this is all done. Maybe we'll have a drink together." I grabbed my pack and headed out.

CHAPTER 14

I left the cave. The freedom of the air was running through my flannel and into the crevices of my skin. It felt good. I rode straight downtown to the bridge.

"Elise, my heart and soul. I'm sorry. I know this is fucked-up. I'm fucked-up. I hope you are still waiting for me in this life or the next, my love. No matter what happens."

It sounded crazy, just saying it. Standing at the bridge again. The first time we'd said, "I love you." Right here. We'd promised. We'd made a vow to never be away from each other.

"I will find you."

I felt like a fool professing my love over the side of the bridge, but I needed to. I needed to talk to someone, even if that someone was just the memory of love, of what Elise's embrace felt like around me. It was warm and kind and honest. None of the things I felt when I allowed myself to be seduced by Epiphany's majestic body and mysterious spirit, but it wasn't time to feel guilty.

I started to replay that day on the bridge. I remembered running so fast to catch Elise. She'd been so stoic in the air above the cement, like she'd been frozen in time. I tried to remember the rest, but it was fuzzy. The conversation we'd had when she tumbled off the ledge and back into my arms had faded from my mind. I couldn't connect the dots. I couldn't remember what we had said to each other anymore.

My memory was nearly broken and gone.

I needed to get to the Café Revelation and figure out the next step. I turned and saw the bleak, marmalade-colored sky trying to burn through the smoky air. A few strands of light pierced it, and I could feel its warmth on my face. The particles of smoky debris and ash clung to my cheek.

I paused to confirm I was still alive. The rest of this was just a sadistic nightmare. I tried to convince myself without any success. I didn't belong here.

The clouds ate the rest of the light up, making sure no fragments existed to breathe hope into any living being. The bike was running low on fuel. I cruised back into my old garage to siphon more gas. The minivan was still there, as was the hose I'd hidden behind the tarp.

I grabbed it and felt a nasty sting on my finger. I lifted it up and saw a large black widow scurrying away, back into the creases of the tarp. "Fuck me." I hated spiders and hoped that this thing's bite wasn't going to cause my whole hand to swell up in agony. I acted quickly and squeezed my finger around the base of my knuckle, took the axe off my back and aligned my finger on the ground. I made a large slice in the tip, right over the two-pronged bite mark, and stepped on my finger with my boot. The blood squeezed out onto the concrete and looked purplish and oily. It felt good, a blunt pain, and the pressure started to release.

I got the remaining gas siphoned right into my tank. I fired up the motorcycle and went ripping out toward the Café Revelation.

I got to the café and I could hear a familiar bass line from an overplayed song from the 1980s. It sounded good to hear it, the Cure. Inside was the same crowd. I recognized a few of the faces from my last visit to this dump.

"You made it back," Ezra the bartender said, surprised.

"Needed more of that saucy booze you got lying around here."

"I'm sure that's not the only reason." Ezra was smarter than he looked. Or he was just a great bartender and could read his customers' motives. "He's over there in the corner." Ezra nodded.

"I'll take a mug of moonshine."

"All right, but you might need your wits with that one." He pointed to the guy in the corner, passed out facedown on the table.

I took the mug full of the heinous-smelling alcohol. I glanced to the corner of the room and my eyes fixed on him, the mole-faced man in the corner. He was bald, with eyes orbiting in dark circles, and adorned in leather holster straps over a vintage T-shirt. *Looks like a fucking BDSM goblin.* I didn't know it would be Cabal in the flesh.

"That's far enough. Put that axe behind the bar." I forgot I was still toting my axe everywhere I went. It had become part of me, so I didn't feel the bruises it caused around my spine, except when it wasn't strapped to me.

"Yeah, yeah. All right. I didn't know if you'd show up." I could feel his beady eyes beating down on my back as I headed over to Ezra at the bar.

"Keep this close, friend." I gave a nod to Ezra, though I didn't really know whose side he was on. I expected every living human left was out to avenge something or someone and take it out against me or the Beast on the other side.

"Now, that's better." The small man was drinking a concoction of green chunky liquid. I stared at it.

"You want one?" He choked down a couple sips and chewed on it in his mouth.

"Nah. I'm good. Got my own elixir right here. Ezra makes you that, too?"

"No, BYOB for me."

"You look different."

"We are all different on the other side. Why do you think I helped you?"

"I don't remember you helping me. It was more like leading me up to the only structure on that remote island."

"Whatever you saw, or think you saw. I am here to help you."

"So... help me, then."

"It doesn't work that way. We need to go to the other dimension together."

"When do you want to take that trip? I thought we were still getting to know each other."

"I'm sure they told you."

"Who?"

"Oh... Hiram and the filthy Washouts up in the caves."

"They are good hosts, though, I gotta say..."

"Do you think this is a silly joke? That we aren't all here suckling off a poison tit? You really don't get it, do you?"

Cabal grabbed my arm and put it on the table with my palm up. His tiny hands were strong; his nails latched into my skin, drawing blood.

"Look, look at it."

The blood started to trickle over my wrist where the strange written characters projecting from the silicon chip glowed, and Cabal started to outline archaic symbols in the blood on the table. Suddenly the patron next to us reached in swiftly and shoved a long knife in Cabal's direction. It missed his heart and struck him in the shoulder. I turned around.

"Kyle!"

Ezra tossed me my axe, and in one motion I spun and sliced into the assassin's neck.

Shelle-e-ewack! was the sound of the axe hitting him.

It hit with more blunt force than I'd imagined. It didn't just slice his head off. A large piece of it was still there; the neck was jagged, and it felt more like cutting into the bark of a rotting tree.

It was a hell of a lot messier than cutting down a tree, and the air reeked of spoiled milk.

I looked in the eyes left on his head, still half-stuck to his body, toppled against the table. His eyes were black circles. I didn't recognize the face, but the eyes. The eyes, I remembered, like Reamus's in the other dimension. The pupils never ended and looked like vibrating waves of neon-blue electricity.

"One of your buddies?" I looked at Cabal. He was bleeding in the corner, his back against the wall. I was also exhausted and breathing heavily.

"You know who sent him," he stated the obvious.

"Come on, cut this creepy mystical shit out. Now he's in the real world, too? I don't buy it, man. He was probably just a degenerate who didn't like the way you were looking at him."

"Ha! If only that were true." He was panting heavily.

"You gonna make it, man?" I saw the blood starting to leak from his shoulder wound.

"You might have to go there alone. The Beast won't let me pass the gate. He knows that I'm trying to help you. I've betrayed him."

"Just get me to that damn island again, Cabal."

"There is no island, don't you see?"

"I'm lost." The final mutterings coming from Cabal were all I had to cling to. The stink in the bar was starting to get to me. A Tom Waits song came on, and I was really starting to feel depressed, like this might never end. I took a massive swig from the glass on the table. I needed to settle my nerves. Waits' voice came over the bar about "easy street" and I knew it was far from easy for me.

Right now, the most complex poetry sounded simple.

"So, you gonna live?" Cabal was starting to cough up something nasty.

"I've had much worse." He motioned to the flask and I handed him his green serum. He guzzled it down. It seemed to help. "All right, I'm out of here. Going to find that Beast. Settle this thing."

"Wait." I recognized the voice. I turned around and there was Epiphany.

"I've been thinking about you. And look who I found," I said.

I figured she was here to lecture me about how I could not pass into this other dimension, or tell me that I was not ready.

"I'm ready to do this alone, but I could use your help." I leaned over to her and nodded.

"It's not that basic." She grabbed my arm and nuzzled up close to me.

"I'll handle it," I whispered in her ear.

"He will use everything and everyone you love against you."

"I don't have much left." I didn't have any more witty remarks.

I was heading off into another dimension to face the epitome of evil.

I was willing to go because I didn't really care enough about the reality of fear. I didn't feel the same fear as other people in the wasteland. The fear that clung to their faces, their insides, reeked of it like I was off to see the Devil himself. I pictured the Beast they talked about as a diabolical human behind all the madness, just sitting there playing with a model city where they could pull the strings and manipulate us like computerized dolls. Maybe it was like that. Or maybe I was making it up to quell the fear building inside me. The beast must be a disgusting creature.

"Hold me close," Epiphany said. Maybe she could smell the fear in me that I was doing my best to rationalize away.

I kept convincing myself that it was all a game and that was the truth, which lessened the reservations I had about carrying out this mission. But I knew this was the truth that I had to find and fight against for the preservation of humans everywhere.

I wiped the axe on a dishrag at the end of the bar and then finished my mug of moonshine that had a reddish tinge from drops of blood-splatter in it. It helped settle my stomach.

Epiphany was at my side. She put her arm around me and I pulled her closer and kissed her passionately. Time froze, and I felt like a statue with a woman in a loincloth clinging to my ankles after a great battle, like a Frank Frazetta painting. Just romantically fantasizing the shit out of the moment.

I held the pose while I finished off the last of my drink. I turned to leave, and she kissed me again. Her tongue pushed seductively in past my teeth. It grazed the inside of my mouth like sharkskin, but it felt powerful and good. I wrapped my lips around hers.

"Take this. Memorize it." Cabal reached up and gave me a piece of the table that was splintered on the floor that had writing inscribed on it.

"OK." I took it and read over the few lines. It was about death not being real. I flung it back to Cabal.

"Don't forget any part of it."

"I got it. It's no poetry." I walked out and gave a nod to Ezra.

"You better have it memorized. Or you won't make it back with your mind intact." Cabal's words echoed as I headed out of the café. Epiphany followed me out to the bike.

She stood there waiting for me to say something. She didn't let the pause last indefinitely. She grabbed my hand and put it into the waistband of her pants. I guessed she wanted to get one in before I vanished into the other dimension. In case I didn't come back this time.

Instead, she stared at me. She was glowing.

"Yes." Then she started to nod up and down coyly while I stroked her abdomen. She batted her eyelashes. I realized she was not really glowing. There was glitter on her cheeks, and it sparkled dully beneath the light coming in from the overcast sky.

I wasn't sure what the nodding meant. She did look sexy as hell, and I wanted to take a moment to understand her, but that could take time with Epiphany. I continued rubbing her abdominals and her stomach, which was bigger than I remembered. She kept looking down and at my hand and putting hers on top of it.

I had to get going. I jumped on the pedal to kick-start it while standing on the side of the bike. It fired right up.

"Take me with you," Epiphany said. I could hardly hear her over the sound of the engine.

"I can't—I thought about it and I don't want you to get hurt. You know that."

"Thank you, Kyle. OK, but I'm riding with you all the way to the wormhole."

"Please, get Cabal patched up. We might need him."

"You don't understand. I love you." I stared at her, my hand still in her waistband.

"I love you, too. Thank you. For everything. Let me finish this."

I jumped on my bike and tore off to the overpass on the Interstate 5 Freeway, leaving Epiphany behind. I felt an insane urgency inside me, and a deeper connection to her.

I rode fast down West Sunset Boulevard. The chunks of asphalt and potholes forced me to slow down so I didn't crash into any fatal obstacles. I cut right through the city at the base of the Hollywood Hills. I pictured Hiram and the other Washouts up there.

The cluster of human beings lived in those caves like animals. This must be our future as a species. I started to question it over and over again as I sped up over the uneven asphalt.

I still thought about Elise, but the image of her started to waver in my mind. The specter, the imagined version I saw of her on the beaches of Malibu, was as close to real as I could picture her. I reached up with my left hand and felt where the picture of her was tucked into the front pocket of my flannel. It was enough to make her real again. I took it out to look at it, but it got caught in the wind and flew away. I tried to grab for it in the air and nearly lost control of the bike. I steadied myself and realized she was probably gone forever. Tears came from the corner of my eye, but I didn't know if I was crying from the loss of Elise, and the memories, or from the wind blasting my face because of the bike's excessive speed.

"I'll miss you." My heart hurt.

I took Sunset all the way through the rest of Hollywood, in case the Washouts were tucked away in Beachwood. It was safer to gun it all the way through Los Feliz to the 5. I cut up to Griffith Park and then over the Shakespeare Bridge directly toward the wormhole and rode straight into it.

CHAPTER 15

Sticky air coated my face as I pierced through to the other dimension, and there was violent rattling all around me. The dimension was different than I remembered. The desert horizon had morphed into a pastoral landscape. It appeared to be moving, like watching erosion and tectonic plates shifting in stop-motion; layers upon layers of earth molting and moving with the tides of the inner core of the earth's magma.

Inundated with curiosity, my eyes began to wander, mirroring my shifty thoughts. Life was so crude in the Wasteland. Here I could almost feel it breathing. It was alive again and changing itself. It made me think about how many times the earth had transformed its surface, and maybe even its species.

I looked around. My motorcycle was gone. The grass was growing up around my boots rapidly. Spiny nettles clung to the laces.

Rolling hills filled the landscape. I took my first step and the ground crumbled below my feet. I started to run and follow the shifting earth beneath me, eyeing the ground as it slid off into the sky below. My legs carried me weightlessly across it, hovering up the hills. Pastures of the purest green filled the horizon—effervescent, the blades of grass sparkled. The grass looked so sharp that if my feet had been bare, it would have cut them open, bled me out from the bottom of my limbs, dripping blood into the barbed soil.

This dimension seemed to be governed by a natural frequency of electricity. The undercurrent was so powerful, I could feel it pulsing. *How did someone create such a terribly beautiful masterpiece?*

I reached the end of the hill. On the top was a churchlike structure. The steeple extended; an onyx pyramid outstretched to the sky. A road appeared that swirled around Tuscan-style trees, manicured to perfection. I had no choice but to follow the single winding road to the one symbol of humanity placed inside the grassy fields.

"On the highway to hell."

The magnetic pull from the building was enough to cause the hairs on my arm to stand on end. It pulled and manipulated the blood inside of me. I was charged up by a surrounding energy field. It pulsed and radiated like a wave I'd once surfed before in a perfect swell in the Pacific Ocean before it was unrecognizable from the pollution. The wave had highlights of blue and transparent white, crashing overhead in a foamy elixir. I wanted to be back there, but I felt a pure purpose now. I knew this was my fate—to walk into the Gate of the Beast.

"I'm no savior. But fuck it."

I was a good man to the woman I loved. I'd never questioned that. I'd never questioned much until after the lab, after the meeting with Michael—I didn't believe in chance anymore.

What mattered right now was that the desperate population in the Wasteland was depending on me to fulfill a prophecy—to kill the Beast.

My body moved mechanically, controlled by the pulsing waves of energy channeling through me. It moved me up the hillside at a controlled rate, like a conveyor belt, until I reached the entrance.

There was no door, no neon welcome sign, only rigid stones carefully placed in perfect symmetrical succession. The balance of each delineated only by the most miniscule line between them. The masonry was exceptional; it had to have been constructed by an otherworldly form, or gods.

I ran my hand over the polished stone. It felt soft—handwashed with a rag thousands of times to give the perfect sheen.

My eyes started to roll back in my head. I faded from consciousness, and in my broken vision I saw a cloaked figure. He came close to me and handed me a large silver-and-blue key. I took it from him, only it wasn't me taking it from him physically. My energy field, a dark-colored matter, seeped out from my body to accept the key.

It was like I was seeing myself through my third eye. The shadow version of me continued to walk away from my body. I'd birthed a silhouette of me moving with the help of imaginary strings.

My mental state was void and navigating the mechanisms of my unconscious. While my physical body was sitting there unplugged, I was a static target for the demons. The undercurrent of the physical world pulled at me, trying to get me out of this parallel dimension. I could feel the g-force tugging at my intestines, even in my deep state of barbaric hypnotism.

The cornerstone started to move as the key was slotted into the structure. The stone looked more like scales that peeled back. I went inside and the congealed, shadowy particle version of myself crawled back inside me. I felt it slither into my skin. I was whole again, but didn't feel like myself.

"You have reached the event horizon," a voice echoed. It was familiar.

"What do you want?"

"You know why you are here." The voice did not question, just understood my point of existence—something far from my capacity.

"But I'm just a nobody. Or am I now a savior? A Rider?"

There was no answer. It was a dead frequency. My mind scurried to find another answer, a better response to cover up my mission. *The reason I am here?* I thought about that in my head. There was no answer.

"There is no 'here,' all of this," I blurted out into the shadows.

"Doesn't it look real to you?" The inside of the building looked like human loins and tendons stretched like fishing line in crisscrossed patterns. It was grotesque and made me queasy.

"This shit is real." Beams of light, a milky yellowish-white, illuminated corners of the space.

"You remember what you cared about before you came here?" I thought about it. I couldn't really remember. It was blurry; thinking about the past made my head hurt and my mind bend in frustration, trying to find an answer. Now even the simplest memory was gone.

"See what you love and let it go." I looked around, and there in one of the beams of light, lit up so eloquently but posed like she was in pain—it was my love.

"Elise!" I struggled to free my body.

My body was so heavy with straps of my thought tying me down. I was paralyzed and wanted so badly to break out and touch her, free her. I couldn't. The resistance caused me to sweat and shiver. I was a prisoner to these temptations. I'd die in pain if I couldn't release her.

"Elise!!!" She did not respond to my voice. Zero recognition. She flailed around against the post she was tied to with leather bondage straps.

I could see that the leather restraints were cutting sharply into her skin. They were so tight, she bled.

"Let her go! Fucking maniac." Tears trickled down from my eyes. I wiped my face against my arm, still unable to lift my hands. My tears were bloody and smeared over my rough, pale skin.

"Elise!" I called out. My ribs contracted, forcing the sound out of my throat like a bleating horn. It trailed off just short of Elise. I could see the soundwave, its color metallic, fizzling out in the thick air of the quadrant.
"I... love." I tried to force more words out that used to carry meaning. They, too, fell flat. The ominous voice came back above us. It poured down through the sharp angles of the pyramid.

"Your face is in the Beast's hands. His nails are thorns on your cheeks, playing your every emotion. He is not the Devil, Satan, Lucifer, or the many incongruous translations of the 'bringer of light,' but the one who lives inside you. The knowledge that he lives as a figment, in a dark corner of reality, is enough to breed the fear. Now, let that go..."

"I believe you." I believed the voice. It made sense to me now. Maybe my desperation had died from the pain of trying so hard to reach someone that I loved. The only force holding me back seemed to be death. I let go of the anxiety that crept in.

I remembered the shadowy figure that crawled inside of me. I harnessed it, pictured the Beast and the carbon molecules flowing in and out of me like onyx locusts coming from the depths of my innards.

The insects flew out towards the light that still illuminated Elise. She was heavily drugged. She flailed forward as the black molecules poured into her mouth. She snapped out of the sedated state and yanked around violently. Whatever force had inhabited me now possessed her. She was losing control. Like a transplanted organ, her body rejected it.

Elise broke free from her restraints. The leather straps left bloody circles from where the harnesses on her wrists and ankles were tied. She staggered around, off-balance, and wandered toward me. It was the first time she was real—not a specter on the degrading beaches of Malibu. She reached out to me. Her fingers extended and touched my cheek. Her nails glided through the stubble on my face and touched my skin. I felt her for the first time in a long time.

The moment was still vacant, even with this contact. I couldn't attach any emotion to her touch. It didn't feel the way it was supposed to. Like when we'd been on the bridge, or the feeling I got every time we would argue and I would just go paralyzed. I didn't feel anything but the scratching of her nails against my face. She gripped tighter into my skin.

Blood seeped out from under her nails as she squeezed me harder. The blood and the digging of her fingers into my skin were the only things that felt human. I looked into her eyes and they were endless; this first love of mine was gone forever.

"Goodbye, sweet lover of mine. I loved you to death."

She was not mine anymore, but belonged to another force, inside the Gate of the Beast, where I knew in my heart she would stay. I was unable to move, even with my mind running rampant. I started to get sensation back in my body.

The air around us was alive and pulsating with dark energy.

Elise leaned in aggressively and pressed her lips against mine for one final kiss. She opened her lips and pushed mine open for me with the tip of her tongue. I could feel an immense force coming from inside her. She didn't kiss me; instead, she purged all the particles back into me. My body inhaled them like they were lost and I welcomed them back inside their home.

When the last particle was funneled from her mouth to mine, her eyes turned pure-white.

"Goodbye, Kyle. Don't forget me."

Her body went slack and my arms worked again. I caught the dead weight of her body against mine. It almost made me fall.

"I love you." It did no good. I laid her down gently. Bent over her, I tried to cry. Nothing came out. My eyes were dry, but filled with pain. I heard footsteps in the shadows. The voice came back.

"Can you see it now?" I looked around, trying to trace the source. I couldn't see anything. The voice reverberated and was hard to follow.

"You made it this far. All alone now, Rider." I recognized the voice. From the shadows came Michael. He was no longer in his suit and tie. He was wearing a long, dark-brown cloak, but his voice and presence made me remember him. I remembered how we met, the Chinese food; it all came back to me how I'd gone into that program, and the lab...

"Why did you do this to me?" I asked.

"You were more than willing."

"Yeah, but then LA fuckin' exploded. I'm sure you didn't plan for that."

"Our research showed the Rapture coming. Comets. Massive comets coming toward earth."

"Are we half-dead? Stuck in this dimension?"

"I was always in this place. Waiting for you. This is the future. The other side of the portal," Michael said.

"I wouldn't believe that bullshit. What I've been through, man, and seen. You weren't always here. That's for sure."

He walked steadily toward me and lifted the hood of the cloak and revealed his full face. It looked different than I remembered. His hair was nearly silver.

"Damn! You aged." I looked closer as he approached.

"Now you remember me." He reached up and pulled at his face. The tissue turned soft and almost melted right off into his hands.

Underneath the mask made of skin was my face. He looked at me. His eyes matched mine—the blue streaks were an identical replication. Every characteristic of his face was a flawless replication. His eyes seemed different, but as I

218

looked at them reflecting my own features, the two versions of me blurred together. I grew dizzy.

When I stared at my own mortality in the face, and recognized it, it burned. I forgot which person I was. My inner voice was the only thing that separated me from this replica.

My face was being pulled up by Michael's hands, only he was gone. His body was gone and there was nothing left in its place. The room had gone completely dark. The spotlights that had illuminated the space were gone, and the darkness consumed every square inch of me. I reached down on the floor, trying to feel Elise's body, to give me the sense of where I was, and take her with me. I felt nothing. The darkness seemed to be moving, rolling like a thick liquid.

I dropped my head to the floor, but there was no floor, just weightlessness, and my body tumbled, somersaulting down a cylindrical tube of gold streaks of light.

"God, help me!" I tried to cry out, but no sound, no whimper could escape my lungs. The pressure around me was heavy and warm.

"G-O-D." I finally purged the three letters from my mouth. I was curled on a wet surface in a fetal position, covered in sweat.

I reached for the dagger that Hiram had given me—I knew why I was here. To kill the Beast.

The Beast was inside of me. I stabbed wildly into the air. Then I stabbed into the duplicate image of me. I stabbed him right in the heart. Michael's caricature warped and bent inside, and I could not figure out which one of the two persons was me anymore. We were one. I wanted to absolve him and yank his artificial skin from inside of my body and shred it. I saw blood on the floor.

I must've killed him. I felt freed from his possession of my soul.

The dagger fell beside me, and I wilted into the wet tube— a hallway shaped like a chrysalis. My breath chanted out again the memorized phrases from the Café Revelation that I could hardly articulate before. The ones Cabal told me to say. The words now seemed so clear, ingrained in my memory. They tickled my throat. The different tones escaped my lips abruptly and sounded like incantations.

The chanting didn't disintegrate me from this nightmare and free me, it just stopped the darkness from coming in all around me. I didn't see my life pass before my eyes or my own mortality. I was battle-hardened from my dream. A dream that had become real.

"I'm ready to come home now." I got it out. The English language felt different. The words carried meaning and each letter had renewed power behind it.

I had never felt this way before.

CHAPTER 16

I fucking did it!" I yelled out when I walked into the Café Revelation. I expected cheers of joy because I'd basically just saved all of humanity.

I could have used a round of free drinks. It would take me back to my local watering holes downtown—the tilted neon lights of beer companies that had since lost one or two letters to age. Seeing a Miller High Life 'Champagne of Beers' sign right now would have been enough for me to call this home.

Even a simple, "Thanks, you are the greatest human!" would have been good enough. But there wasn't anyone here. The place was deserted. Almost like no one had been in here for years. Time seemed to have stood still. The light coming in from outside was creamy-white. It was filled with dust. Each time I moved, the dust pile on the floor spouted up into the air. I tried to walk carefully on the busted floorboards and kept the haze in the air to a manageable level. I pulled my shirt up over my mouth to minimize the taste of salty crud in between my teeth.

I went looking in the back room. I pulled back the curtain: nothing. The walls were naked, with smears on the exposed sheet metal that looked like grease from a broken-down engine. The oil was a dark, rancid color that I'd seen in the basin of many excessively used toilets.

"Where's Epiphany?" She wasn't here, either. Her presence still lingered, like right beside me, so close I could almost feel her calloused hands wrapped around my waist from the motorcycle ride up the coast to Malibu. Her grip under my shirt pressed firmly against the top of my pelvis and the other hand dug past my belt and down into my pants.

The memories caused sweat to form on my forehead. It dripped down my face and across my eyelids like tears. Only they weren't salty; they tasted like alcohol. It gave me all the encouragement I needed to go scavenging in this place for a few drops of booze.

Behind the bar, in the shelves, were a few leftover Mason jars. I grabbed one. It was sealed tight as hell. I twisted harder, but it was no use. I held on tightly. I couldn't afford to drop this one, as the inventory was depleted. I grabbed a dirty dishrag and wrapped it over the lid, prying it open with a jerk. It unsealed and a breath of the trapped air inside burped out. The alcohol spilled a bit and burned my skin, but it felt good.

I took a swig and wiped my lips with my forearm. The serum crawled into my body. It stung and soothed me.

"I've missed you."

It tasted so good and burned just right. My taste buds popped and my gums receded in harmony, letting the dirty air rush in over them. I licked my lips and tasted the blood from my chapped lips. It left a sour aftertaste.

The memories of the lab started coming back again. Constant images of IVs being stuck in my veins pounded in my head. I looked at my wrist, the scar burned underneath from the heat of the microchip. and saw the green LEDs still there, muted below the surface of my skin. The scar was real, the burn was real, and the human testing I was subjected to in order to travel into the future was real, too.

The horror of the memories was broken by sounds outside. I heard someone scuffling. It sounded human and not animal.

"Could be a sewer rat the size of a person." I remembered chomping down on that fur in the sewers while escaping the lab. Thinking about the clumps of fur made me nauseous.

I stayed on-guard for whatever was coming around the corner and into the café. The alcohol was dulling my senses. I felt drunk already. The door to the café started to open. I looked around for a weapon, or anything that could be used to spear anyone who trespassed. I lost my balance and the room started to spin. My arms slid down the bar. I tried to regain my balance, but tumbled onto my back like a submissive dog. I passed out.

I opened my eyes. Above me was a longhaired figure. It could have been a boy or a man. I couldn't tell, but his hands were nimble, and he lifted me up by the front of my shirt. I was helpless. Goddamn, my tolerance sucked. I couldn't remember feeling this wasted since I'd been a teenager.

I was loaded into a covered wagon-looking truck. It was an old pioneer thing from the Western frontier. The engine started and I had a strong suspicion this truck was not going to paradise.

There was no fear left in me. I had been purged of the ability to conceptualize my fate on any level where physical pain existed. I was an exile. The lack of fear gave me a sort of freedom that I'd never felt before.

I woke and I was strapped up. My hands bound and feet chained to rivets. I dozed off under the tarp in the back of the wood truck bed. There was no point in trying to escape, so I started dreaming.

I pictured the world as it had been before, only nicer. It was a place that felt like Utopia. There was no government control, no media manipulation, and people said "hi" to you on the street when you passed them by, giving little nods and waves, acknowledging the underlying human connection. This dream felt good. The sidewalk underneath my feet glittered in the warm Cali sun. I dreamed of the old ways that seemed so far away now. The simple pleasures of feeling the rain on my skin, and staying indoors with Elise watching movies. Even the rain coming from leaks, finding its way along the exposed steel beams in the loft. Tracking them to their source and then collecting them in pans or buckets. This simple life was comforting.

I hoped that I was not alone in this feeling of freedom. The death and destruction that was inevitable made me run toward the light. It took blinding dedication and recklessness to encounter the end of this life and the beginning of the next with no pain. Joy was not the feeling, or pleasure. It was pure passion for the life burgeoning ahead of me.

I felt vindicated by having purpose again.

I would liberate the tortured humans in the Wasteland—the lost angels whose shadows careened in and out of the city. They were betrothed to the Rapture. They would feel the fire when I released my words and announced what I had seen in the other dimension. I'd seen the future, and I could save them.

The Beast used a light wave, pulsing at intermittent tones and emitting a frequency that served as a beacon to all the wandering souls to come and get born again. When the people realized it was a trap, it was too late.

My theory was that it was like a battery made of human souls. It trapped all the energy and could only be used and harnessed by a select group of people, the Riders. It had to be the Riders because they fed on the weak. They were like predatory birds picking at the remains of humans in the aftermath. They wanted our energy, our life force; it was the only thing that was more powerful than the sun. If they could really harness it, where would its collective energy field take us?

I believed in something greater. The richness of the human spirit was a banner held high above the manipulation of our minds. This was not a random dream, or romantic bullshit ideal; the thought was becoming our reality.

When I woke up from my elaborate dream of paradise, there was a group of boys—I suspected Washouts, by their appearance—standing over me. My dream was about a utopia, but it was short-lived.

They examined me like I was a cadaver. My body quivered because I was not dead. I could feel internal organs, like my liver inside of me, that I hadn't felt before. I adjusted my body, but remembered I was restrained. The ties looked like they were made from horsehair around my hands. The mane was tied together in bundles, and it was scratchy as hell. A rash was developing on my skin.

"What the fuck? Is this really necessary?" I had to ask.

"You'll find out soon enough." One with a snaggled front canine tooth spewed the words out. Age spots covered the sides of his face. When he squinted, it looked like he had on a painted mask around his eyes made of brown-colored spackle.

"Give me a hint. The suspense is just killin' me." My sarcastic charm came back. It had been dormant, but maybe my optimistic nap had brought my personality back.

I remembered the best part of this human world that remained intact. Her name was Carmella. The image of her olive skin and dark-colored lips—a slightly different shade of brown than the rest of her body—filled my mind. I started to obsess about her and shut my eyes. I remembered every detail of her. She had on a silver armband. I remembered it because it stood out from everything else here, all the dullness here in the caves, the blunt edges and the muted colors. Her silver band reflected light, and you could see the metal was well-polished and looked foreign to everything else around us. It was even more bizarre to see something of monetary value. The only currency now was objects that sustained life, like food, or which could be used as weapons to defend or attack.

When I opened my eyes there was a chalky white powder covering my skin. It smelled toxic, like ammonia or bleach, and looked like powdered milk.

"You guys dip me in a cocaine bath, or what?" It was wishful thinking.

"You have been cleansed." The large man with snaggled teeth was serious and shrouded.

"Well, finally someone tells me real shit that's useful, not just spoken in tongues," I said sarcastically.

"Now you are ready for the ceremony."

"I'm honored, man, really I am." He looked at me from under his white hood. His eyes were transparent blue. His skin, nearly as white as mine, was covered in the chalk. His eyes were so clear, like the light had washed away the solid colors all the way down his veins that connected his eyes into his skull.

"I'm sure you get this a lot, but your eyes are a trip. Kind of fucking creepy."

He didn't respond and started to paint with a reddish substance on my forehead. It dripped into my mouth. I licked it off my teeth with my tongue. It was blood.

"Am I being sacrificed or what? Damn it! You're going to eat me, aren't you? I knew you were cannibals." He didn't respond. I struggled to get up.

"Throw me a bone?"

"This is the blood of the calf. You will cross over today."

"I've already been to the other dimension. In fact, a fucking lot of them."

Maybe they would put me out of my misery, euthanize me. I didn't know what the hell this freaky man was talking about. I was finally back to the Wasteland. It felt realer here than all the other crazy places I'd been, and yet I still couldn't get any straight answers to my questions. I just wanted to be able to make sense of the words. They always sounded normal, but the meanings escaped me like a foreign language I was raised on, but could no longer understand.

I tried to release the urge to control the situation, but the blood markings on my face were starting to itch, and I couldn't scratch them.

This was a ceremony. It had taken a lot of planning. I'd ride this one out, then escape from the cave. And as much as I hated to say this, I'd go find Epiphany. I'm sure she had the answers. She was the only one who kind of had a normal existence as a telepathic nymphomaniac. But that kind of worked for me.

Now I knew why Michael wanted to see what was in this portal, what this other dimension was. It was incredible, and I might be the only one with answers about what the future really lookcd like.

I saw the cave. I didn't remember the scale of this place. It was a fully working city inside of the hills. It was an endless maze throughout Hollywood, the relocation spot of everyone who was still human after the blasts. These hills existed below the sign, Beachwood and Laurel Canyon—even the houses around Lake Hollywood had slid right into the reservoir. The caves seemed to be the largest refugee encampment in the city.

They propped me up on the wooden table. Sitting up gave me a rush of blood to the head. My temples were throbbing. The blood pumped unevenly. My hands gripped tightly to compensate for the painful gurgling in my stomach. I was in between throwing up and choking down the taste of bile in the back of my throat before it triggered vomiting.

"Where's Hiram? I need to see him. He'll understand." I pleaded and tried to demand his company.

The Washouts were laughing spastically. It was fucking weird, but I went with it. I saw their faces quiver and their cheeks contract and expand. It made for a depressing synchronization of facial expressions.

I swiveled my legs off the table. I jumped, nearly falling into the crevices of the bedrock. The Washouts grabbed my arms above the elbows. Their touch was balmy. They directed me down the passage of the cave, entering the main city area. The city was shoddily constructed, and there were bridges interconnecting the different parts.

We walked down one of the bridges toward the top of the rock to the same place where I'd first spoken to Hiram. The city was kinetic with excitement. I could feel a sense of hope wash over everyone in the cave.

A young boy, missing a few lower front teeth, waved his hand and flashed a nearly toothless smile at me. The remaining lower teeth pressed against his lip in more of a snarl than a smile. He ran off.

Another boy of about fifteen was in a wheelchair made of old auto parts, a used seat from a '90s car sitting on bicycle rims. The spokes were a little bent, but completed with a couple cards spread throughout the rims to make a flapping noise as he trawled alongside of us over the bridge. It sounded almost like automatic machine-gun fire with fake paper bullets.

A dulcimer started to play loudly, and the hairs on my skin stood on end. The melody was a cryptic version of a traditional song I couldn't quite identify. The dulcimer was slightly out of tune, making it sound even more demonic. The notes were all-too-familiar, and spread eerily throughout my bones and into the rest of the caves.

I looked up to see a row of five Washouts without shirts, covered in reddish paint—it was smeared across their faces. They were banging on skinned drums. The pounding bass was all muddied together in a wave of beats. I looked closer to see they were using large bones as drumsticks. The look of the drummers made me question whether this ceremony was cannibalistic.

230

As we approached, flowers and grains were thrown all over us. I saw Hiram standing there next to a veiled woman. The tan, olive skin of her arms let me know it was Carmella. I felt uneasy. The taste in my mouth from nearly throwing up still lingered. It was bland, but smelled earthy and left grit stuck between my teeth.

I was enchanted and my body felt in a trance. My compulsion toward Carmella was like a tiny voice at the bottom of my stomach, behind my pelvis, that was telling me secrets about her. These secrets seemed to pull me unconsciously into her. The closer I got, the more powerfully the combustion inside of me hammered away, like an engine struggling to the end before it dies.

Every person in the Wasteland was a messenger. They had all given me purpose. Now I was starting to listen. Maybe they were embodiments that destiny took to guide me through this world. I questioned it, but also believed the mantra. The words repeated in my head: *This is your fate, embrace it.*

Still, my instinct was to turn and run back across the bridge. The human instinct to escape from danger was so powerful, I almost went blind. My body twitched to the right, trying to pivot 180 degrees. The teenager in the makeshift wheelchair swerved in front of me and the other young, blue-eyed guard wearing an old Boy Scouts uniform gripped even tighter to my bicep. My arm throbbed. The air was sweaty and vacant like a cheap coffin. The last Boy Scout squeezed my arm and my equilibrium shifted. I felt drugged on ketamine, as if I had vertigo. The two feelings were intermixed and indistinguishable.

"Did you drug me? Because I feel like I'm walking on marshmallows." There was no response.

I didn't have solid control over my muscles. I couldn't move my feet except in a sluggish dragging motion. I was stuck following this path. I kept walking forward until I was standing across from Carmella. She was a true enchantress. I didn't think about it before our last encounter, but she really was perfect-looking. Her skin was so tan, like a Peruvian princess with the cheekbones of a high-fashion model. She didn't need makeup or anything to be flawless.

"Hi, there. So, maybe it was worth it," I said to her through the veil.

Hiram looked at me strangely.

"We heard you did it," he said.

"It was fucked-up. Once I saw a duplicate of myself in that place, I knew what had to be done. It was like I was programmed for it."

"I knew you would either remember or die trying in selfish misery."

"Thanks," I shrugged.
I didn't really know how to respond. I thought about the other dimension and looked around me to see how many onlookers were observing our conversation. I felt their eyes on me. They were assessing every movement, every twitch of my skin, and following the droplets of perspiration as

they rolled down the sides of my cheeks and onto the hairs of my arms.

Carmella just stood looking at the ground until I took her hand in mine.

"You're good with this?" I thought it was right, even if only a formality, to ask if this was her choice or an arranged marriage.

Her eyes met mine. They welled up with tears. The puffs under each eye looked like little caramel macaroons. I hadn't realized until now that one of her blue-green eyes was discolored. The corner of her eye was fading from greenish into white. I couldn't tell if her tears were from joy or out of sadness—I was too focused on the discoloration in her eye. I was fascinated by the imperfection of what was otherwise the most perfect woman. Her pupils looked like scorpions preserved in a Mason jar of green formaldehyde. I put my arm around her lower back. Her skin was soft and buttery. It felt so different than I remembered, like it was soaked in olive oil. My fingers massaged her muscles. I could feel them loosen. She turned to me again and her energy shifted. It didn't seem to be a completely forced union sanctioned by a religion.

The deacon or whatever the hell he was started in on his own version of a wedding service. He had lowered his white hood and put on a big top hat and a lot of silver vintage turquoise jewelry. His white button-down shirt was in tatters underneath his tuxedo jacket, with smears of an unidentifiable liquid on the right lapel. The thing that stood out most was his teeth. They looked like boar tusks filed down into miniature daggers. Every time he lifted his arm, the jewelry clanged around and his turquoise ring passed by his fierce bony teeth.

This wasn't the Vegas wedding I'd pictured with Elvis, the King, marrying me and my sweetheart. I tried to relax. Having my hands on Carmella set me at ease. If it was drugs I was on, I decided to just enjoy the trip and listen to this voodoo witch doctor of a priest unite us forever.

"This is a union we have been waiting for," he started. His voice was much clearer now. It still had the guttural vibration I'd felt earlier when he'd been dabbing my face with the blood paint. I was expecting him to speak an incantation that had subtextual meanings, but it was partially clear he was speaking English.

"In the wake of the collapse of the Beast, a soldier was born unto us. He has transformed the path to reach the other dimension."

I couldn't take my eyes off Carmella. She looked like a real-life princess. The priest's words faded into the background, spreading over the crowd but not distracting me from my thoughts. I pictured us away from the cave. I continued to daydream and think about all the exotic locations we could travel to. I wasn't sure what else still existed beyond the Wasteland. I'd seen the edges of it—the Pacific Ocean turned black, eating away the landmass.

There had to be another way out of here. Another civilization: survivors must also have escaped the blast, as it had seemed to mainly affect Los Angeles. Maybe it finally detached California from the rest of the continent. We couldn't exactly flip open a *Travel + Leisure* magazine and dog-ear the pages of destinations and book our tickets.

"We join them for eternity. They will give us the continuation of our civilization, transcend the dimensions, and bring back what we need to survive." His words finally pierced through.

The words were intensely spoken, but I swallowed the simplicity of the benediction. It didn't go down as easy as a vanilla milkshake from In-N-Out, but it had a subtle coolness to it. I remembered seeing an In-N-Out sign half-buried in the caves, with a string of white lights wrapped around it, illuminating the sides of the red rockfaces. That's what made me think of it.

I was standing again, balancing on my own two feet, and I could see the world around me. I could sense it, too—the humanness of it all, the contagious energy that swept through a crowd of people gathered for a purpose. You could almost hear the hum of emotional electricity like the sparks from a fluorescent bug zapper cage. *Zzzzp. Zzzzz.* I could hear it crackling and popping.

I turned to the crowd; their faces were not recognizable. I tried to distinguish a few of them, but with certainty I did not know anyone. Los Angeles was a big fucking place. Before the blast, even within a few square blocks, I didn't know too many of my neighbors; I barely recognized their faces on a daily basis.

The chance of me recognizing anyone's face now, when everyone was altered by starvation, with sunken cheekbones and covered in dust, was next to none. It was past the static of their eyes, behind it, that there was the strongest will to survive. That was where the beauty lived inside them.

"You may now unite for eternity. Kiss the bride." These were the only words I heard, breaking my focus on the presence of everyone to look at Carmella.

I lifted Carmella's lace veil, spun from what felt like spiderwebs—it was so sticky from the humidity in the caves. I leaned in and kissed her lips. Her lips felt so good. Their warmth was perfectly squishy, and the sweat on her skin made them taste salty.

I was already addicted to her with carnivorous fervor. Whatever personal secrets she had in her past seemed trivial now, and so did mine. We shared a certain collective misery. Our fingers molested the pulse of life, pressing against it like sandpaper, and grinding away until our fingerprints were obsolete, and our identities became anonymous. We felt hope again.

She took my hand in hers and we turned around to face the Washouts. Our union connected by the pressing of our palms against each other. The point of our hands, skin against skin, felt magnetic. The pulse inside her was prominent against the vein in my hand.
We had hope again. We could give that hope to everyone else here who had survived. They had similar stories of misery and needed to believe in a brighter future, too.

236

The crowd clapped and blew kisses into the air. This was a bigger affair than I would have imagined. The applause echoed through the caves and then came back at us. It made it hard to discern where the sound was originating. It just felt like a blanket of noise that was all around us. Hiram looked at me again and took my arm before I could fully move from our perch above the rest of them.

"You know what you must do. Don't let us down. We don't have a choice but to believe in you."

I wanted to agree with him, nod and say, "No problem, sir," like any normal groom would say to appease his new father-in-law, but I couldn't. I couldn't because I didn't know what was next.

I didn't have what it took for all these missions and prophecies, and didn't like the idea of going back into the other dimension. I was taking in the idea of my new, beautiful bride, which went down uneasily because Elise remained on my mind.

We started walking down the stairs and into the crowd. The different groups of people parted away from us. I felt something wet on my leg. I looked down and saw a cattle dog that reminded me of Chico. He was probably dead now. My eyes got watery. I couldn't imagine he had made it out of their nets. I couldn't. I hoped that mutt had made it out of the Wasteland. Maybe that Washout kid might have scooped him up. I bent down and he licked my face. His breath smelled like salmon. As I rubbed his head, it looked like he was talking. I tried to make out the words. I heard them in my head, too: "Be careful. She is here." I wasn't sure if the dog was really talking, but I heard it.

I stood up and squeezed Carmella's hand, clenching it. We continued navigating through the crowd. Near the bridge, that's when I saw her. She was standing there. The only one wearing black clothes: Epiphany. Epiphany looked at me sharply. Her bright-green eyes saw right through me. Her gaze stung me a little bit inside. I tried to avoid her, but she was in me now. Her voice was in my head, crawling around. It interrupted the enchantment of this moment.

I continued walking, but couldn't avoid the impulse to look at her again. I needed to confirm that I was not hallucinating. I scanned her body. She seemed swollen, her cheeks puffy like she'd been crying. *She looks thicker than I remember, not nearly as athletic.* Her curves had been so proportionate before, and her skin fitted around her muscles. You could feel every shape of her body, each individual stomach muscle defined in a tight six-pack. She looked softer now, gentler. She looked really good.

A mesh veil covered her body. It was see-through, and below the fabric I noticed it. It was subtle, but it was a bump. When I focused on it, it was not a small bump, either. I thought about the last time we'd had sex. It was insane. It felt like it was so long ago. Time was on an accelerated rotation here.

I connected with her mind again, and we were speaking telepathically to each other. She was transmitting her thoughts into my head that she was pregnant. I remembered again about the last time we'd had sex. I saw it now very vividly. She'd held me so deep inside her, and I hadn't been able to pull out. Her face had morphed into Elise's; the flashback caused me to get dizzy again and nearly fall.

My grip on Carmella's hand tightened so much she nearly let go, jerking her arm back in response. She held on to me despite the pain of my grip and helped me regain my footing. She knew something was wrong, but didn't change her expression of contentedness, maintaining her royal disposition to the crowd of people.

She was royalty here, and her demeanor showed her strength as a woman. She was honoring their new way of life, but I knew she deserved better than me. Carmella was a woman who deserved anything she wanted. I saw her as the warrior she was, and in comparison, for the first time I saw my own weaknesses.

I tried to block Epiphany out. I laughed inside. I shook off the image and thought it was a residual effect of all the weird serums I'd imbibed. The alcohol wasn't helping either. Right when the alcohol subsided, I had always taken another drug to counteract the pain of my existence.

There was a welcoming party for our wedding reception. It felt good, except I didn't know anyone. I continued to think, and the whole wedding celebration didn't become real again until I took a sip of grain alcohol. It burned and felt just right going down my throat. The burn traveled delicately, making me conscious of all the inner workings of my organs again, and sizzled my lips.

"What is bothering you?" Carmella finally asked me.

"Oh, nothing. Thought I recognized someone. Maybe past-life-type shit."

"Really, who?" She was prying. And so intuitive; I knew I couldn't hide a damn thing from her.

"Someone I used to know."

"A past love? Or just someone you slept with?"

I was not sure how to answer the question. It was all short-lived love in this place, pure passion. I had to admit to myself that I craved Epiphany. Her body, and something more... something moved my heart again. It continued to gnaw at the inside of me. The second glass of alcohol masked the constant discomfort, the thoughts about my past that bubbled up into my brain.

My past life of love, those memories, and the guilt was so nauseating that I thought I would die. I finally realized I'd never have Elise again. Up until this very second in time, I still believed I would be together with her. Even throughout the ceremony, I'd still felt that tiny flashlight bulb of hope revealing the love we'd had. It was almost gone now. Admitting to this was the hardest part of it all.

The marriage had gone from being a dream to a nightmare. I slugged down another mug of alcohol. I was still not thinking straight, and my focus was on losing everything and not my new wife. *Shouldn't I be happy?* I craved the feeling of being in the loft with Elise. The feeling didn't come back to me—the feeling that you called home. I was in a new place where I had to evolve and exist within the caves above Los Angeles, or what was left of it. This was my new home. This was my life.

CHAPTER 17

I heard footsteps outside of our tent. I didn't remember falling asleep. My eyes were covered in a crusty paste, and my throat was chafed from the high-proof booze. The bed was covered in calfskins, and it wasn't very comfortable. Inside of my body, the dehydration crackled like a fire going out and the embers left a spicy acidity as an aftertaste. I shifted gears into hunter mode and tracked the sound. It got closer and closer, moving from right to left. I found an opening in the tent where light was pouring in. It was a slit in the canvas in the shape of an upside-down V.

A hand pushed back the opening of the tent. More light poured in. It was Epiphany. She looked different. She had removed her veiled clothes and was wearing white fabric draped and tied around her body. She put her finger over her mouth, telling me to be quiet. I couldn't make a sound if I wanted. My throat was still so fucking dry I couldn't swallow.

I leaned over and coordinated my feet to touch down softly on the dirt floor. The blood rushed down to them and I got lightheaded. The spots and pixels poured into view in repetitious waves, nearly blinding me until they settled. I stood and walked over to her. I rested my hands against her tough skin. I tried to lean into her and direct her out of the tent. She resisted my weight with hers.

"So much time has passed," she whispered into my ear.

"Yeah, crazy shit happened."

"I know. I saw it when the lion ornament fell from my tree."

"What?"

"Feel what we have created."

She placed my fingers on her chest and slid them down to her distended stomach. The baby bump threw me into a fucked-up tailspin. I lost my balance and fell into her. She caught me. I heard more commotion outside.

"Come with me," she said.

Epiphany pulled my hand with hers. Her grip was so tight on mine. Part of me wanted to run with her; the other wanted to stay here, protected by my new life inside the caves. The confused voices inside of me felt like multiple personalities. The visible facial expressions must have been changing on the surface of my skin.

"Let me go," I said. Her eyes turned scary serious.

"You have to come with me." I shook my head.

"I belong here. I think."

Epiphany looked at me. She looked over my shoulder and saw Carmella, her naked body sticking out from underneath the calfskin blankets. She pushed me aside and headed toward Carmella. She grabbed an iron candlestand like a spear. I couldn't get my footing on the dirt floor in time to stop her momentum.

I barely caught her and grabbed her arm; she had slung the makeshift weapon at Carmella like a javelin. Because of my interference, it landed just short of the bed. I grabbed her arm and restrained her. Carmella rolled onto her side and woke up. She jumped to immediate action.

"What the hell! How did you get in here, witch?"

"His baby is mine."

I was looking at her, Epiphany locked in my arms. Carmella didn't understand what was happening. The candles on the floor had started to ignite the draped sheets and sashes in the tent. Carmella jumped up and didn't look at us again. She grabbed the bathwater from the basin and doused the sheets on the floor. It put the fire out.

I restrained Epiphany. She was still struggling to get at Carmella, grabbing in the air, trying to attack her. She was relentless, her arms frantically clawing.

"What does she want with you?" Epiphany squealed.

"I'm married to him. We are destined for each other."

"You have no idea."

"Is she possessed?" Carmella said.

"Maybe she is, but she saved my life on the outside."

Before anything more could happen, a few of the Washouts came into the tent.

"Are you guys all right?"

"Yes," Carmella said.

"Yeah, I guess," I said.

"Please get her out of here. I don't want her near us again," Carmella ordered the guards. I was shocked, still confused by what was going on.

"I'll kill you," Epiphany screeched at Carmella as the Washout boys dragged her out of the tent.

"I fucking love you, Kyle," Epiphany continued to yell outside of the tent, her voice drowned out through the canvas.

Carmella got into the bed. She turned her back to me. I didn't know if she expected me to come hold her or get out of the tent.

"I'm sorry." They were the only words I could find.

I would have been appalled by the whole scene if it had been the other way around, but it didn't seem to bother her. I was stuck in my head. It was spinning, thinking about the life growing inside Epiphany.

I paced around the tent. It wasn't a lot of distance, but the repetition felt good. I knew my path and each step felt right. The dry, dirty bedrock under my toes was gritty and reminded me of the beach sand. The air was stale and smelled like sweat and burning wax.

I tried to calm down and got back in bed. Her body was warm. She felt so good, but something was pulling me down into the ground—a weight I couldn't describe. It felt like a burning chain endlessly pulling through my bowels into the rock.

"What will they do to her?" Carmella mumbled. It was a precious whisper. I couldn't understand what it was. "What did you say?" I asked. She rolled over and looked me in my face. Her sleepy eyes were glowing.

"They will probably tie her up. Question her and then kill her." She said it so damn casually.

I'd never seen this callousness in her. I realized that I barely knew her. I marinated on the thought.

"They can't do that!"

"You don't want to defend her, do you?" I did want to protect her. I owed her.

"Are they going to kill me if I do?" I asked again, questioning her about my own fate.

"No. Stop worrying. It'll be all right." She rolled back over and looked at me with adoring eyes. I looked at her, but I thought about my baby inside Epiphany.

"You can't just kill her! She's done nothing wrong."

"She tried to mess this whole union up. Try to get some sleep. It's OK." She put her finger on my lips and then kissed me gently.

"She saved my life!"

"That witch! She's lying to you." Carmella said it convincingly.

I almost believed her, but everything Epiphany had said just felt truthful. I'd seen the oversized bump. It had looked like she was almost six or seven months pregnant. She looked nearly ready to pop. It wasn't small or unnoticeable. She just hid it well with her fit body and thin profile until she was in the tent. It had then been unmistakable and huge.

I couldn't decide what was worse: the thought of Epiphany literally getting burned at the cross, or the idea that she might be carrying my baby and they still would sacrifice her.

"Fuck, Carmella." She looked at me, sullen.

"It will be all right. I promise you. We know her. She's full of shit."

"What do you mean you know her?"

Carmella gave a glance to the corner of the room.

"They're all the same. She's creating an illusion. Manipulating you."

It seemed like Carmella was the one lying to me.

It was impossible that someone could create an illusion of being pregnant. They were or they weren't. She might not have taken a drugstore pregnancy test with a plus or a minus on it, but who in the fuck cared? I could see it with my own eyes, and felt it inside me, too. I felt a protective instinct sprouting within me that was unexplainable.

I replayed the whole wedding and the moments of darkness, of lacking consciousness in between. None of it made sense.

The images of Carmella in the wedding started to come back to me. I saw her face up-close. She had an inner pain that I could feel in my heart, like the longing for someone who would never come home again. It was in her eyes, a certain vacancy. The existence of it inside of her made her even more powerful and her beauty overwhelming.

We were married. That was true.

Carmella kept pulling at me to get back in bed, so I got on top of her. I stared into her eyes. They were deeper than I remembered, and her beauty was so imperfectly perfect. I was transfixed and kissed her. My tongue licked her lips and slid inside of hers, our tongues licking together, and I lifted her legs to her head and I fucked her so hard. She ached for my touch. I pushed even harder inside her. Then over and over again, I didn't stop until she came so many times she passed out.

I lay awake on my back. It took me a few minutes and I made a decision. It came to me as a voice in my head. I felt really guilty about fucking her. Epiphany could've been telling the truth. It wasn't the first time her prophecies came true.

"I'm getting out." It was like I'd broken the spell of the caves. The mystical brooding of the Washouts had served to hypnotize me from the reality outside of here, and the whole reason I'd been sent through the portal in the first place.

I got up and put my clothes back on—not the weird tunics and fabrics they'd draped me in, but my old dirty-ass jeans. They didn't fit right anymore. My skin was swollen and fattened by the heavy air in here.

I crawled outside from the yurt and saw that most of the Washouts had crashed hard.

The aftermath of the wedding ceremony had everyone sedated and had put them in a deep celebratory slumber. It was what the world would look like if everyone continued to drink booze and take Xanax all day. They were near-comatose. A vivid image of the old Los Angeles resurfaced—the superficiality and lackadaisical attitude—and then it faded fast.

I had to sniff my way through the cave air to find Epiphany. I might as well have been on all-fours like a bloodhound, with my heightened senses from enhanced instinct. A big part of me wanted to just get the fuck out of here and leave the caves behind, but I couldn't. I had this pulling sensation inside of my heart. It was so strong I was nauseated by it. I choked up bile into my mouth.

The feeling made me chase after Epiphany. *Where the hell did they take her?* I thought about it. I retraced the scene of the wedding. Nothing there made sense as an entrance to purgatory. There had to be a prison, a hold where they took outsiders and locked them up. I closed my eyes and pictured it in my mind. I could see the sandy edges of the cave surrounding the bars—a primitive facility built by the Washouts. The vision of it led me down the halls past most of the village and up into the catacombs. The blended noise of the sleeping city started to dissipate down the caverns as I got farther from the center of town.

The cave I was in didn't seem to end. I was out of breath, and my heavy breathing circulated the disgusting taste of leftovers and bile in my mouth. The hope of finding Epiphany subsided. I was standing still, half-drunk in a cold cave. The air carried sounds and echoes of voices, but the words were muddled together like whispers in a foreign dialect. I was not alone.

As I traveled through the caves, I spotted a couple Washouts around the corner. One of them had a bald head covered in tattoos. The other was smaller and wearing a bunch of chains with locks on them. The chains were probably his weapon of choice more than a restraint. They were holding mismatched coffee mugs in their hands and swilling the leftover booze from the wedding. They seemed drunk, but still, there were two of them, and it could go either way. I grabbed a jagged rock the size of a small cantaloupe and held it behind my back. The blunt object would work on at least one of these fuckers.

"La la la..." I started singing, which turned into a drunken hum of "Jolene" by Dolly Parton. It was the only thing that came to mind. I kept staggering like a drunkard toward the two guys. I dragged my left foot, hobbling and playing it up. They took a minute to notice me. I raised my hum to incorporate a few words from the song: "Please don't you take my man." They didn't grab any weapons. I continued down the hallway.

"Hey! What are you doing there?" They started to get inquisitive. I felt the tension rise.

"Chill out over there, buddy. Go sleep it off." They must not have recognized me. The shadows in the cave covered me with anonymity.

The bigger guy walked toward me. He had purpose in each step. When he got closer, I leaned into the wall of the cave to further conceal the rock in my hand. He came in closer to me, and I twisted and snapped my fist at extension, clocking him in the side of the head with the rock. He staggered and blood came from his nose and leaked over the tattoos on the side of his head and over his ear as he buckled at the knees in front of me.

"What the fuck is going on down there?" The other Washout came sprinting down the cave toward me. I grabbed the rock again and hurled it at his head. It was too late—he avoided it by diving into my chest, knocking me onto my back. I felt his fists smashing into my face. The left side of my face went numb. I looked up through the blood mask over my eyes and saw him raising his fists again. My instinct took over and I stabbed him with the dagger. I stabbed him again and again. He collapsed onto my chest, then lifted up again, hovering blank-faced above me.

I pulled the dagger out one last time and thrust it deep into his kidney. He paused mid-swing. The aggressive strength of his body went limp, and the aggravated look in his eyes retreated to a state of confusion. His body twitched and he attempted to refocus. I twisted the dagger deeper and withdrew it only slightly. The blade stayed stuck in him, protruding from his side like a dorsal fin. His warm blood leaked onto the exposed skin on my stomach. I shoved his body off of me and onto the floor next to his comrade.

"Fuck." I couldn't say anything else. I was exhausted, and his death still made me feel guilty for a minute.

I rolled onto my side and lifted myself up to my feet. I was covered in the silty dust of the cave floor. I kept walking down the cave and saw Epiphany. She was tied up with ropes made of animal sinew. I got on my knees. Her face was gentle when she looked at me. It was like she was looking into my childhood memories, deep into my soul, asking for help. Every part of me wanted to free her. *I owe her.* She might have gotten me into fucked-up scenarios, but she also got me out of them with her insane advice. *Not so insane now.* I tried to release the restraints from her hands. She was tied to the rack made of welded metal rebar embedded in between the boulders. There was no way I could pry her out of it.

"Wait, I'll be right back."

"Don't leave me, please," she pleaded.

I wanted to hold her. I had never seen her so vulnerable, and it looked good on her. Her eyes were softer than usual, and the oversized circles of her pupils had receded, revealing the pale, transparent streaks of green. It looked like interwoven emerald. The strands seemed to be moving inside of her glassy eyes, interconnecting and weaving themselves right before me like jellyfish that were alive.

"I'll be back, I promise."

I ran back down the hallway and flipped the dead guard over. I yanked the dagger out of his body. I wiped the blood off on my pants and returned to Epiphany. She was pulling her arms toward me. The tension on the restraints was taut. I took the dagger and sliced the cords, and she fell like a freed marionette into my arms. I held her close to me. Her heartbeat was warming. I pictured the baby inside of her and that heartbeat fluttering rhythmically in harmony with ours.

"Let's get out of here."

"They'll never let us leave."

"Don't worry, I'll get us out of here. Can't you see in your mind's eye the way out of this maze?"

"They block us from hearing them. The walls in here are insulated by metallic emitters that confuse the wavelengths from telepathy."

"Bastards!"

We had to resort to the old-fashioned way, and looked for a light at the end of the tunnel. Being reunited with Epiphany and running away from this strange place made me remember being back in Los Angeles, when humor had made more sense. I had been much more sarcastic then. We ran toward the entrance and I could hear voices getting closer in the distance. There was only one other opening I could see down towards the end. It looked like there was water trickling from between the shale rock.

"Let's go!" I grabbed Epiphany's hand and led her in between the crevices of the rock.

"This is too small." She was so curvy that she barely fit through. She couldn't suck in her baby bump. I worried it would crush the baby, but we didn't have a choice. Her belly dragged against the coarse rock surface and got small cuts in a few places.

"C'mon. We have to." I helped guide her body around the boulders. Once past the opening, it was huge inside. Through the other side was a hidden water table with multiple streams flowing into it out of the rock.

"Look at that. Fresh water."

We stood in awe of the flowing brilliance of the sight. The sound soothed us, and we forgot about fleeing from the Washouts who would soon discover that Epiphany was no longer tied-up for their sacrifice.

"Give me your hand." I took it and we scaled down the rocks. They were slick with pinkish-colored algae. "Ow, fuck!"   I   slip

ped and scraped my arm on the rocks. I looked up at
Epiphany, and she was being careful with every step. She
carried two lives with her. She didn't have the belligerence
that I did.

Past her shoulders, I saw lights coming down the
passageway. They were followed by voices escalating in
their urgency.

"Epiphany, come on. Please, we have to go." I reached my
hand out again. Blood from the scrape on my arm trickled
down over our fingers as they clasped. We shared the
moment in this embrace; the prolonged pause was welcome
in this chase.

I slipped down the rest of the rocks and into the water. It
was cool. It tasted like volcanic rock and salty minerals.
Epiphany carefully stepped until she slid off the last rock
and into the water with me. Her dress was heavy and the
material was pulling her down with its weight. I pulled the
bottom part of her dress off, the sound of tearing fabric
inaudible under the water. It made it more difficult to rip,
and I nearly yanked her under the surface with my force.
Finally, I got the weighty material off so that I could pull
her under my arm and paddle us to the other side of the
spring without drowning.

We reached the other side, and the Washouts were already
descending the boulders behind us. Carmella was there and
she was yelling, but I couldn't hear her as my head bobbed
in and out of the water. I climbed out and dragged

Epiphany onto the shore. It wasn't a far swim, but I was exhausted. I felt lightheaded and Epiphany seemed to be fading out.

"Hurry up!" I yelled at her. She started to keep up. She was breathing for two humans, and the depleted levels of oxygen were taking their toll on her. I prayed we would make it into the next cave and that fresh air would be freely pouring through it. If not, there was no way we'd survive.

"I can't go any farther, Kyle. My heart, it feels like it's exploding inside of me." She gripped her chest. Tears started to come from her eyes. The eyeliner she had painted on smeared down her face like war paint.

"We have no choice. Please!"

The Washouts were diving into the spring water and swimming a powerful freestyle right toward us. I propped Epiphany up. She started to walk with me. The weight of her body leaned into me and it dragged me down. I was limping as we struggled to get through the cave. We saw dusty beams of light coming through a crack at the end of the rocks. We got to the source, but found the hole was too small for us. I began lifting rock after rock, hoping to dislodge one of the larger boulders. It sounded like shards of metal against a grindstone. The cave echoed the cracking noise bouncing all the way down the cavern.

The boulders began to break and crumble out, and we could see the Wasteland. We were perched above it. The polluted air that rushed in still felt good, even though it was probably toxic. It poured into the cave. Traces of the soot in the air came rushing past our faces. I could still hear the voices, but we had nowhere to go. I looked down and the cliff was steep. There was nothing we could do. The fear set in again. *We are going to die in these caves.* They would never forgive me for deserting this marriage and freeing Epiphany.

"It's the end of the tunnel." Epiphany pointed. She was nearly falling and pulling me to the ground.

"It's a wormhole..." She barely spit out the last words. "Look at your tattoo, it's glowing. That's how you know you're close to it."

I knew what she meant. Another fucking portal, but I didn't have many options left. I looked up and saw a few of the Washouts, running at us and carrying spiked bats. The image of our impending fate, the metal prongs from the bat sticking through Epiphany's head, was grotesque enough to strip me of my fear and bring tears to the corners of my eyes. We turned, and I dragged her off the sandy floor and somersaulted forward into the dark matter of the wormhole.

CHAPTER 18

We embraced in the oblivion of the wormhole filled with our memories. It felt like all human consciousness in this dimension was unified by a sticky web of thoughts. Every person left in the world was connected by this matrix. Whispers of all human thoughts vibrated across electromagnetic lines of communication.

Time passed at an indeterminate speed. I got lost in it. My thoughts were crippled, and I could not help but fall victim to my lost love—the sentiment that still burned so fucking bad. I wanted to rip it out from inside my chest and disarm the feeling, pull my ribs apart and tear out the hurt, the longing, and the feeling of true love that beat inside of my soul. It wasn't so easy when I was paralyzed physically in another state of existence. It was the same frustration—like in a dream, the kind where you felt helpless and couldn't even lift your arms to protect yourself. I was time traveling and I didn't have the option to reach down, check the time, or tie my shoe—the normal shit we took for granted.

The thoughts were purged from me, and I could do nothing other than pray I'd gotten a good memory and was stuck in a perpetual repeat of that memory. For me, it was the one of Elise on the bridge. The air felt so distinct. It lifted her hair and flicked the corners of the blonde strands against her face in rhythmic precision. It felt magical, and the memory was more vivid than real life. I could smell her—the lilies and the taste of salty perspiration that was on her neck just below the hairline. It mixed with her natural aromatic oils and caused part of my tongue to go numb. It played on repeat, and each time I noticed a new detail. This time, it was her beauty mark she would draw on, the placement of it, and how tightly pressed her lips were in that last moment. It felt so real I could breathe her in, kiss her desperately.

It was Elise. She was there again, so solemn and upset. Her hands clenched. A blush of blue from the cold air was darkening her cheeks.

I remembered the day her soul had been taken away from me. She had lost it to the wretchedness that had swirled around her since the time she'd moved to Los Angeles. The uniqueness of her soul was what remained a constant untouchable beauty, a black rose.

I'd still had hope. Hope was a cosmic fire that I thought burned inside both of us. I never wanted that to go out. I wanted to protect that at all costs, even if that meant giving my life for hers. I was prepared. My heart was in her hands. And then in one day, it was gone. Her soul was stolen from her and the fire extinguished. I wanted to say I was surprised. I wanted to pretend like I hadn't seen her running away when I looked into her eyes and read her future, but that wasn't what I'd seen. I'd known in my heart that when she left that day, I would never see the real her again. I'd been in denial from my depression.

It tore me up to think the person I'd spent countless hours divulging the secrets of the world to could spiritually die so quickly. All the wisdom and protective spells could never save her in this city. When the darkness came, it was swift and invaded her spirit like a serum injected into her veins.

The poison took so little time to take hold. It poured the shallow warmth throughout her body until every last stitch belonged to it.

I cried inside. The memory was too real. It became an awful hurt.

I woke from the journey inside the wormhole with Epiphany in my arms. There was no trace of Elise. I had to look around and get a grip on where we were. I heard a faint cry that sounded mechanical. It was getting louder. I looked up into the burning sky and there was a seagull. It was covered in ash and looked more like a raven overhead. It cawed out above us. I wouldn't have recognized the species if it hadn't left a dust trail of ash in the air behind it. It was probably just as surprised to see us there as we were to be alive.

I looked down at Epiphany. Her clothes were shredded, and she was covered in sweat. I was compelled to lick it off her, but I didn't. I used my sleeve to wipe her face. The memories were still lingering, and it didn't feel right. I didn't have any of my morals left, and I decided to rely on my primitive instincts now.

"Where are we?" Epiphany woke up.

I saw through the channel of light. "I think we're next to the LA River."

The smell was worse than I remembered. It smelled like all the sewage from the city had been gathered into this confluence. The river was gushing and pouring over the sides of the concrete retaining wall.

"We can make it to your place."

"I can't move." She tried to lean herself up, and the shredded fabric revealed her distended stomach. It was even larger than it had looked in the cave.

It was hard to carry her up the street and over the rubble. Her weight had nearly doubled, and the lopsided distribution from her baby bump made it even harder. We got up to the place on the hill where her apartment building had once stood. There was nothing there. It was a vacant lot. In the center was a cross hammered into the ground. It was made from wood and tacked together from white picket fence posts. The paint layers were peeled back, and a piece of cloth clung to it. It had been blown onto it from the trash that was covering the city, traveling on the cyclone of wind gusts that arose without warning and coated everything in dust from the debris.

We staggered up the hill and got closer to the cross. I saw a figure coming toward us, but I was blinded by the dust in my eyes. Tears trickled out—not from despair, but as a natural reaction to cleanse my eyeballs so I could see again.

Epiphany was panting heavily and covered in sweat. I could see she was in brutal agony. Our child had grown at a rapid rate. I looked at her eyes and they were dilated. I took my flannel off and put it over her body. I wrapped her with it, but it didn't seem to help her shivering from the pain. I looked down and the remains of her dress were completely soaked and stuck to her leg.

"My water. It's broke," Epiphany spewed the words out.

I knew what she meant. My words didn't come out, but I nodded. She pointed for me to go get something. Her legs were covered in a mucus-like substance; it was yellowy and got on my chest. The fluid was warm.

"I'll be right back, I promise. Hold on, please," I begged. My words trailed off and I sprinted toward the remaining structure of a house.

The side was ripped off it. I thought about what the city had become after the blast. LA was a place of painful emptiness no one should ever have to experience.

I returned to the muddy hill after mourning the city's death. My boots were slipping and sliding on the uneven terrain. The topsoil was sandy from the ash, but below was a gooey, dark mud. It was the guts of the planet all mixed together. I could feel how soft and fragile this place was now that it'd been destroyed. It was even more tragic that we had never cherished this place when it had been filled with all the pristine buildings, perfectly trimmed lawns, and strategically spaced palm trees lining the streets.

I looked inside the house and saw the remnants of a bathroom. There was a large clawfoot tub inside, still intact.

I removed the debris from inside of the tub. I flipped the handles and the sprayer worked. I hosed down the sidewalls of the porcelain before sludge started to mix with the clear water. I shut it off and ran back to the hill. Epiphany was lying on her side. She was passed out.

"Wake up, please. Wake up!" I shook her and she moaned.

"Ahhhhhhh. I caaaaaaan't do it." I picked her up. She weighed a ton. Her full weight and the weight of our child were almost more than I could carry.

I placed her in the clawfoot tub. It was the best place, insulated from all the filth. Epiphany was fading fast again.

"Please. Epiphany. Wake up!"

I slapped her in the face. Her skin felt feverish. I slapped her again on the other side of her face and cupped the water residue in my hand and splashed her. She started to come back to consciousness and opened her eyes.

"Stay with me forever?" she asked, and caressed my face.

I thought about this life here. It was so fucking crazy that I couldn't imagine being stuck here forever. I saw her and the tears in her eyes. No matter what, she was carrying my son inside of her. I couldn't tell her I would leave. The comfort of being back at the loft sounded so good, but maybe I wasn't meant to go back.

"Yes, I will be here for you." The words felt eternal.

"I... I love you, Kyle." She started to wince. She was having another contraction.

"Puuuuuuuuuuuush!" I held her hand and she started screaming and white-knuckled the side of the tub. The world around me was a blur. I tried to clear my thoughts as I stared straight into her vagina. She was shaking from the gut-wrenching pain. Her legs trembled, bent at the knees and wrapped over the walls of the tub.

"Uhhhh... it hurts. Fuck! Oh, my god, it hurts." It was trauma, watching all the blood and tissue pour out from between her legs. I couldn't imagine the pain she was feeling. I prayed she was all right and that all of this was normal. It looked like a massive amount of blood loss.

I splashed more of the dirty water on her face to cool her off.

"I can't do it." Epiphany seemed defeated. Her body let go.

"Just a little further. You're almost there." I just wanted her to feel relief.

"I need to catch my breath." My anticipation was starting to wane, too. It felt like it was never going to happen. I started to hum a Metallica song, playing the riffs with my fingers on her enlarged stomach. "Dn Dn Dn, DnNn," and then I repeated it aloud.

I kept going with the rhythm, and Epiphany woke up.

"What are you singing? That's a good song."

"I know, but I need you to focus, mama. Please push as hard as you can."

"OK, I will. I will." She agreed and situated herself again for the next stretch of this painful birth.

I'd never seen someone endure so much pain in one sitting. It made me sweat, watching her push so hard. Her pregnant body was contorting and the skin on her arms looked oily from sweat over her tendons. I noticed all the freckles I'd never seen before. When I looked at her face, she was covered in sweat. It was dripping down onto her body. Her thighs were pressed against the top of her stomach as she pushed one more time from deep inside her abdomen.

It was a long, deep push. I placed my hands on the inside of her thighs and pulled her legs back toward her head. It seemed to help. A rush of blood and tissue came pouring out from inside of her. It was the smell, the earthy scent of the blood—the reminder that we were from this earth and would return to the ground when we died. The thought of mortality brought me back to witness the birth.

I didn't know how long we'd been in the tub, but it felt like forever. I couldn't help but think we were all probably going to die. I accepted that thought and had to swallow it down. Suddenly, I could see the hairy little top of the baby's skull starting to push out from between her legs.

"It's coming!! A little more. Just a little more..." The head was starting to fully emerge now. I reached my hands inside of her warm body and around the head of the baby. I gently gripped its body and pulled it up and into my chest. The rest of the placenta pulled out from inside of her. It was still attached to the baby. I grabbed the flannel off Epiphany and wrapped the baby in it to keep him warm.

The boy looked beautiful. His face looked older than a newborn's. His forehead had little wrinkles and he was nearly bald except for blonde peach fuzz. He must have been an old soul. I thought about him and the circumstances he'd endured to be here, in this dimension with us. A life in the Wasteland didn't seem like much of a life, but we would make it our life. The moment he came out, so did tears come from the corners of my own eyes. It was a miraculous moment in time. Everything stopped when a human being I helped create came into the world before my very eyes. It was the most beautiful thing I'd ever seen.

Epiphany was nearly awake, coming in and out of consciousness. I took out my knife. Epiphany's eyes widened until she saw me, and trust returned to her expression. I heated the knife with my Zippo lighter and cut the umbilical cord from our baby's belly button. It bled slightly but was cauterized and clotted almost immediately. He was crying. Epiphany held our boy close to her chest and fell asleep.

I couldn't sleep from the adrenaline. My back was propped up against the edge of the tub, and I felt Epiphany and the baby's breathing together through the porcelain. I had drifted off for a few minutes when I heard a rumbling noise far-off in the distance. I staggered outside, but didn't see anything. I looked down the cliff's edge. It was a long way down. The lights from fires covering the remnants of Los Angeles sparkled in the distance underneath the cloud cover. I heard it again, the low rumbling. Sounded like a helicopter.

"Holy shit!" I felt hope growing inside me.

I ran into the open lot. I felt bad abandoning Epiphany, but if I could get their attention, we could be saved. They would have blankets and medical supplies.

"God! Please help us." I dropped down to my knees and prayed. I didn't know how we'd survive in this place much longer.

I looked down and pressed my head to my chest in prayer, but when I looked up, there was nothing. No helicopter. No rescue party to take us away. The glimmer of hope was put into a bottle and tossed out over the ocean waves.

I jumped up, defeated, and started yelling belligerently, "Help! Help!" I screamed it over and over again. The sound continued to drown out my cries. It got louder and louder.

The rumbling got closer. We were saved. This whole thing was done. The game. Maybe we were going home. I got my hopes up again. Then the sound... it got close enough to recognize. I realized it was a lot of motorcycles. Different types of bikes, the sounds of the engines stacked on top of each other—Panheads, Sportsters, and dirt bikes all joining in the flurry of noise.

"Fuck. We're not going home." My survival instinct kicked in. The melancholy expression returned to my face. I ran back to the house.

I looked out through the crack in the dismantled wall that still stood from the destruction of the house. I could see the bikes approaching. Riders filled the streets, far vaster than any other motorcycle club. This was an army here for the reckoning. I wanted to go challenge them, but this wasn't a joke. They would destroy me, and then take our child. I couldn't let that happen. I hoped that maybe they were just passing by, but then the bikes came to a halt at the end of the road next to the empty property.

"We're fucking dead." I put my hands to my side and gave up. Epiphany was awake and our newborn was starting to cry in her arms.

"Kyle. Please take us back home."

"I can't. They're covering the block. They're going to kill us."

"They want our son," she said.

The words distorted. They didn't make sense to me. *They want our son.* I kept thinking it over and over until the sound *DRRRRrrr* from the dirt bikes came closer. *They are riding up the dirt lot right at us.* My body didn't want to move; it was too intense, the feeling of paralysis. I wanted to unlock my legs and make them work. The empty lot seemed huge. Really it was only about 20,000 square feet, but it looked endless. I saw Epiphany; she was frightened.

After giving birth and becoming a mother she looked like an angel, holding our newborn son covered in dirty smears from the water and caked dried blood. The image burned heavily into me.

The primal instinct to protect my offspring kicked in again. I jumped up and saw the dirt bikes motoring closer to us. They didn't see us yet, but sensed our presence. The Riders were doing wheelies around the building, trying to look inside, their heads just below the bottom of the remaining window of the rubble. It was only a matter of time until they dismounted and came in like savages. I didn't want to imagine what they might do to us. They sprayed dirt around the lot like a demonic motocross event. I looked out and tried to make an assessment with all the elements at play. I didn't have enough time to consider my options.

I grabbed the side of the clawfoot tub and started pushing it. It didn't budge. I got on the other side and pulled it. It slid slowly. The weight of the tub, and Epiphany inside it, was too much for me to yank off the concrete pad. It was stuck.

I saw the connection to the water line and kicked it hard as fuck. It snapped on the second try, and the remaining water filled with sludge, and rust painted my face with overspray. It smelled like raw sewage. I dragged the tub off the pad and onto the dirt. One of the Riders, his face covered in tattoos, saw me and came zipping over to us. I dove into the dirt at the last moment before he could knock me with a bat he was swinging in the air. He was so close I could see his bloodshot eyes squinting. The corner of his face was covered in tattoos of old gas station logos.

"Mama, hold on. Hold on to him. We are going for a ride." I dragged the tub to the edge of the hillside before the Rider made another pass. He was about to hit us again when I ducked behind the tub, and he slammed into the side of it and went flying in a superman pose over us. I dragged the tub another inch, and it started to slide on the crumbling earth. I jumped in and covered Epiphany and our son. I held them tight as we picked up speed down the hill. Epiphany was writhing in pain. I could see it on her face.

She was barely able to remain conscious because of all the blood loss and exertion.

I ducked inside the tub and held Epiphany and our baby boy down tight to the basin to avoid toppling over. I heard the sound of the motorcycles fade off and I knew we were far down the side of the hill. The hill was steep. I could hear the dead bushes being torn apart as we ripped through them. We got to the bottom and the tub connected with something solid and sent us rolling out onto the ground. I stayed holding my family, so my back and shoulder absorbed the majority of the blunt force trauma.

I looked at Epiphany. She was moaning in pain. And then I heard it. The baby was crying, and I was relieved. At least I knew he was alive after that crash. I looked up the hill and couldn't believe we had made it down without dying. Then I saw the same Rider; his face looked like mud at a distance with all the tattoos. He was ripping down the side of the hill on his Yamaha. I looked around for a weapon, but didn't see anything I could use.

"Fuck! Mama, get down."

I saw a piece of rotted wood filled with old nails clinging to the bottom of the tub. I grabbed hold of the wood, and it splintered into my hand. I clenched it tight and waited patiently.

My other hand was on Epiphany and my son. I could feel both of their hearts pulsing in a synchronized rhythm with my own heartbeat. I knew this was my family. In my other hand, the pulse against the two-by-four piece of wood beat faintly inside of my palm.

He got close, but swerved off to get another angle. He turned and sprayed mud and dust everywhere. It was hard to differentiate his silhouette through the cloud. I just listened for the 450cc engine sound coming closer. It wailed and screamed as the engine revved and he shifted into second gear. I waited patiently until he was close, like a hunter waiting for a predator that was stalking him instead.

When he was close enough, I leaped up and shoved the splintered stake into the chest of the Rider. It snapped everywhere and drove the splinters into my hand, but knocked the Rider onto the ground. He was unconscious. I walked over and stomped on his Adam's apple, over and over again. He stopped breathing. His spirit left his body. I hoisted Epiphany up and dragged her. Her weight was pressed against my skin.

"Your hand. It's bleeding." I looked down. The splinters were large stakes and had pierced through the center of my hand. It was starting to go numb.

I reached down and yanked one of the large pieces out. "Fuck, that burns. Goddamn!"

Epiphany pressed her finger against my lips to hush my demons and soothe my pain.

"Can you stand?" I asked her. I put my arm under her armpit to help her balance.

"I, I am fine. Just get us out of here." She was right. It was only a matter of time before the rest of the Riders figured a way down through the streets to get here.

I propped the dirt bike up and jumped on it. The gear was stuck in second. The bottom of my boot slid off the side foot peg from the mud clod. I got off and squeezed the clutch and stepped hard onto the gearshift until it popped back down into first and then up into neutral. I jumped down on the kick-starter and it fired up. Twisting the throttle was painful. I could feel the remaining wood in my hand, and the blood trickled faster every time I pulled down on the throttle to keep the fuel flowing and the bike running. I had to ignore the pain. The flap of my skin hanging from the side of my hand was wrapped over the rubber throttle on the handlebar—it stung less and less with each rotation.

I got Epiphany on the back and tucked our son into her shirt. She held him close to her large chest. They were about the best makeshift car seat we had right now. I got on and we took off. I didn't know where else to go except the Café Revelation. I knew there would be provisions there and maybe clean water. I was hoping we could get something more than we had now, which was nothing.

CHAPTER 19

The café still looked deserted from the outside. The wind knocked around a few of the empty beer can chimes hanging from fishing line outside the door. The air was stagnant and heavy, but we'd brought signs of life with us. Our stirring awakened the place, and even the faint sound of music from inside came trailing out from the cracks of the soldered-together Airstreams.

"Let's park around back. See what's going on here."

I parked behind the café. It was the same place where I'd had to kill that kid before. It seemed like déjà vu. I wasn't sure what to expect inside this place, if Ezra was going to still be serving up homemade shine, but this was the only spot I could come for answers and a real drink. Besides, Ezra was like a damned prophet.

We walked in through the back door and the place was jumping. People were everywhere— Washouts, Telepaths, but no Riders.

"I thought you'd never make it back!" The words from Ezra were warm and welcoming, the best feeling.

"I'll take one, please, maybe two of whatever you got back there. That moonshine I had before would be good."

"Of course! And I see you've added company this time around."

"It's been a long-ass day."

"Here, take this for that hand." He tossed me a dirty dish rag.

"What's the celebration?" I shook my head.

"You. You've done it! We are celebrating—take a look."

He held up a handwritten menu on butcher paper that read, "Death of the Beast Happy Hour: 2 for 1 on all homemade sarsaparilla and scoot monkey cocktails."

"Man, that sounds good to me. I'll try that, then, the scoot monkey."

"Sounds exotic," Epiphany muttered, and sat down.
"On the house. Right, everybody?" There was a cheer, a weird, orchestrated barrage of sounds that hit me hard. An internal alarm went off like a hammer hitting metal, and I couldn't see straight. The ringing didn't stop until I took a swig from the mixed beer and moonshine concoction. It was like a supercharged black and tan. My hand steadied and I could see straight again. The medicine was working. Alcohol always worked its magic on my sick mind.

"What's the plan, Kyle?" Ezra looked at me, expecting an insightful response. I didn't really have much to say. I'd seen so many crazy things happen that this place felt normal.

"I have no fucking idea, my man. I'm pretty tired. I'd love to wake up tomorrow sleeping off a bad hangover."

I craved the normalcy of a bad hangover. That world was gone. I was wrapped up in a serious engagement with Epiphany.

"Y'all thinking about getting married?" Ezra broke my trip.

"I already got married in the caves," I said with sincerity, but I was starting to feel buzzed, and the marriage seemed like a hoax. The whole concept of marriage was a sham.

"Well, I'll be damned, Hiram got to you after all."

"Yeah, you could say that. It was wild shit, but we're happy to be out of there."

"You're in good company. Well, shit, if you can't get married, you should at least celebrate. You know, consecrate your bond."

"We are spiritually married, Ezra, thanks." Epiphany was breastfeeding the baby. She'd finally spoken more than two words. She had been silent since we'd gotten back into town after the clash with the Riders. The birth had taken a toll on her. She had every right to be drained. It had been the most intense shit I'd ever seen. The birth trumped the run-in with the Riders tenfold.

I grabbed a handful of beer nuts on the table and gave them to her.

"You must be starving. Chow on these and I'll find an animal I can kill and roast up for you."

She took the boiled peanuts and shoved every last one in her mouth. She chewed ravenously, with her mouth open. My nerves were starting to cool, too. The alcohol helped bring my adrenaline down and my eyes grew heavy. I felt relief. It had been a close call.

"Why did they want our son so bad?" I looked at Epiphany, but she motioned for me to keep quiet.

"What's his name?" Ezra asked us. The question was directed at both of us, but I didn't have any name in mind.

"His name. His name is Apex," Epiphany broke the pause. I was content with her response. This wasn't a typical birth, where the parents huddled over a baby book with five thousand plus generic names and just selected one at random. I knew whatever Epiphany's logic, it made sense.

I nodded and agreed with her. Inside, it felt right because his birth had now become the most important moment in my life. It brought a certain light into my soul that had never existed before. *Love.* It was the word that filled me and gave me a feeling of happiness I had never felt before.

"That's a great name. Here's another one on the house for Apex." I drank it down with ease. Everything started to blur again. I regained consciousness, but then the pulse of microdots returned.

"I gotta get some air." I staggered and walked toward the back entrance. I looked at the corner table and remembered the incident with Cabal. All the memories came crashing back down on me.

276

I couldn't escape the sensation that his presence was still here. He was my guide to get to the Beast, and he must have still been lingering, looking for the next spirit to inhabit. He was like my own personal ferryman across the River Styx. He had taken me to the other side. That figure never left. He was just another mystical person in a series of urban legends until you found out that he was real.

The polluted air outside still felt fresh. The café had been getting thick with people's odor and sweat; it'd been getting to me. Epiphany came out shortly after with our son, but first I had a moment to myself, and my mind wandered back to Elise. I couldn't rid myself of her memory. I couldn't help but feel close to her. Maybe it wasn't meant to be with her, but it just didn't feel that way. Standing on the bridge that nightk looking at Los Angeles and thinking of her slipping away from me, made me cling so tightly to her. I clenched my hand and thought about holding her. I thought about Valentine's Day and how it had changed everything. Only days after that I'd been gone, implanted with a new existence. That was my identity now.

"Are you OK? You're acting weird," Epiphany broke in.

"Yeah, as good as I can be."

"You want to see our baby boy?" She held him out, wrapped in my flannel. There was dried blood and other fluids caked to the outside. The fabric felt crusty in my hands. I pulled back the covering off his face. He was sleeping. His face looked like mine but pudgier. His cheeks looked like two perfect circles, and his eyes were almond-shaped, closed. He was resting peacefully.

"He's my son."

I was startled and it felt like electricity in my blood when I came to that realization.

"He looks just like you," Epiphany said.

"He really does."

"Here, hold him." She passed him to me. His body was warm. He was so peaceful and sleeping in his own little world.

I felt weak. The homemade moonshine was twisting up my stomach, but something didn't feel right inside of me. I almost puked but held it back in my mouth. Apex started to wake up and open his eyes. It was like I was looking into my own eyes. I could see all the way through him and into me. A shiver inside me ran like a serpent of light in my blood. I loved him. It was a new love that I had found. A real love and not the delusion of love.

"I'm going to get cleaned off." I nodded.

Epiphany wandered to the back of the building where there was a garden hose slung over the side of a piece of plywood. It was hooked to a filter and pump. When she turned it on, a loud screech came from the motor, and a cloud of gray smoke rose from the gears firing up in the industrial sump pump.

"We should have consecrated our bond," she said from behind the planks of wood pallets. It was hard to hear her—

she was nearly yelling over the sound of the compressor pump.

"Didn't we? Look at the beautiful boy you conceived. It's a fucking miracle."

It was miraculous. It didn't feel over yet, just a moment of respite where the solitude in the parking lot of the Café Revelation felt good. My nerves were calm.

"And your fake-ass marriage to that Washout whore." She called out the ritual with Carmella.

"I don't know what the hell that was. I went through with it out of survival. It's not like I wanted to. Or knew her. Not like you, not like the way our spirits continue to find each other."

"It didn't feel that way. I saw the look on your face. You were numbed out but smiling like a fucking asshole."

"Don't blame me. I drank the Kool-Aid, you know. It was temporary, and the shit they had to say was similar to the stories you were feeding me about the Beast."

"They don't know. I've seen him. I know he's still in you."

"What the fuck..." She came walking out from behind the wood planks and corrugated plastic siding, completely naked and dripping wet. She used her clothes to pat herself dry. Her body was swollen and stretched from carrying Apex. She saw me staring at it and covered up.

"Yeah." She nodded and gave me a sly grin.

"You don't know what you're talking about. That thing, or whatever shapeshifting energy shit it was, broke into thousands of particles. I'm pretty sure that means it's gone, baby. Bye-bye birdy."

"That's what he wants you to think."

"Oh, really? Listen, I feel fine. A little buzzed and hungry, but no weird shit swirling inside me."

I couldn't take back what I'd seen. It wasn't a dream anymore. It was implanted in me like the device stitched into my skin. You couldn't tear something like this out of you. It never leaves you, no matter what.

Letting go of the past hurt. Not like a Band-Aid, but an inner stinging, the salt-in-a-wound kind; it hurt and then soothed the skin when the pus seeped out. The memories of the lab still filled my head. The loft, Elise. It all was growing dark inside. I needed to accept this new reality and embrace my own flesh and blood. This was the family I needed to protect now. I had to sacrifice my life for theirs and never look back. The past was the darkness. The Wasteland was the present, and it was undetermined if there was anything after this, if humanity had a future less grim than this one.

"Where should we go?" I looked at Epiphany, and there wasn't any place left that I knew. My old loft didn't feel right, even if the building was still standing.

I felt something on my free hand that was not holding my son. It was moist and wet.

"Chico! Holy shit, puppy. Where you been, boy? I missed you." He was a real companion. Tracked me down. It was like my long-lost family member had come back to complete our crew. Yeah, it was a motley group, but damn beautiful.

We walked together out from the Café Revelation's alleyway and down the street and found an old Buick. The interior was completely stripped out of it, probably being used for bedding in a lean-to.

We got in and checked the damage. Crazy thing was, the keys were still hanging in the ignition with a plastic keychain that was in the shape of a heart. I gave it a couple turns, but it was dead. I jumped out.

I tried to pop the hood to check the engine. It wouldn't unlatch. I had to jimmy it open with a piece of metal until it released.

"We still have an engine!" I troubleshot it visually. Everything seemed intact. It even had a battery in it. I figured the starter was probably bad. I grabbed the same piece of metal I'd used to pop the hood and wedged it between the screw on the solenoid and the other screw. It made a bridge. This was an old trick I'd learned a long time ago from my old man.

"All right, turn the keys." I saw Epiphany slide over to the driver's side and give it a twist. Nothing.

"Again!" I yelled. I pressed the metal harder against the screws.

Vrrrrr. The engine turned over. It sputtered a bit, but it was running.

I got back in and we drove away.

CHAPTER 20

The Buick was choppy. The back right tire was flat, so the ride was real bumpy. Every rotation of the axle caused the car to bounce up and down. I saw Chico in the back being thrown around and Epiphany next to me with my newborn son. I reached over to keep Epiphany glued to the seat. She was sweating.

"You OK, mama?" She looked at me funny and then passed out.

I drove faster, not knowing where to go. Then it hit me: into the other dimension. I thought of the danger of going back into that world, but we needed supplies and food if we were gonna stay alive much longer. We couldn't survive on the diet of alcohol, meat of scavenging rodents, and bar peanuts.

I thought again about the other dimension. I veered to the side of the road and nearly caught the tire on rubble stacked in a sculpture-like form on the side of the road.

We headed back toward the freeway. My idea wouldn't work if we couldn't get enough velocity to penetrate the wormhole and jump the fold of space.

Epiphany's health was wavering. I was still coming down from my buzz after drinking all the moonshine at the café. I could feel my heartbeat in my temples. The thumping of the flat tire exaggerated the pounding. It got louder every mile we drove down the 5 Freeway, until I didn't hear anything anymore.

The metal frame of the seats underneath us felt cold. The car must've been sitting for a while. It was a recycled prehistoric creature now. Most cars had been burned to pieces or salvaged for usable items. This one ran, barely. I was still shocked, but maybe it was Ezra's car.

I tried to imagine music playing as we drove along. I scrolled through tracks in my mind that I hadn't heard in years. "Mother" by Danzig came on in my head.

I could only remember one verse. The rest I hummed aloud to keep my spirits fired up. Epiphany was still passed out, her arms clenched around baby Apex. The flannel he was wrapped in was coming undone. It still had blood and mucus caked on it. I could see his pudgy legs. They were so cute, so innocent and unexposed to the elements. I wanted to get him the hell out of this crazy and fucked-up place. The other dimension was dangerous, but food and all the other shit we needed was there, and plenty of it.

I sang out loud as we reached about sixty miles an hour. I knew if we didn't get through, we were going to spin out of control and die.

"Until the wheels fall off." I pressed the pedal to the metal.

I closed my eyes at the last minute and held my breath. My hand was wrapped around something wet, and I didn't know what it was. The sliminess felt foreign to me. Like it was inhuman.

"Hang onto him."

I kept the pedal pressed to the floor. The Buick didn't move any faster with the distressed rotation of the axle. It could barely support the frame. I was worried the car was going to come apart piece-by-piece until we were sitting on the floorboards, holding just the steering wheel like in a twisted cartoon, with the brass squeeze horn strapped to the window.

"Mama..." I looked at her. She was nodding off again. "What is it?" I held my expression of concern.

"We're gonna make it." I looked down at my wrist to see the symbols lighting up, so at least I knew we were close to the wormhole.

Then it hit. None of this felt right. I could feel the engine starting to cough. It was seizing up. I knew it was too good to be true to find a car that ran in the Wasteland. I looked down and the fuel gauge was bouncing up off the white empty line.

"Just get us to the other side." I smacked the steering wheel.

I looked down and baby Apex had his mouth locked around Epiphany's large breast. He didn't know what was happening yet. I prayed it stayed buried in his subconscious and it never resurfaced later in life. A late surge of repressed shit like this could be too traumatic.

"All right, here we go!" I saw Chico curled up on the makeshift seat in the back. He didn't seem too concerned. Epiphany held Apex tight to her chest.

I jammed the accelerator with all the force I had. It didn't
do much, but enough. We went through the spot on the 5
Freeway where the wormhole had been before. I didn't feel
the same sensation.

I felt pain and nausea. It didn't stop until there was only
darkness all around me.

We crashed. It was the smell that woke me up, the smell of
gasoline mixed with flames. I didn't see what I was
expecting in the other dimension. I just saw the Beast
staring at me from behind the flames, coming toward me.
He had infected me with his fear. All I wanted to do was
kill him.

He came over to me and there was darkness all around, and
a burning sensation in my chest. I couldn't look him in the
eyes. He just kept walking over to me and I was rolling
around on the highway bleeding. My heartache felt like
someone had surgically cut out everything inside me, all
my organs. I knew that he was going to leave me for dead
on the side of the freeway.

"Are we dead?"

The question continued to arise in my mind while darkness
ensnared me. I couldn't process what was happening. The
alarming ringing came back to my head. The pounding
inside was getting louder and blinding me from the pain.
I lurched my legs back to the vehicle. I crawled on my
hands and knees over the broken safety glass of the
windshield. Shards lodged themselves into my palm. My
body felt like it was swollen, pumped full of sand and

nearly impossible to lift off the concrete surface. Blood dripped from the corner of my mouth and nose, splattering swirls on the ground. I tried to lift my torso upright. Then I felt it in my left arm, the needles burning through to the bone. It was broken, shattered throughout the limb. The serrated bones were only held in by the outside sinews of skin.

My arm fell dead at my side. I staggered to the passenger door of the car. I could not see anything clearly. There were globs of fur strewn out all over. My mind did cruel things as I thought about my newborn and Epiphany. There was no sign of them.

"Have mercy on my fucking soul!" I yelled at the top of my lungs. The sound vibrations were so loud I could almost see the wavelengths in the air. Then I saw her.

Epiphany was lying there on her side—she had been thrown from the car. I rolled her over, and in her arms, happy as a little wrapped clam, was Apex. He was crying, but stopped suddenly. I couldn't figure out why. He looked at me and I swore I saw him smile. It melted my heart, and for the first time in a while, I felt happiness so deep inside my soul. It gave me a slight feeling of hope.

I helped them get up. I held Apex in my arm and lifted Epiphany up with my same hand. She struggled to get up, but seemed OK, for what we had just gone through in the accident.

"Chico!" I called out his name but didn't see him anywhere. I was hoping he'd come out from the rummage and be alive.

Then I saw his body. It was unmoving on the far side of the car. I bent my head down and shook him.

"I'll really miss you, pup."

Baby Apex was in my arms and I supported Epiphany as we turned to walk away.

I heard sounds in the distance. The low, rhythmic beating of the drums. *Ba ba phm, Ba, Ba, Ba.* It was a deep banging, and vibrated up the walls of the cement river basin.

I couldn't find the source of the drumming. I felt it inside of me. It was like a subtle incantation. My own lifelessness had been repelled, and my spirit had been called back for a purpose.
Then I saw them: masses of Native Americans, a few in ceremonial headdresses, walking up the LA River. They were translucent spirits of this earth that were roaming through the chaos. They were the ghosts of the world that had existed here before the Wasteland. This was their land. We owed them an undying gratitude.

I saw the medicine man—he walked around me and Epiphany and then made his way over and did a figure-eight around Chico's limp, lifeless body. "Wani wachialo, wani wachialo, wakankatanka..." He repeated the incantation over and over, shaking the red-tailed hawk feather secured to the antler with tanned leather wraps and silver beads. He shook it purposefully, gestured toward the sky, and continued to chant. His eyes looked white, rolling back in his head. He was in a trance.

288

There was a ghostly image of Chico, and Epiphany and I walked beside him. He looked like a blue flame enchanted out from his physical vessel and into the spiritual astral plane. The blue flame wrapped itself around us, too. I touched it and my hand cut through it like a mist. There was a substrate that my fingers penetrated, but it had no permanence on my skin. Apex was in my arms, and we walked up the cement pathway on the side of the riverbed.

Chico's spirit ran out ahead and surveyed the land. I watched him. His energy was renewed. He was no longer just a street dog scavenging. He was part of a pack. We all fit together and had become spirits of the land. It fit us, and we fit together in this family, despite our differences. In the afterlife, we all belonged, and the astral plane of existence was not the same as it was in the physical world filled with so much judgment. The eyes that watched us as we traversed along the riverbed were hollow and didn't contain the same criticism that I'd felt in life.

A young Indian warrior came and circled around us. His face was painted with streaks of yellow-and-white pigments. It was caked on his cheeks, and I could see the bones underneath the clotted colors that were starting to crack from the dryness of his skin.

His eyes were like chrome mirrors floating inside. I could see my reflection in them. I looked much older and more worn. I was sure it was a more exact replica of who I was now than who I had been before—I was battle-hardened. Silver hairs lined my beard and eyebrows. I'd aged considerably under the layer of dirt ingrained in my skin's complexion. I looked further inside them and disregarded my age—I thought about the memories. It was all a vacant past that didn't amount to much when I saw my altered appearance. I was a completely different person, ready to sacrifice myself for the ones I loved.

The reflection in his eyes shifted and I could see my son. He was awake and staring off blindly into space. The warrior faded into the white blinding light, and all I could feel was the heat that emanated from inside of the warrior's body.

He jumped up and down wildly, channeling something even greater. I saw him wave his hands over Apex. The paths from the movement in the air looked like sparkles behind falling meteors. I was grateful for the warrior's energy that he put into my son.

Apex seemed like the only real part of me that was left. He wasn't a dream or part of this vicious world. He had been untouched by the violence that flowed through the veins of the transients who'd happened to make their way to the City of Angels.

I was not in denial of our perilous fate. I dropped to my knees and bowed to the earth. I was hoping to catch the mercy of a passing eagle that would carry my offspring to another planet. There had to be another place out there that would sustain life, without brigades of interdimensional motorcycle riders with the intent to kill.

We were at the lowest level of purgatory, and yet my love for my family grew stronger. My spirit joined them, and our energy came together like a scaly serpent weaving up the central nerve of the city. The LA River was now a spiritual causeway of the undead—the centrifuge of lost souls making their way up the valley to the headwaters of a toxic flow that poured into Los Angeles.

Apex barely made a sound. He was wrapped in Epiphany's arms. He was the only one from the next generation of humans left alive in the spiritual pilgrimage of the ghosts of the past. I felt an inner compulsion to get him to the gate for his survival in the next dimension. There he would find the same abundance, and not be subjected to the mutiny and degradation that society had taken. My instinct to protect my kin superseded all other impulses in this state of decay.

"Where are we going?" I asked the chief.

He looked dead into my eyes. He paused and raised his staff and pointed it northwest. I glanced upward and saw it now. I could only make out the outline of it, forming out of the winding particles of soot. I recognized the face that formed from the ash and dust. It was the Beast. It was his elongated, demonic face, and it covered the vast landscape and drowned the sun's rays.

The mouth of the face, formed from ash and debris, opened into the river tongue. The flow of filthy water looked like a stream of vomit pouring out from inside of the Beast. It opened and closed like the entrance to a creepy amusement park ride.

"This doesn't feel right." I looked around for Epiphany and grabbed her hand.

She wasn't saying a word and just stared at the baby. We walked at the same pace as the rest of the tribe. The warriors walked out ahead. They spun and yipped into the air as they passed to the other side. They were swallowed up by the Beast and didn't come out, their souls consumed and digested into the other dimension.

We continued to walk with the sea of souls that were the lifeblood for the Beast. He could not survive without the beings that found their way into his open breath to live eternally.

The tribe dissipated into his mouth. Epiphany and I walked hand-in-hand. Our son started to cry and resist the warm, liquid feeling inside. It pulled us, our hands splaying apart. I saw Apex floating inside of the vacuous portal next to me. Our energies split apart into molecules in our own fractional existence. It was only temporary. I believed in the greater good that we would reach the same destination. We would be together, never ending this journey until we could be rejoined together without all these deviled distractions to the truth.

"Apex..." My voice trailed off into the wormhole.

My arms felt like they were spread wide-open, encompassing the plane of this travel to the other side. I could touch the slimy walls. They were alive and pulsing, too. All the veins inside of the portal contained a soul traveling through the fold in space and into another dimension. We could be split atomically, shredded apart and never pieced back together again. I had known that when we'd walked through to this dimension, and that the Beast wanted to take us together.

CHAPTER 21

I was spat out onto the ground, covered in an organic matter like mucus coating every crevice of my body. I was totally naked this time.

The landscape looked rocky and the air was cool. I was sitting on shale ground and there was a small lake. I could see to the other side, which gave me hope. A multitude of capsized rowboats were sticking out of the water, their noses like dead metal dolphin heads.

"Apex!"

I looked around frantically and slapped my hands against the ground in a sweep of 360 degrees. He was nowhere to be found.

I didn't break down yet, but the tears were heavy, ready to flood out. The pockets under my eyes were saturated and bulbous. The caves reminded me of the Washouts and a strange familiarity seeped in.

There was a rowboat. It sat idling on the tide which lapped against it, knocking it against the rocks. I crawled over to the boat. It was tied up with string that looked like braided horse mane. Inside the rowboat was my son. He was wrapped in the flannel and snoring. He must have been put to sleep by the transport into the other dimension.

I was relieved, but in my heart, I felt that we had lost Epiphany. She had gone away. Part of me believed that passing through the wormhole was determined by a judge with a big gavel who decided who would enter the forbidden paradise and who would be banished from Eden. I didn't have a clue where she was, and I didn't see a trace of her anywhere.

I got into the boat. I untied the makeshift rope and sat in the center of the wooden dinghy, balancing the centerline. Apex was peaceful and quiet. A long stick with prongs at the bottom was lying inside against the rail's edge. I pulled it up with my good arm and leaned back in the dingy and forced the stick into the water like a gondolier.

The current was strong beneath the murky water. I sliced through it and found a notch in the rocks to push off from. The boat glided through the surface of the lake. Navigating this darkness was hopeless, but my hand continued to work unconsciously and forced us toward the center of the body of water and away from the shallows.
Then I heard it. The voice. It was gentle-but-guttural. I recognized the voice, but couldn't place it.

"You've found him, ma boy."

"Who's there?" I called out. My voice echoed inside the caverns and came bouncing back at me.

"We made this trip together before, you and me."

"What?" I looked around, still uncertain of what direction the familiar voice was coming from.

"Remember the emerald island? You saw him in the glass pyramid. I took you to him."

It came rushing back to me. My blood thickened. The fear started to set in. I remembered him: Cabal.

He was my own personal ferryman. Cabal had taken me to the other side and had expected me to end this dimension permanently. He'd had me believing normal life would be restored to Los Angeles if I followed all these cryptographic directions and slayed the Beast they talked about in hushed voices.

While hope still burned inside me, this dismal place seemed more like the real future of this city. It would continue to be desecrated and fold into the ground below it until we were all living in these caves permanently. A pale light illuminated the rock faces of the cave. I pushed toward the far walls—there was an alcove, and I got out of the boat. I made sure Apex was sleeping. On the cave were drawings illustrating an ancient ceremony. It looked Egyptian, almost, the triangular heads and the ornate gold around them, with Cleopatra-style cat eyes on the figures. There were two huge statues of sphinxes carved out of the rock on the sides. They looked almost real, from the detail in their eyes.

In the cave art, it looked like they were making an offering. There was a sarcophagus wrapped in cloth, ready to be embalmed. It must have been a sacrifice to the gods. I thought about how the religious cults and other powerful organizations out there in the world had resulted in this nightmare of an egomaniac. Collectively, they had decided it would be worth watching us all suffer into our own demise. They had known we would come crawling back, looking to escape our grim realities, and enter into another

dimension or go to another planet from the fear they had
instilled in us.

There was writing carved into the rockface. It was hard to
make out in the darkness, but I read it carefully, going over
each letter to make sure I was reading it right:
"OF ALL that is written, I love only what a person hath
written with his blood. Write with blood, and thou wilt find
that blood is spirit."

I didn't know how to interpret it. It was beyond my
comprehension, but I knew I needed to figure it out.

"You know what the Beast wants..." The voice echoed.

"What the fuck are you talking about?"

"He wants his own blood back."

"Damnit! What do you mean?" I started to lose my shit
completely.

"He wants his son." I looked at baby Apex. Cabal couldn't
possibly mean my own flesh and blood. My baby boy I'd
made with Epiphany.

"If he means my kid, he can never have him. Fuck the
Beast."

"See for yourself—you were both chosen to make his heir
come back to life."

Another beam of light moved across the water's edge. I fell
to my knees and looked into the water. In horror, I saw
Epiphany's face staring back at me. She was bloated and

frozen in time underneath the surface. I recoiled backward and pulled Apex from the boat and onto the rock. I leaned against a few boulders in the center, nearer the inscriptions in the rock that I still could not figure out.

"You must give him to the Beast." The voice of Cabal was becoming shrill.

"Fuck you. You will never take my son." I looked frantically in both directions for a passageway out of here.

"Put him on the altar."

I stood up with Apex braced in my arms. He started to wake up and began to cry. I knew he was hungry, but I couldn't do anything about that. I felt helpless.

"Put him on it now. He will be taken care of like royalty." I saw that I was in no position to negotiate. I would sooner give my own life than the life of my son. His innocence was the last pure thing left in this world.

The altar was cold, and the face of the rock was the darkest of grey. The paintings on the cave wall began to come alive and move. The figures on the rock continued their process of turning the embalmed figure toward the archway in the drawings. They were trying to take my son's soul and put it into the body of one of their own. The heir to the Beast. My heart skipped rapidly, and my legs didn't seem to work. I was near-paralyzed from the waist down, but I'd been preparing for this moment.

I saw Epiphany's stoic face. I could almost hear her voice. It awakened my muscles. My broken arm mended itself and started to work. Cabal kept yelling through the cave.

"Give him to us, give him to us!" he kept repeating. My arms stretched out and the pounding in my head was also getting louder, with the volume of his voice, until I couldn't hear anything anymore.

I saw a shiny, jagged stone on the altar. It had a different luster than the rest of the shale. It looked like obsidian. I grasped it in my open hand. I could feel the thin, sharp edges slicing into my skin. I squeezed the serrated knife in one hand and my son in the other. My hand started squirting blood, yet I couldn't stop squeezing the sharp stone tighter and tighter. My wrist started to light up again with the symbols.

Inside of my head was another voice. It was a female voice, so soothing, deep inside of my head. It was like a miniature person was standing in my brain, talking to me. It was Epiphany, her telepathic abilities magnified from under the water in the state before death took over. She was whispering, but the words were so clear. Each syllable sounded like it'd been rehearsed to get the perfect tone.

"Save the beautiful life we have created. He is the savior. Protect him and write with your own blood. Remember what I showed you. Write the symbols." Her words continued to travel through me. They were the same words she'd said to me back at her apartment that I hadn't understood then, but now they were the truth.

My instinct took over, and I started smearing the symbols—a cross, a skull, and the sun—with my bloody hand over the shale altar. The symbols were a mess, but light from my wrist was transferring to inside of the rock face. Light started to break out through the cracks of eroding stone.

"No! Stop. What are you doing?" Cabal's voice was enraged. I could hear the shock and fury inside of it.

"Writing in my own blood," I said as I finished transferring the last symbol from my wrist onto the altar. My smeared blood pooled up and started to boil, and a bloody mist evaporated from it.

"Damn you! You must sacrifice him to kill the Beast!" His voice trailed off in the distance, and the inside of the cave began to rumble. I knew he was lying.

Then I saw him. It was Michael again. He walked out in his same slick suit. It looked like the suit had turned into a million tiny dots, like pixels were crawling all over his body, just like I'd seen before in the desert.

"You are here to kill me. So do it."

"You, you are the Beast?" I looked at him again. His flesh was not real; it moved differently. Every cell of Michael's body turned into dots. His face morphed from his human face into a goat's. His eyes were red and burning inside the angular mouth that bleated at me. The sound was so disturbing and shrill, it cut into my heart with a coldness I had never felt before. I tried to use my hand and stab him in the side, but his shadowy figure slid away from me. I

300

dropped the blade. The blood was still pouring from my hand and Apex was crying uncontrollably.

I remembered the advice that Hiram had told me. I reached my hand into my pocket and grabbed the obsidian blade he'd given me. I closed my eyes and heard the words Epiphany had told me to say. I was in a hypnotic state. I was possessed. I stabbed the air in a semicircle and caught the supernatural animal in the center of his forehead. The pentagram etched into his skull eroded, and milky white light poured out from inside the shadowy being.

It sounded like the rocks were moving. Boulders started to drop from the top of the cave. Huge splashes of water washed over the embankment we were standing on. Apex and I were washed clean.

The cave paintings started to bleed off like melting crayons down the rockface. The light flickered and the pale beam came pouring out of the altar and onto the rock. It illuminated a small door with wings painted on it.

I walked toward it. My knees were weak from the blood loss. I held Apex high above the flooding water. I could hear a new voice.

The voice. I recognized it. It was distorted, but became clearer. It was Elise. "Come back to me," she said, and we walked through the door together.

CHAPTER 22

Waaaah... wahhh." I woke up to the baby crying.

"Where the fuck am I?" I looked around. It looked like I was back in the loft.

"Thank god." I couldn't believe it. I closed my eyes again tightly, and counted for a few seconds and then opened them again. I was still in the loft.

I wanted to get up, but I couldn't manage. My legs felt like they were fastened down with a strap. I looked around and confirmed I was back in the loft. I couldn't remember going back through the wormhole to the real world. I hadn't gone through the portal this time. I tried not to remember the horrifying moment at the altar, and Michael. But I did remember him.

I felt different. Nothing was the same, and it wasn't just another massive hangover from binge-drinking. "So, this is what time travel is," I said affirmatively, but didn't know for sure. The images of the future were grim, if it was true.

"Waaaaa." I heard the crying of the baby again.

"Can you get him?" I rolled over, but didn't know who I expected to see staring back at me. The bed was empty. I thought I heard her voice coming from the other room.

The baby's crying stopped.

My feet curled up and I scratched my toenails against the sheet. I liked the noise it made. The familiar combination of cotton, remnants of sweat, and my bed was comforting. The air was a little stinkier than usual today. From the Johnnie Walker and multitude of Modelos I'd consumed the night before. My usual "night night" formula if I couldn't fall asleep. I could still taste pieces of the pulp from the limes inside of my lips between my gums. My skin felt different, too. It almost looked like it was covered in chalk.

"It's dry. Must be the Santa Ana winds fucking everything up."

Lying in bed with the hot air blowing through the pull-down glass windows reminded me of the times before the baby. When I had been done sleeping and could lie around all day in that comfort of perspiration and fabric and fill the day with day-drinking and sex. It didn't get much better than that unless pancakes were thrown into the mix.

I could never object to banana pancakes, even if Elise used that wheat flour she preferred. She always said it was healthier, as if pancakes could be healthy. If she'd used bananas, we'd always call them "bamcakes" instead. It was our little joke, but she always laughed when I said it after a long night. We would wake up and she would roll over and I'd say, "I wish I had bamcakes right now."

No matter how hungover we were, she would laugh, sleep for a few more minutes, and then whip them up. It was really one of the best dishes that she could make. It was also the hangover cure if she mixed a little Southern Comfort liquor into the syrup. *Yum.* They still tasted like cinnamon and the abundance of syrup could soak anything up, even those party nights we had doing drugs and having sex until sunrise.

Now things were different. No lazing around in a stupor. I had a baby now.

"I have a baby now." I couldn't feel my body when I said it like that. It was like I was hovering in between the sheets. I wanted to roll over and get out of bed, see if the lights worked by flicking them on and off. Maybe slap myself in the face. A good hard slap would reassure me that this life was real.

I heard her voice again in the other room and felt her presence. But she didn't walk in. I still pictured her, though—Elise looked so perfectly put-together. Her hair was dyed a dark brown, almost black, and cut in a bob. It looked good on her. I tried to lift my arm to run my fingers through it, but I still felt paralyzed. It was surreal to see her again. She was weightless. My hand passed through her like she was a ghost.

I raised my hands in praise, doing the cross formation over my heart. I thought it meant the Holy Trinity, but the only thing that played inside my head was the nursery rhyme, "Stick a needle in my eye/cross my heart and hope to die." It was morbid, but the melody of it inside of my head was comforting.

Most of the nursery rhymes I could remember from Sunday school were concocted in a way to make you afraid and full of fear. If you didn't follow the word of God, you wouldn't survive. The idea of going to Heaven escaped me, too. I figured by the time I took my last breath there wouldn't be anything more than pictures and romantic notions of what I could still remember. None of which were an accurate resemblance of who I really was.

I romanticized every moment. I thought I did it because I knew the end was coming, and what came next didn't amount to all the glorious narratives about the four white horses and the trumpets blaring. The future I saw was the Wasteland. The comets that lit up the sky and wiped everyone out. Society was going to be fucked if it was real. It felt real. Maybe that was why I'd been inside the portal, to warn everyone about the impending doom on the modern world.

"Oh, my god! I need to warn everyone." I panicked and went into the bathroom to look for my medicine, but I couldn't find the pill bottles.

I looked outside to take my mind off the prophetic thoughts. I knew my whole trip into the Wasteland had been real. I'd gotten a glimpse into the future, and now I needed to warn people. But would they listen? I didn't want to start to spread the fear, like the doomsday preparers with thousands of cans of food and pickled meats beside their arsenal of weapons made for killing zombies. I didn't want to impress that fear on the world, but I needed to tell people what I saw. If it saved a few people, maybe the Washouts could prepare more. Maybe Los Angeles wouldn't become a total Wasteland if people were ready for the explosions that were coming.

The sky was filled with gray clouds. They weren't rain clouds, but dark and cinder-filled from the fires on a few local hills in the San Gabriel Valley.

I stood by the window above the fire escape and lit a joint. I loved when you first flicked a shitty plastic lighter and the sparks looked like mini-fireworks going off. It took me a few times of missing the flame to get a good little show going on, until it worked and lit up. Then the end of the cone lit up in a flame. I blew off the flag of paper, leaving the hot ash.

The weed was good. It always tasted best a few hits into it, before the smoke saturated the rest of the leafy, lime-green flowers. The strain was an LA kush, and it always made me feel relaxed and let me escape my body for a few hours.

Apex started to wake up again from his nap. I snubbed the joint out and went over to him.

I picked him up out of the bassinet and carried him to my favorite place on the couch. I turned on the screen and started perusing through different programs.

"Isn't that weird, programs? Like I want to be programmed." A flashback hit me. It was of a laboratory. It shocked me. I nearly fell backward.

I started thinking about the politicians, and the propaganda and posters plastered all over Los Angeles. I couldn't shake the fear, though. The image kept taking its toll and distracted me from thinking about the wheat-pasted posters carrying advertised meanings from a street artist, talking about how the end of the world was here, trying to have a sliver of influence. Everyone wanted to be an influencer. It had no real effect next to the monsters who controlled the media and were willing to watch us all slide away into the abyss. We had become the experiment. Our lives were just manipulated over and over by talking heads that dictated the news on all the different broadcast networks and virtual membranes.

"Damn, this weed is strong."

It was getting to me. I always overthought and came up with these elaborate conspiracies when I got high during the day.

I started watching a nature show about the ocean. It was incredible—my eyes twitched with how fast the schools of fish darted around, trying to escape the bill of a swordfish attempting to stab them in the side and wound them before eating them. The school of yellowfin tuna spiraled in perfect unison, finding breaks in the water to maneuver away from the agile swordfish.

It was a dance of predator and prey that was so elegant, you forgot it was nature that designed the perfect hunt. An ecosystem that was built on instinct and forms of communication so advanced that even our military modeled sonar after the dolphin's telepathy-like abilities.

I looked down at Apex. He was snoring again, these cute little snorts like a baby pig.

I returned my gaze to the screen and watched as the sharks started circling on the outer fringes of the schools of fish. The blood in the water dripped like iodine curls around the tinge of the deep blue. The swordfish had gotten its fill, or was intimidated enough by the presence of the serene killers approaching in the distance, that it darted off back into the deep.

The first attack by one of the mako sharks was quick and calculated. It took a huge chunk from the side of a large yellowfin. The meat looked charred, pink and beige, like the shark's teeth had seared the sides of its flesh underneath the scales. As the mako came back in for another bite of the immobilized tuna, it stopped in mid-glide, and the head was locked inside of a much larger set of rows and rows of serrated jagged teeth. It made me jump a little into the couch. A great white shark had grabbed the mako, making the mako look as small as the tuna.

"Damn, it's all relative."

I couldn't help but think about the food chain. It seemed so wrong when a shark ate one of its own, even a different species.

The thought electrified me. My brain went into shock, and the lab came back to me again.

"Fuck. Stop it." I suppressed the horrible flashback.

It was from the video-conditioning. The nature images that were more violent than my little ocean video thrashed around inside me.

Apex started to cry again.

I snapped out of the lucid dream and held him to my shoulder. He was my only focus now. I loved him more than anything else in the world. When I became a father, nothing else mattered. I would have given my life for my son and done anything to give him the world.

I knew he was hungry, so I grabbed the bottle from the fridge and put it in the microwave. I squeezed a little in my mouth to test the temperature. It tasted pretty good, and soothed me, too.

The phone rang. I set Apex in the bassinet and ran over to the phone, still holding his warmed bottle in one hand, and placing a rag over my shoulder for a burp cloth with the other.

"Weird. Only Elise ever calls this number."

It was the vintage telephone, one we picked up from a flea market and mounted on to one of the steel support beams in the center of the loft. We'd hooked it up as a kind of novelty and not a real utility. I answered it.

"Elise?"

"No. Kyle, it's me."

"Ummmm." My mind drew a blank. I couldn't place the voice.

"Who is this?" The line was silent. I could only hear her exhale on the other end.

"I'm coming over." She sounded insistent.

"Who the fuck is this?"

"Are you taking your medications?" she asked, unnerved.

"What do you mean?" I asked. There was no response, only a loud click and the sound of the dial tone on the other end. I fell to the floor convulsing, and the flashbacks continued.

I saw Hiram and Carmella, the wedding, and then I saw her face, Epiphany.

"Is it fucking Epiphany? It can't be. She can't be." I wanted to say 'real,' but I couldn't. That would make her real. I remembered what Hiram had said about saying the name of the god and controlling them.

"If I say her name, will that give me control over her? How in the fuck did she get this number?" I tried to reason with myself aloud.

CHAPTER 23

I started to question if I was really back in the loft and not still in the lab. There seemed to be a nocturnal experience buried in me that I was slowly beginning to realize was not a dream at all. I knew now it was fucking real. The urgency to escape crept back in. I felt like I needed to report back to Michael, even though I knew who he was. I had to let them know how many dimensions were on the other side of that portal, all the chaos that was coming for us.

I got myself up and walked over to grab the bottle of formula. A few drops of the substance had dripped from the rubbery nipple. I smeared it with my fingers and licked it.

I walked over to the bassinet to feed baby Apex, but he was gone. He was nowhere to be found.

"Where is he?" I started breathing heavily in a nauseating panic.

There was a banging on the door.

"What do you want?" I said loudly.

I avoided the door. I grabbed the couch pillows and put them over both ears and ran frantically around the loft, looking for the baby.

"I can't fucking hear you!"

I ran around the loft until I fell onto the bed and pressed the pillows as hard as I could against my head. The banging seemed to stop. I released them slowly and there was peace. A moment later the banging on the door started again. I heard keys being taken out. I threw on my favorite jeans and the sleeveless jean jacket with the band patches sewn all over it.

I headed toward the window with the fire escape. I knew I had to get out of here and escape.

"They're coming for me."

"Kyle! Stop right there." I turned for only a second and I could never mistake her face. It was Epiphany, standing in my doorway. I didn't know how she got there, or what was happening. I went totally numb and my body stopped working. I was frozen in time and Epiphany started walking cautiously over toward me. Then I saw her pick up Apex— he'd been back in the crib. She held him and he stopped crying immediately.

"Where was he?"

"What do you mean? He's right here. Come back inside, Kyle."

"Don't worry, I'm not going to jump." I reassured her of that much, even though it was like I was seeing a ghost.

"Do you know who I am?" she said.

"Of course! I know who you are, Epiphany."

312

"Kyle, I'm your doctor. Doctor Rosen, Jessie. Don't you remember?"

"I don't remember. Where's Elise?"

"Kyle, she's gone, sweetheart. That day on the bridge. She jumped. Don't you remember?"

The image of her on the bridge flickered in my head. The static picture of the terror on her face returned as the memory fast-forwarded to her slipping off the ledge. The shrill sound that had trailed off below me as I'd reached for her to grab her pale hand in mine. The flurry of ambulances and police that had showed up shortly after.

"Am I crazy?" I asked her sincerely.

Epiphany avoided the question, the same way I had avoided the questions from the police that day on the bridge. I hadn't been able to look them in the eye. It was like they'd stripped duct tape from my eyelids. They'd stayed open, staring, burning. I went back and combed through the memory. It was buried behind my denial and the excessive amount of alcohol I'd imbibed that night to let the liquor help me forget. It hadn't worked, and the spiral had gotten darker and darker until I'd gone to the facility to meet Michael.

I remembered I had nothing left to lose. She was my doctor. The one with the dark hair in the bun, Doctor Rosen. Now I remembered. She'd said I was having an epiphany. So, that was what I called her. *Did we really have a child?* I had flashbacks of our 'sessions.'

This was our child. Oh, my fucking god. I'd lost it and was stuck in my own nightmare.

"It all happened after coming back through the portal."

"What?"

"You're suffering from advanced paranoid delusions. When you take your medications, you're harmless, but if not, you keep screaming about being a Rider fighting the Beast. We've been keeping daily watch to make sure you're OK. Besides, your time with our baby is limited. I thought it would help you."

I was convinced what she'd said about Elise was a blatant lie. The present version of reality was glitching. She had been here this morning. I could still smell her scent in the loft when I'd woken up. The smell of lilies. Or was she really gone this time? Was she just the specter I had seen on the beaches of the Wasteland?

The world that included the Wasteland seemed more real to me now. The doctors and the lab—that was the real part. I must've lost my mind to the point I needed a shrink who was more twisted than me.

"What the fuck? Are you serious? And what? You fucked your patient? You're fucking crazy."

"You're fascinating," she said with a creepy smile.

"So, I'm a goddamned science experiment you get to have sex with in between my delusions. Have a baby with."

"We needed to produce an offspring. Remember, Kyle, you told me our child would save the world. Like the opposite of the Anti-Christ, a savior. Kyle, come back to me, please."

"Hell no. You're not Epiphany."

I leaped out onto the fire escape and climbed down the metal ladder fast, nearly falling off the last part of it that wasn't fully extended. I dropped onto the lid of the closed dumpster at the back of the restaurant. A stray dog ran out from underneath the dumpster.

"Chico?" I paused for a second and called out after him. It couldn't have been him.

The window was open to the restaurant and I climbed through it, hoping to blend in with the other patrons.

I jumped right into the dining room. A couple customers started screaming, scared I might be robbing the place, or just another homeless lunatic who'd strayed from my cardboard shelter on Skid Row.

I brushed myself off to look a little more presentable, but I was barefoot and didn't have a shirt on underneath the jean vest. I looked around for Pascal, the owner, hoping he would validate my existence as another one of his artsy tenants in the building. He was nowhere in sight. Then, at the corner table, I saw him. I couldn't believe my eyes. Michael was sitting there. I'd never forget his face. My eyes met his. He got up and casually walked out of the back door of the café. He was different; he was carrying a cane and cupping the left side of his belly when he walked.

"Hey! Come back here."

Everyone was looking at me like I was crazy for yelling at the well-dressed customer. I ran out of the back door and saw him already walking down the street.

I ran after him. I stepped on a few glass shards, but I didn't care. I had to get to him. I caught him halfway down the street. He turned around.

"It's not over. Your mission is just beginning. You'll know when we call you."

"What are you talking about, man? What the fuck did I sign up for?"

"You know what you are doing. Kill the Beast."

"The Beast. The Beast is dead, man. The Beast was you."

"Let me see your wrist," he said. I held it up. He pulled a portable scope from his pocket and put it over my wrist, and I watched the symbols morph again in the projection like they had before at the Café Revelation.

"I told you it's real."

"What are you? God? The Beast? What the fuck is happening?" I started to lose my shit.

He turned and got into a Lincoln Town Car that screeched to a halt next to us. Then I felt it. The pain in my right foot. There was blood leaking onto the dirty pavement. It was bright red and smeared all over.

I lifted my foot and removed a triangular piece of green glass. I felt momentary relief without it jammed inside me. I heard a voice calling to me in the distance. It was Epiphany, Doctor Rosen, or whoever the fuck she was. I couldn't place her as anyone else. She wasn't the same, though. Something was very different about her. She was so normal, and her mystical aura was gone. Reality seemed distorted. It was a version of itself that didn't make sense with the connections happening in my brain. I grabbed my head with both hands and shook it out of frustration, trying to extract the thoughts out of it like a thousand molecules that made up a whole.

My only compulsion was to run. I ran with a limp on my right side. I aimed straight for the bridge. If what Epiphany had said was true, then I was going to be with Elise one way or another. Our souls would be reunited in the afterlife. I convinced myself that death would feel good, that plummeting to the ground would be beautiful. There would be a few seconds of floating free in the wild LA air, before my corpse got sucked down the river basin and on into the suburbs. The heart of the City of Angels would push me into her veins and drink me through the channels of her contorted body, and ultimately out into the Pacific Ocean with the rest of the garbage.

I'd fit right in. I wanted to float out with the tide. I wanted to be in the ocean and see the whale again like I had in Malibu with Epiphany—the timekeeper, she'd called it. I believed he could help me. Maybe the whale would reset time and I could go back to the beginning. I pictured the mako sharks swimming underneath me, and the great white shark gliding in the shadows. The fear almost took over, but I kept running at full clip toward the bridge, trying to get to Elise and my spot in the center of existence.

CHAPTER 24

I was almost to the bridge. A group of motorcycles came roaring by. The band of riders was an old motorcycle club that haunted this part of downtown. Their leather vests were covered in a huge patch of an ancient Chinese warrior cutting the head off a dragon-like monster.

I continued staggering up the street, waiting for a clearing to cross to the other side, where Elise and I had last stood. Part of me wanted to feel her again and remember, and the other part of me wanted to follow her same fate. As the last few bikers went ripping by, I connected with one rider's eyes. He was a big-looking dude whose eyes were piercing. He cut into my soul. I could feel a pain in my heart like I'd remembered in the other dimension.

The cold feeling continued until the biker looked away and gunned the throttle on his Harley. I hobbled across the street, the blood thickening on my foot. I grabbed hold of the railing and there was a chain-link fence attached to the other side now. I tried to climb it. The small lattice of diamond-shaped gaps in the fence hurt my feet so bad that I could barely fit my toes through the holes.

I was close to the top of the fence now, using just my upper body to propel up and over, when I felt two pairs of hands grabbing my legs and yanking me off the railing. I came down hard on the cement. It hurt and knocked the wind out of me. I watched my breath kick up piles of dust on the ground. Every time I exhaled, it hurt my ribs from the hard landing on the concrete.

Epiphany was standing over me, and a man in a lab coat. I closed my eyes until the pain in my chest subsided. It went numb and eclipsed any other compulsion I had to escape.

They lifted me up. I was dead weight. They struggled to get me onto the gurney. I shook free and pushed one of the EMTs to the ground. Then I felt it. It was an electrical current pulsing up from my lower back area. I reached around to try and tear the sensation out from the source, but I couldn't. My hands squeezed the wires extending into my back, connected to the taser probes that were lodged in my skin. My grip slackened and I folded limp onto the ground.

I was on my back in the ambulance. The siren wasn't on, but the inside was filled with breathing devices, a defibrillator, and an IV that was already hooked into my arm. I didn't remember them spiking a vein with the PICC line. My eyes moved slowly across the interior of the ambulance.

The equipment seemed so modern and all high-tech. Even the heartrate monitor on the screen pulsed images of a pinkish heart at the end of the miniature frequency wavelengths. The only things out of place were gauze rolls that were half-used. My eyes continued tracing the interior and made their way to the EMTs.

"Remember, I told you how to get out," the small dude said.

"What are you talking about?" I muttered.

"Cut the head off the Beast and the rest of the body dies."

"Yeah, I killed him, man. I killed the damn Beast," I muttered. He just stared at me.

"Wounded him," he responded disapprovingly.

I passed out for the rest of the ambulance ride.

I slept until I woke up strapped to a table. The stainless steel underneath me was cold. I was back on the operating table. I remembered it like yesterday. This was when the images started, and the music. It was hard to forget the piercing robotic symphony that played in the background. I wasn't sure if it was supposed to torture me or lull me into a nocturnal state of mind so it would be easier for them to manipulate me.

"Get me the fuck out of here!"

I got a burst of energy. My screaming plea was met with a syringe into my IV. I struggled, but the nude-colored straps didn't let me go. They held me tight to the table, so tight that I was unsure where the skin of my back ended and the table began. The serum intoxicated me and caused my vigorous body to go totally slack. My legs didn't work, and I started getting sleepy again, too.

I could feel my heart beating wildly, like my organs were eroding inside. I wanted to tear my skin off and let the flame out of my soul to burn brightly.

I couldn't discern between the last time I'd been here and now.

"What did they call me?" I whispered under my breath. "Whalen, Kyle," I yelled out. My last words were my name.

I couldn't open my eyes; they felt sealed shut. An ointment covered them, or maybe they were crusty from exhaustion.

A video projected onto my eyelids. It went through them and showed a big cave. It led into another cave. Inside of it was a small town. It looked like a makeshift shantytown that I remembered so well, but it was different. There were fires consuming all of it. It burned with a vivid glow that made it appear four-dimensional, surrounding my face. I could nearly feel the warmth from the flames on the sides of my cheeks.

I recognized the village burning. It was the home of the Washouts. Hiram and Carmella. I cried out, "Nooooo! What in the hell are you doing to them?"

They were using these artificial images to get me enraged. I thought they must have been digital manipulations of the truth, but they felt so real, I couldn't help but become maddened beyond restraint.

I used all my strength to pull away from the gurney. I pulled again and again. My neck was affixed to the table and propped up by a pillow. It was scratchy, and irritated my cheek as I jerked my head around from side to side, trying to free myself.

"Ahhhhhhhhh!" I screamed out, but nobody heard me.

I continued to thrash around until I got enough momentum that the gurney toppled over. My legs fell to the side and the weight of my body pulled the neck restraint so hard it felt like I was being hanged. I couldn't breathe and the blackness set in.

I woke up staring at him. It was Michael. He was there. I saw a man and not the Beast. I was free from the restraints. We were in the room together. It was just us. There was no one else around, no weird visual illusions. It was just us two in a room alone. He was sitting in a large, ornate chair with wooden moldings extending past the top and red velvet cushioning. There was only one table, and on it sat the knife I had used to stab the Beast. An oily substance was still caked on the blade. It looked like squid ink.

"Welcome back," he said.

"I'm really happy to be back," I said sarcastically.

"You passed all the tests. Congratulations."

"I don't care about your tests. I want my life back."

"What if I told you I can give it back to you? Everything, your old life, Elise, the baby, all of it."

"I'd say you were a liar." I started to get my bearings. The drugs they had given me were wearing off, and I could feel my feet underneath me. One of my feet was bandaged up.

I ran to the table and instinctively reached out to grab the blade.

"Why shouldn't I just kill you?"

He looked at me in disbelief. He shook his head. The images started playing above him. They were of Elise and me. It was like a visual scrapbook of all my memories of her. It was everything from the day we'd met downtown, to the first time we'd made love, Valentine's Day, everything until the day on the bridge. The point of view looked like the camera had been lodged inside of my forehead for all of it.

"What did you do to me? Is this a game to you?"
"I told you I could give it all back to you, Kyle. I can bring her back into your life. If that's what you want?"

"Yes! That's what I want." He looked at me again with similar skepticism.

"It will take you back to the beginning. Are you sure you want that?"

I didn't understand what he was saying, but every cell in my body sang out for Elise. I wanted to get back with her and play out our love affair and not this deranged reality.

"Yeah. Send me back. Put me in the other dimension or whatever you need to do."

"I'm not sure you are ready."

The anger inside me was building. I lashed out and put the blade to his neck.

"Do it, man. Fucking do it," I ordered him.

"What if I say no?" He couldn't possibly think I was joking.

The images were still playing of Elise and me in the background. I glanced up, my eye started twitching again, and I stared at Elise through my good eye. She was crying. When I looked down, Michael's head had morphed into a goat's again, and he was laughing that same disgusting guttural laugh. I couldn't handle the sound of the bleating laughter. I sliced across his neck, sawing through the center part, and his goat's head fell to the ground. His blood leaked out all over my hands.

I staggered backward. The television screen above went blank.

On the ground where the goat's head had fallen sat the face of Michael. His head was human again and his eyes gazed off into the distance with no life left in them.

I walked past his severed head on the ground to the back of the room. In the corner was a door. As I got closer to it, it illuminated from lights embedded around the frame. I pushed it.

The door opened back into the streets of Los Angeles. The city continued to crumble, and the buildings had almost completely turned to dust. I took one step outside. I thought about all that had happened, and where I had been, but mostly I thought about the love I had for my son. A love that would last forever. I thought about how I would always be traveling through other dimensions. *I'll be here with you forever.*

I sighed and realized who I was. I was a Rider.

www.ingramcontent.com/pod-product-compliance
Lightning Source LLC
Chambersburg PA
CBHW030937120726
47906CB00002B/610